From #1 *New York*
Audrey Carlan, discover The
One…

Three women and one man put themselves up for auction in a high-stakes game of marriage, money, and mayhem. The spice is high, the characters intense, and the plot will keep you guessing until the bitter end. This is the filthy, gritty, angsty soap opera you never knew you needed. Welcome to The Marriage Auction.

Meet the candidates:

Maia Rhodes – A twenty-four-year-old pickpocket with a tragic past and one goal: Do whatever it takes to secure enough money to save her family from the devil and his spawn back home…even marry a stranger.

Memphis Taylor – A college footballer who had big dreams of playing for the NFL but dropped out of college due to an injury. He needs to make enough money to help support his five sisters, his parents, and his sassy granny. What's three years of his life?

Summer Belanger – A Californian cannabis farmer with an unorthodox family, a witchy faith, and a desire to find her life's purpose. As a horticulturist, she finds solace and peace in plants and nature but doesn't know the first thing about running a successful business. Her kookie parents suggest the auction so she can find a businessman who will help her succeed and also handle her pesky lack of orgasms.

Julianne Myers – Was raised in the lap of luxury, until her parents and their best friends were killed, leaving her brother and her childhood crush their empires. Her brother and his new fiancée attempt to take it all. Lost and utterly alone, Jules enters into the auction in order to make a huge amount of money fast. Only she didn't expect her godmother, aka Madam Alana, to meddle and create a match she never dreamed possible.

Continue to Book 2 to meet the Bidders…

***

Disclaimer: This serial can be read as a standalone but is best read after TMA 1. Recommended for individuals 18+ as it contains graphic depiction of sexual acts and adult content that may trigger some readers. Please visit my website for a full list of sensitive content.

THE MARRIAGE
AUCTION
BOOK 1

Audrey Carlan Titles

The Marriage Auction
Book 1
Book 2
Book 3
Book 4
Madam Alana
A Christmas Auction

Soul Sister Novels
Wild Child
Wild Beauty
Wild Spirit

Wish Series
What the Heart Wants
To Catch a Dream
On the Sweet Side
If Stars Were Wishes

Love Under Quarantine

Biker Beauties
Biker Babe
Biker Beloved
Biker Brit
Biker Boss

International Guy Series
Paris
New York
Copenhagen
Milan

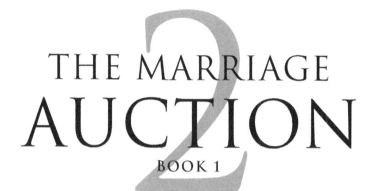

THE MARRIAGE
AUCTION

BOOK 1

By Audrey Carlan

The Marriage Auction 2: Book One
By Audrey Carlan

Copyright 2024 Audrey Carlan
ISBN: 978-1-963135-17-6

Published by Blue Box Press, an imprint of Evil Eye
Concepts, Incorporated

This is a work of fiction. Names, places, characters and
incidents are the product of the author's imagination and are
fictitious. Any resemblance to actual persons, living or dead,
events or establishments is solely coincidental.

Editorial team: Liz Berry, Ekaterina Sayanova, Stacey Tardif,
Suzy Baldwin

Cover design by Asha Hossain

Dedication

To Amy Tannenbaum, because you listen to my dreams and help me make them a reality.
You are one of a kind.

Episode 1

Lying is for Losers

NAOMI

"Men are dogs." I whispered to myself as I looked at my most recent text message. Every last godforsaken one of them. I ground down on my molars as the muscle in my jaw worked overtime to help cool my jets. I stared down at my cell phone, reviewing Jamal's last infuriating, but not altogether unsurprising, text.

> *From: Jamal Watson*
> *Sorry, last weekend was fun, but I'm not looking for anything serious right now. You're a beautiful woman. You deserve better. If you want to hook up again when you're in town, hit me up.*

I pressed my lips so tightly together you'd think I'd just sucked on a lemon wedge. The nerve of this man. Led me on to believe he was into me. All the way up until I gave him the honey pot, then poof! Gone. He got what he wanted from me. And now I was just the next in what was likely a long line of women he'd fucked and then ditched with a single text.

You deserve better.

Wasn't that the damn truth? Not that I needed a player to tell me that fact. I wasn't one of those simpering women who needed a man to tell her that she was beautiful in order to believe it. I knew I had a pretty face and a killer body because I worked hard to keep fit, and the good Lord above graced me with stellar genetics. I was also rich. The kind of wealth 99% of the population would never reach. I'd not only been born into generational wealth, but I'd made money on my own. One couldn't say I was self-made, as my family absolutely fed me from a silver spoon and provided me with a trust fund I tapped right into once I graduated from Princeton. Still, I was successful in my own right.

There weren't a lot of women in the precious gems business. My company purchased the finest quality gems from all over the world. My team then evaluated, tested, cut, shaped, and provided certificates of authenticity with all the appropriate metrics for all of our jewels. Our best clients were retailers such as Harry Winston, Cartier, Tiffany's, Van Cleef & Arpels, Piaget and more. Though my passion lay in designing one-of-a-kind pieces. Those took me months to make and went for obscene amounts at private auction.

None of the men I dated online had any idea who I was or what I was worth. This was intentional because I had hoped to find real, true love. Unlike my parents whose marriage had been arranged. The top one percenters of the world loved to pair like with like. Money with money. Very few in my circles had a love match. My father believed me wedding a man from the upper crust of society, handpicked to continue the upward trajectory of our generational earnings, was absolutely necessary.

I disagreed. Thus the entire reason I was in Las Vegas in the first place.

To choose a husband.

I tossed my cell phone onto the bar and made eye contact

with the bartender just as a man smoothly approached to take the only seat available, the one next to me.

"Were you saving this seat for someone?" His voice was low and deep, reminiscent of my mother's favorite actor, Mr. Morgan Freeman—the man, the legend.

I glanced up, readying a polite half smile when the scents of leather and spice hit my nose. My gaze settled on the striking, chiseled face of a startlingly handsome Black man. I opened my mouth and then clamped it shut, forgetting what he'd asked after taking in the grandeur of his good looks. He was at least six foot three with the build of a football player. Exactly the type of man I needed. One who would not only look exceptional on my arm, but strong enough to protect me from people who might want to hurt me. In my line of business, having a lover who could be both was ideal.

The man smiled wide, his bright, perfectly white teeth on full display as he gestured to the seat. "May I?"

"Oh, uh absolutely. I'm sorry. You…looked familiar for a second." Fat lie. He looked like no man I knew because I would remember someone that handsome. He turned the barstool to the side and wedged his massive frame between me and the seat.

I inhaled deeply, letting his magnificent scent fill my lungs and settle my rapidly beating heart. I put my hand to my chest and cleared my throat. I was positively dying of thirst at the sight of such a gorgeous creature.

The bartender approached. "What can I get you two?" he asked me and my accidental companion.

"Oh, no!" I shook my head. "He's not…" I moved to correct the bartender.

"I'll have an IPA." The man spoke in a sultry timbre that wove deep into my chest like a purr. "Whatever you recommend. And the lady?" His full lips twitched as he leaned a tad closer, quirking his head to the side in what I took to be a challenge.

"I'll have a vodka martini, shaken, two olives," I rattled off my favorite cocktail.

The bartender nodded and left to make our drinks. I turned to the side, putting my legs on full display as I crossed them not-so-subtly. My legs were my favorite feature. They were long, toned, and shined to perfection.

The man's dark gaze dipped to my limbs as if on autopilot, and I watched, satisfied, as he slowly, almost sensually, licked his bottom lip and sucked that bit of flesh back into his mouth. He put a fist up to cover the move and promptly looked away, but I'd caught him in the act of checking me out. I'd crafted the moment. I'd have been salty all night if he'd been too gentlemanly. I liked a man who was chivalrous but also had passion and intrigue in his bag of tricks.

"You didn't have to pretend we're together," I announced.

"Not gonna lie, I saw you from across the room while you were checking your phone. You seemed upset, and my momma always taught me that a kind word or a good deed goes a long way. I figured maybe you could use something to make you smile. A free drink never hurt anyone." He grinned.

"Too true. Thank you. I'm Naomi Shaw." I put my hand out in greeting.

"Memphis Taylor." He took my hand, and like a grizzly bear holding the hand of a child, his swallowed up mine. "That's a mighty paw you've got there," I teased.

He chuckled, warm and deep, the sound causing butterflies to flutter their silky wings inside my stomach.

The bartender approached as a quiet hum settled over us.

"Thank you...for the drink," I whispered, suddenly feeling shy, which was the exact opposite of my normal, overly confident approach to most things, including overtures from the opposite sex.

"You're welcome." Memphis lifted his glass. "To smiling,

every day," he said with his pearly whites clearly visible, proving he practiced what he preached. I stared at his beautiful, kind, angular face. I'd thought he was handsome before, but when he smiled—breathtaking.

"To smiling." I couldn't help but grin myself.

"Aw, there's what I was hoping for. A beautiful smile to go with a stunning woman." He clinked his beer glass lightly to the edge of my martini.

"Flattery will get you *everywhere*." I sipped the vodka slowly, allowing the tang from the olives and the burn from the alcohol to wash over my tastebuds before I swallowed.

"Is that right?" He chuckled. "I'll have to remember that."

I said nothing, preferring to be mysterious rather than give anything more away. I wasn't here to meet a man. Not in the conventional sense. Besides, only seconds prior to Memphis approaching, I'd been kicked to the curb by a man I'd genuinely thought had promise for more.

He took a large pull from his beer and gave a hearty, "Aaaahhhh, I sure needed that."

"Long day?" I asked.

"Flew in from Atlanta today after helping my folks clear the yard, readying it for winter."

"Clear the yard?" I had no idea what he was talking about.

"You know, the yard. Weeding, mowing, pruning, cutting all the foliage back for the upcoming change in the seasons."

"Ah, I see." I lied again. I knew nothing about landscaping. My family had a team of people who took care of the grounds at each of our houses. I didn't even know who took care of mine, leaving the details of such needs to my property managers, of which I had ten. One for each of my personal properties.

"My mother loves to garden. Grows veggies during the spring and summer, on top of keeping an immaculate rose garden." He held up a finger and pulled his phone out of an inner pocket in his sportscoat. "Hold up, I'll show you."

While he scanned his phone I took in his attire. He was well dressed and looked spectacular in light gray slacks paired with a baby blue dress shirt that was opened at his collar. His neck was muscular and thick, meeting his shoulders in a way that celebrated his built physique. The man worked out. And based on the way his shirt stretched across his broad chest, he not only worked out, he *trained*. Perhaps daily, like I did.

It sure would have been nice to work out with someone other than my personal trainer. To have a big, hunky guy like Memphis spotting me while I did bench presses, bending down to steal a kiss as a reward.

"See!" His warm voice burst my romantic bubble as he pressed his phone into my hand.

Suddenly, I was looking at a lush rose garden.

"*Dayum*. Your mother is gifted." I complimented.

His pretty-boy smile went supernova. "Agreed. She's the shit," he added.

"Ah, are you a momma's boy?" I teased and flicked from page to page on his phone, viewing one incredible rose after another in all varying shades of the rainbow. The last image however happened to be one of Memphis and a statuesque woman dressed to kill in cocktail attire. He was wearing a fine suit and she a slinky black dress with a slit straight up to the hip. They stood cheek to cheek, looking like the perfect couple.

Now, I knew I was no slouch in the beauty department, and had had my fair share of compliments by both men and women, but his companion was in the leagues of the famed Ms. Riri aka Rihanna, aka one of the world's most beautiful women. At least in my not-so-humble opinion.

"Damn straight, and proud of it." Memphis reached for his phone, and I handed it back to him, the reminder of the woman he was clearly so comfortable with simmering at the forefront of my mind.

"Nothing wrong with a man who respects and loves his mother," I agreed.

"What about you? When I approached you seemed as though you'd just received bad news. Care to talk about it? Sometimes it helps getting things off your chest."

"By confiding in a stranger?" I could feel my eyebrows rising toward my hairline.

He shrugged and took another pull from his beer. "Sure, why not. What do you have to lose?"

Well, I supposed nothing, now that I had an inkling he was spoken for.

"I was just blown off by a man who I believed I felt a spark with." I pressed my lips together, holding back the snarl I wanted to express at Jamal's obvious immaturity.

"No!" His eyes widened. "You?" He scoffed as though he couldn't believe it.

"Yes, sir." I ran my finger around the rim of my martini as I remembered that men sucked.

"I don't know. I find it hard to believe that any man would let someone like you slip through their fingers." His gaze was heated when he not-so-nonchalantly took in my body from my spiked Louboutins, up my shiny legs, past my Versace cocktail dress to the cleavage I boldly displayed. He lingered there for a solid ten seconds before he roamed to end at my face. "There is no world in which a smart man would let a queen like you go."

"Is that right?" I playfully asked, thinking maybe the Rhianna look-alike was not his woman. Maybe she was a family member.

"If it was me...not a chance." He lifted his hand and wiped along his bottom lip in that sexy way men did that I personally felt as a physical throb between my thighs.

My heart started to beat harder, and my temperature rose as arousal swirled in the air around us.

"Mmm-hmmm," I hummed, grabbing at the four-carat

diamond that hung between my breasts. I often wore a gem I worked with prior to deciding what to create. I found it connected me more fully to the stone, readying my muse for whatever design I'd eventually come up with.

Memphis's gaze set on the stone. "Your, uh, ex buy you that?" He lifted his chin, and I dropped the length of the necklace back to fall between my breasts.

"Because I'm not capable of buying it for myself?" I countered.

He shook his head so fast I worried he'd give himself whiplash before he held up his hands in apology. "Sorry, my bad. I saw the ice around your neck and assumed a man gave it to you."

"It's all right. Not everyone lives by the edict of the great Beyonce' Knowles."

He frowned. "Her edict?" He sounded confused.

"Who runs the world?" I sang lightly.

"Girls." He laughed out loud, and I shivered at the sensual sound. Damn this man had a strong effect on me.

"So, what has you braving Sin City?" I asked, steering the conversation to something more present. I surely didn't want to think about why I was in Las Vegas. I still hadn't made up my mind if I was going to go through with it or not.

He looked down and away. Red flags popped up and started waving in my direction. Usually when a man couldn't keep eye contact with me that meant I was about to be lied to. My heart sank. And I'd had such high hopes.

Memphis inhaled a full breath and let it out slowly as though he were thinking about how he wanted to respond. That was new. "Honestly?" he confirmed, as if I wanted to be told a lie.

I cocked an eyebrow and took another slow taste of my drink. "Would be nice for a change."

"Do men normally lie to you?" he quipped, a non-answer if I'd ever heard one.

"Honestly?" I repeated his question and batted my fake eyelashes with intention. "Yes. You'd be surprised how often men lie."

And cheat.

And steal.

And do a whole host of unseemly things that I wasn't about to share with a stranger I'd met in a hotel bar at a casino a good friend of mine owned.

"Lying is for losers," he stated with such disdain that I actually believed him.

Maybe my radar was off and he was actually the first solid, honest man I'd met in a long time.

"Then be the change you want to see in the world, Memphis." I challenged with a smirk. "Tell me why you're in Las Vegas."

He pressed those beautiful lips together in a way that made me imagine him pressing them to mine. Until he laid out his truth in black and white.

"I'm here to meet the woman I plan to marry."

Episode 2

A Kiss to Last a Lifetime

MEMPHIS

"I'm here to meet the woman I plan to marry." I admitted the truth to Naomi. My mouth felt like cement as I did so, because while I did have plans to marry another woman, I also felt an incredible connection to the Black goddess I'd been speaking with.

There was no sense in evading the reality of why I was in Las Vegas, sitting in the hotel bar at The Alexandra. She'd just been dumped by a man who very clearly didn't deserve such a fine-ass queen. I, too, had no right to lead her on. Nor would I ever want to treat another person that way.

Tomorrow I'd be standing on a shiny stage being bid on by strange, exceptionally wealthy women, in the hopes of securing a three-year contract worth millions.

At least I hoped I would.

My family was counting on me. There really was no alternative.

My mother and father were the epitome of a middle-class American family. Mom was an elementary school teacher, and my father was a veteran who'd served two terms, then became a career trucker. Unfortunately, after nineteen years of safely hauling goods all over the South, he had a bad accident. One that put him on disability for the rest of his life. Disability did not pay as well as being on the job, nor did it come with awesome retirement perks. Something my dad had been just shy of prior to the accident. And my parents had several mouths to feed—not including their own. Not to mention, our granny who was getting up there in age, with a multitude of health problems, even if she was sharp as a tack.

It was up to me, the eldest child and the only other male in the family, to pick up the slack. My sister Sydney, who was two years younger than me, had also been helping the family ever since she got signed by one of New York's top modeling agencies a couple years ago. She should have been living in a beautiful pad in the heart of the city, but instead, she split a place in Hell's Kitchen with two other models so she could send home as much money as possible.

I held my breath as Naomi became quiet and still. It was as though I'd shocked her numb.

"I see." She lifted her drink and sucked back the remainder in one go. "Proves my point. The best ones are always taken."

"I'm sorry if you felt I was leading you on. It wasn't my intention, but I can't lie. You are an alluring and incredibly beautiful woman. I couldn't help but flirt a little. It's in my nature." I grinned, feeling my cheeks heat with a mighty dose of embarrassment.

Naomi waved her hand in the air nonchalantly. "It's fine. Like you said, lying is for losers. I'm happy to sit here and have a drink with a handsome man that has no ulterior motive—like getting into my panties."

I chuckled, relieved that she wasn't angry with me. "Now I didn't say that… If panty removal is on the table, we may need to have a different conversation," I joked.

That had her laughing out loud and back to smiling.

She lifted her hand to get the bartender's attention. While she did so, I checked her out further.

Naomi was something special. Unlike any woman I'd approached in the past. She was confident, straightforward, and absurdly attractive. Legs that went on for days. A toned body that I could tell she worked hard on. Her biceps were nicely defined but not so much that she looked like a bodybuilder, just that she must appreciate weight lifting and regular gym attendance. The dress she wore highlighted every lush curve of her hips and breasts, but also hinted at an athletic body beneath.

Exactly my type.

There was a lot I'd give up to woo such a fine woman into my bed and possibly my heart, but not at my family's expense. I had too much riding on my securing a bid in the auction tomorrow.

"So, where is this wonder woman you're planning to marry?" Naomi asked, bringing the conversation back to reality.

"I'll be meeting her tomorrow." That wasn't a lie, even if I was omitting the full truth. We weren't allowed to discuss the finer details of the auction with outsiders. It was part of the NDA I'd signed. And besides, if I was chosen, I absolutely would be meeting my future wife tomorrow, directly following the auction.

"Well, let me be the first to congratulate you." She grabbed the fresh martini the bartender had delivered. A second IPA sat in front of my nearly empty glass.

"To you and your bride. May you have many happy years together."

I lifted my pint and clinked it with hers.

* * * *

We spent the next few hours together seated at that bar. We ordered dinner and shot the shit as if we'd known one another for much longer than mere hours. It was the most fun I'd had with a woman in years, outside of my sisters. Speaking of my reason for existing…

"Five sisters!" She cackled and smacked the bar top a couple times. "Dang, your parents were getting busy!"

"Right!" I agreed through my laughter. "Every two years, boom. Momma popped out another pretty little thing I was determined to protect with every fiber of my being."

"Awwww." She pushed at my arm playfully, then leaned into my side deeply, half her body resting against me. "You're a good big brother." She patted my arm as she looked up at me with the sweetest expression on her face. She reminded me of a doe from the Georgia backwoods. God himself must have sculpted her features because no woman had such incredible bone structure. Her skin was all sleek and shiny, and in the deepest fawn color. But it was her eyes that had a vise lock on me. They were mesmerizing, like an obsidian gemstone with a golden sheen. When she was happy, shimmery flecks around her pupils reflected back like motor oil over water. I had a hard time not getting lost in them.

"Admit it, you scared the pants off of any would-be suiters hitting on your sisters, didn't you?" She rubbed my back, perhaps a bit more intimately than she should have, but we'd both had several drinks and had gone beyond just strangers. We were…friends.

I shrugged and sipped at my fifth—no, sixth—IPA. "Naw, they make it easy. They're all smart as hell. I'm talking 4.0 and up grade point averages across the board, and two of them are still in high school. They put my status to freakin' shame."

"Oh yeah? You have a house full of smarty-pants, eh? Good! They will make sure that any woman who wins your heart is worth her salt, especially if she has to stand up to five other women, not including your momma."

"True that. And my granny. Don't forget her. She's a pistol on a good day."

Naomi hummed low in her throat, and I swear I felt it in my balls as they drew up, my shaft getting hard. It was as if it had a mind of its own and wanted out. Or should I say *in*to Ms. Naomi Shaw.

I took a few deep breaths in order to relax but her every touch sent a shiver down my spine. Every teasing smile made my heart beat double time. And let's not forget about those eyes. The way she looked at me as if she could see me naked and approved…total mind fuck.

I had to stop those thoughts…So what did I do? I drank more beer.

Not wise.

"What are their names?"

I grinned. "You are not going to believe me when I tell you."

"Try me." She sipped her martini looking over the rim at me with those doe eyes that I wanted to look into for a lot longer than a single night.

"First, you gotta understand my mom. She's quirky. So I'm Memphis…"

"What? Is one of your sisters named Nashville!" She hooted and hollered as the drunken giggles took over.

I bit my lip in order not to crack up, but it was useless. I could barely breathe as I said, "No. But close!"

She placed her hands on my thigh and squeezed my quad as she got herself under control. "Seriously?" she asked through her chortles.

I nodded, breathing through my nose so I'd be able to answer. "We've got Sydney, Odessa, Paris, Holland, and Cheyenne," I finally stated, then leaned back in my chair and watched her laugh.

Naomi ran her hands up and down my leg suddenly

distracted. "You have monster-sized quads." She brazenly tried to put her hands around my thigh.

"That's the years of training to be a pro baller for ya."

She frowned and pursed her plump lips, then tried to compare my thigh size to hers. When she lifted her leg up onto the second rung of my stool and slid her slinky dress all the way up to the promise land, I about swallowed my tongue. I couldn't speak. I'd lost all ability to make logical thoughts as I stared at her magnificent bare legs. I watched her put her hands around her thigh to make the important comparison she'd become hyper-focused on.

"Yours is like two or three of mine," Naomi announced with awe in her voice.

I stared at her shapely thigh, and I wasn't proud of it, but I took a gander a little higher. I could just barely see a hint of her fire-engine red panties.

Instinct took over. "Let me see," I stupidly announced. Then I put both my hands around her thigh. I stared at her sinfully well-formed thigh, enjoying not only that she felt soft like she bathed in shea butter, but also seeing my darker skin tone in contrast to hers.

She gasped at my touch. I slid my thumbs back and forth, petting her delectable flesh. It was so warm and inviting, I could have spent hours touching her. My mouth salivated at the desire to bend over and place a kiss there, drag my teeth along the muscle, and bite down until she cried out in pleasure, begging me for more.

I pulled my hands back and cleared my throat. "So, yeah," I said stupidly, not knowing what else to say, then gulped down my drink, forcing those desires aside.

She licked her lips and eased her dress down before pushing a long lock of black hair behind her ear. Suddenly she avoided eye contact.

I'd made her uncomfortable. "Damn, Naomi, I'm sorry. I didn't mean to touch you…"

"You?" she whisper-yelled. "It was my fault. I'm the one who half mauled you. *I'm* sorry. That's not the kind of woman I am. I do not go after another woman's man. Never have, never will."

I reached out and took her hand. "Hey, it's okay. We've had a good time, but it's really late. I have an early day."

"Yes, of course. You go. I'll settle up with the bartender."

I shook my head and moved out of my seat. Then I held out my hand. "It's already handled. When you went to the ladies room a couple hours ago, I added my room number to the bill."

"You didn't have to do that, but thank you." She eased out of the chair and stood next to me. In her heels, the woman was over six feet, which had to make her a cool five feet ten.

I gritted my teeth as I took in the perfection that was Naomi Shaw. I didn't think I'd ever meet a woman as intelligent, beautiful, quick-witted, and confident as I had today. And that pinched my heart, making me feel as though I had a bad case of heartburn.

"I'll walk you to your room," I murmured, and straightened my spine as I reminded myself about what was at stake. I couldn't risk decades of monetary security on one great night with a woman I'd just met.

"You don't have to do that. I can get there myself as I'm staying here in The Alexandra," Naomi challenged.

"I'm staying here too. And once again, my momma would tan my hide if I didn't escort you. We've both had several drinks and I would sleep better knowing you made it safely back to your room. Plus, we're friends. Adults. It's not like anything is going to happen." I said it, and meant it, but my heart felt the opposite.

She simply nodded.

I put my hand to her back and led her through the casino to the elevators.

"Which floor?" I asked.

"Um, the penthouse."

"The top floor?" I choked out, disbelieving. I happened to know that there were only two rooms on the top floor because my friend, Faith Castellanos, whose husband owned the hotel, had told me so. One being the honeymoon penthouse suite, the other being for special guests or people who could afford such luxuries. The room had already been reserved, so her husband, Joel, had gifted me a luxury suite on the fifteenth floor. Not that Madam Alana wouldn't have paid for my room in the host hotel as part of the candidates' fees, but it made me feel closer to my friends by staying in something they owned. And I promised Joel I would provide detailed feedback on my experience since the resort was newly open to the public.

"I know the owner." She gave a half-hearted shrug and looked away.

"Me too. Faith Castellanos is a friend of mine. Well, technically, Joel is too, but I don't know him as well as I do her."

"I know him through the jewelry business," she answered, sounding conflicted, which was odd.

Maybe she and Joel had been a thing in the past. Jealousy tore through me unwantedly.

"Look, you don't have to explain your relationship to me. I'm not your man," I said, and hated it the instant the words left my mouth. They felt like dry sludge on my tongue—bitter and nasty.

Naomi closed her eyes, crossed her arms over her chest, and took a breath. The elevator dinged and the second the doors opened, she jetted to get out of the confined space.

"Naomi, wait. That was rude of me to say." I followed her out. "I'm sorry…" I tried as she approached her door and slapped her keycard against it several times to no avail.

She shook her head vigorously from left to right. "No,

no. You're not wrong. Carry on. We had a great night together. Really great," she said to the door, not to me.

I reached for her elbow and spun her around to find her eyes glassy as though she might cry. I cupped her jaw and ran my thumb along the high, rounded cheekbone. "I'm sorry. I'm saying all the wrong things. It's just…" I let my shoulders slump. "I'm feeling things I shouldn't for you. Things I can't feel," I whispered, and it pained me to admit it. My chest tightened, and I clenched my teeth in order to hold back everything I wanted to say but knew I shouldn't.

She nodded and I watched a tear fall. I quickly wiped it away staring into those endless shimmery black depths. "I wish we'd met at a different time in another place where things weren't so complicated."

"I wish that too," she agreed. "I know you have to go, but all I want to do is beg you to stay."

"Fuck!" An ache the size of a brick hit my gut, telling me I was about to ruin the best opportunity of my life.

"You need to go…because if you don't, I'm inviting you in. And you're not that kind of man, and normally, I'm not that kind of woman. Though I think I could be that type of woman if the end result was making you mine."

"Jesus!" I bit out, cupped both her cheeks, and pressed my nose next to hers. "One kiss. I can't leave until I have at least a single taste to last me."

"A kiss to last a lifetime?" she purred, her breath fanning the flames of my need for her.

"Yeah, Naomi. A kiss to last a lifetime." Then I planted my lips to hers.

It was akin to a bomb exploding. We ravaged one another's mouths. I sucked on her bottom lip, slanted my head to the side, and devoured her whole. The kiss went on and on. My tongue chasing hers, hers chasing mine. We were both breathing hard as I pressed her up against the wall, my hand on her tight, rounded ass, my cock wedged against her pelvis. She moaned and I thrust my hips, grinding along her slinky dress until she mewled.

When her hand came down between us and she cupped my length, rubbing her palm just right, I ripped my mouth away.

We were both wide-eyed and gasping for air as we realized how far we'd taken it.

I slowly extracted myself, grabbed her hands, and brought them both up to my mouth where I placed a single kiss to each.

"I'll never forget you," I promised as I backed away from a woman who could have been my everything.

She lifted her hand to her mouth and stood still as stone as I stepped onto the elevator.

"Goodbye, Memphis." Her goodbye sliced straight through my heart, chopping it in half.

"Goodbye, Naomi."

Episode 3
A Sign

JACK

"Mr. Larsen, Madam Alana will see you now." Jade's voice broke me from my analysis of the budget report I was reviewing for Johansen Brewing. I'd been sitting only a handful of minutes in one of the plush leather chairs outside of Alana's office, waiting to see her in person.

I exited the report, stood, then tucked my phone into my inside jacket pocket before I buttoned my sports coat.

"Thank you, Jade." I offered a smile to the petite woman dressed in a smart, tailored black suit. Her hair was pulled into a sleek bun at the base of her nape, making her seem much more severe. Liquid liner that came to a point at the outside of her pretty eyes added to the ferocity of her overall appearance. She actually reminded me a lot of the Madam. Which would make sense as I'd learned on the flight over from Norway that Jade intended to mentor under the Madam for an indeterminate length of time in order to learn the business.

I walked swiftly into the office. Alana sat poised behind a glass desk, her hands clasped together on top of it. She wore a sharp gray suit with a white silk blouse underneath that buttoned all the way up to her neck. Her shiny dark hair was parted down the center and fell flat against the sides of her high cheekbones and over the front of her suit. The locks so glossy they shined a bluish-black against the natural light spearing into the room from the floor-to-ceiling windows overlooking the Las Vegas strip.

She made a gesture with her hand for me to take one of the seats in front of her desk.

I unbuttoned my coat and sat down, sitting up straight as I did so. Something about the Madam in this setting demanded professionalism. Even though we'd broken bread together, attended a wedding, shared friends, and had spoken on the ride over, it seemed all of that familiarity was pushed aside. Here sat the Madam, not just Alana.

Jade took the empty seat next to mine, crossed her legs, and set a tablet on her thigh.

"Mr. Larsen," Alana greeted. "You requested time with me today. What is it that I can help you with?"

I cleared my throat. "Well, as you know, The Marriage Auction is tomorrow. I was hoping to receive some intel or portfolios on the women who will be participating."

Alana cocked an eyebrow. "Mr. Larsen, I made it very clear in the information packet you reviewed and the multitude of agreements you have already signed—the bidders and candidates go into the auction knowing very little about each other."

"That's ridiculous," I scoffed.

She blinked noncommittally at me but didn't say a single word.

"You're serious? We bidders are supposed to spend millions on a bride not knowing anything about her? Or him, depending on one's preference, of course."

"Of course," she agreed, but once again, didn't share anything more.

"I don't understand. How am I to secure the right woman for me if I don't know anything other than what she looks like?" I clenched my teeth together, holding back my frustration as I'd hoped this would be a positive conversation. One where the Madam apologized for her lack of preparation, and I left her office with a pamphlet or something more concrete regarding the event and the candidates participating.

"That's a very good question. It's incredibly surprising that you waited until the night before the auction to ask it," she countered calmly.

I glared. "I expected you to provide information prior to the event. I was being *patient*. Now in the final hour, so to speak, I'm concerned."

"I can see that." Alana leaned back in her chair, and I could have sworn I caught a lift of her lips before the bland expression slipped back into place. The micro-movement led me to believe she was enjoying my discomfort. Something that instantly set fire to my ire.

"Tell me what it is you expect to get out of the auction tomorrow that won't be exactly what I've promised you, Mr. Larsen? A willing bride and a three-year commitment of marriage. The same your friend Erik Johansen received. That is what I have offered, and what you yourself agreed to when you signed each of the contracts my lawyers provided. If you are not interested in bidding on a person tomorrow, you don't have to. Nothing is set in motion until you've won a bid."

"I have no idea who to bid on!" I barked, then tugged at my necktie to loosen it. The damn thing felt like it was cutting off my airway.

"That is up to you. During the auction, you will receive some general information about the candidate at the same time as everyone else."

"I want more than that," I growled. "And for the millions of dollars I will be spending, I deserve it." I inhaled sharply through my nose and let it out slowly, staring Alana down.

The Madam was a worthy opponent. She didn't so much as flinch or change her expression. She knew she was in charge, and regardless of my dislike of the process, she carried all the cards.

"What exactly is it that you're looking for in a bride? Do you even know?" She redirected the question at me.

"Obviously, I do." I snapped and then my mind went blank. I went from feeling frustrated to angered to nothing. A big, empty hole right where the visions of my dream girl should be.

The Madam waved her hand in a circle. "Then by all means, share it with me and perhaps I can be of some assistance."

"I…" I frowned as a multitude of new, unexpected images flashed across my mind.

The way my best friend Erik looked at his new wife Savannah with such intensity, the love they share filled the very air around them.

How Henrik, the only father figure I've ever really known, doted on his wife, Irene. Lived to make her laugh, so he could simply see her smile.

My friend Troy kissing his pretty bride on their wedding day, with Erik and I standing up as witnesses.

Then the beautiful images changed.

Darkened.

Me standing without Erik at Troy's funeral, holding his wife's hand as she curled her free one around her largely pregnant belly while her husband's ashes were handed to her.

Seeing Erik in the hospital, half of his body mangled and broken after the helicopter accident, believing he wouldn't make it.

Being moved from one foster home to another over the years, losing my newest mother, time after time. No one ever wanted to keep me.

"I want a woman who will stay." I swallowed past the

lumps of cotton coating my throat. "A woman who will be devoted to me. To our marriage."

"And you will have that. For three years. But I can't promise forever, Mr. Larsen. Each candidate enters The Marriage Auction for their own reasons. What I can say is that most of my marriages stay intact far longer than the three-year period. And some end prior to that. It's not often that a candidate breaks the contract and loses everything, but there's always an out. For you and for the candidate."

"Then why do we do it?" I breathed, uncertainty filling my veins.

That time she did smile, though it didn't reach her eyes. "I believe that is something only you can decide. Why are you really here?"

"I want what my best friend has. I want what his parents have," I answered honestly.

She pursed her lips and waited for me to continue. The woman was more strong-willed and self-composed than any tycoon I'd battled in the business arena.

"I want true love."

"Ah, now we're getting somewhere." She smirked. "As you know, I'm in the business of marriage. I've never offered love. I'm afraid you have to maneuver that path on your own."

"But Savannah and Erik, Faith and Joel, Sutton and Dakota. Even the Penningtons, identical twin brothers, both found true love in a pair of sisters."

"They did." Alana dipped her head in acquiescence.

"And you're telling me you had nothing to do with that?" My tone was rife with skepticism, and I didn't try to hide it.

"You can believe what you wish. I can only tell you, Mr. Larsen, that I presented the opportunity, and the universe provided the happily ever after. Not me."

"Now *that* I find hard to believe. You had to have encouraged them somehow. Provided a hint of what was to come." I was desperate for her to admit that she could, in fact, lead me to the right person.

"Is that what you want? For me to choose a bride on your behalf? And give you the opportunity to claim I chose poorly when there isn't a love match? Basically, providing you with a reason to sever your commitment and walk away?" Her eyebrows rose. "I'm in the business of making money by offering a very unique and rather discreet service. A service you claimed to want."

"And I do. But I can't just walk into the room tomorrow and bid on the most attractive person on stage. I want to bid on the right person."

"Only you can determine who that person is."

I closed my eyes realizing that we were going round and round with no hope for resolution. Usually in business I would suggest a break to regroup so that each party could come back to the table with fresh ideas. This wasn't one of those times. Staying the course was my only hope.

"Do you interview your clientele? Ask them what they are looking for?" I asked.

"I do."

I licked my lips. "Okay. In doing that, if you've come across a woman who is sweet, kind, engaging, accepting of her partner's busy work schedule, willing to attend business events happily, not because they are forced, who comes from…"

"Who comes from what, Jack?" Her tone softened when she used my first name.

"A woman who comes from a *good family*. A woman who wouldn't be opposed to this marriage going longer than three years. A woman who wants children of her own one day. If you come across a woman with those attributes, give me a sign."

"A sign?"

"Anything. During the auction, if you believe a woman on the stage fits that description, tap your nose, tug your ear.

I'm asking for your help. The magic of your auctions has worked for people I care about. Brought them the loves of their lives. You've changed them for the better. I'm asking for no more and no less. A sign that will help lead me down the right path."

I stood up, clasped the button on my coat, and nodded. "I appreciate your time and look forward to tomorrow." There really wasn't anything more I was going to gain from this conversation. I wasn't even sure she'd help.

Though I had hope, for the first time in a long time. I hoped for something I wanted to happen. Hoped that I could find a woman who would connect to me the same way Savannah had with Erik. How Irene did with Henrik. I had hope that I too could find the woman who was meant for me. The woman who would choose to stay.

Episode 4

It Must Be Fate

SUMMER

The elevator dinged and the doors opened on the twentieth floor, the one I was supposed to get off on. I straightened my shoulders, readying myself for the last meeting with Madam Alana.

"I can do this," I whispered to myself as I looked up and lost my ability to breathe.

A man stood before me, blocking my exit. I stepped back on instinct, staring at the most attractive human I'd ever seen.

He was dark and light, reminding me of a sun-kissed day where the temperature changed drastically when a cloud crossed over the sun. His skin was the color of toasted honey, paired beautifully with dark-brown hair that had the subtlest hints of caramel. He wore a bespoke suit so dark it could have been black, but it wasn't. It was the deepest midnight blue, the color giving off a slight sheen in the unnatural fluorescent lights of the elevator.

"Were you getting off?" The man gestured his arm to the side as though to allow me to pass.

I shook my head, incapable of speech at the moment.

His full lips compressed into a smirk as he entered the elevator. I watched in silence as he pressed the button for the lobby, which was when my brain came back online.

The doors closed and necessity forced me to take a gulping breath. I wished I hadn't because his scent was intoxicating. An earthy desert aroma invaded my senses. There were hints of bergamot, notes of pepper, and a woodsy walnut scent giving off a masculine, cozy feeling I wanted to snuggle up with. I'd enjoy pressing my nose straight to his neck and inhaling while running my tongue along the warm surface, just so I could have a taste of that heavenly smell.

"Are you okay?" His voice wasn't a rumbling storm as I expected, but the timbre of a man who knew he was in charge. Direct and confident layered with a coating of compassion. And it was accented. Not like a British or French lilt, but definitely European and sexy as hell.

I pressed my hand to my rapidly beating heart. "I-I…you smell fantastic," I blurted, mentally chastising myself for being so lame. This was why I didn't date. Men made me nervous and socially awkward.

The stranger's lips lifted into a smile showing a neat row of white teeth. "Thank you," he stated as his eyes seemed to trace the features of my face and down the boring, plain black dress I wore.

I must have looked like I was going to a funeral. I wasn't usually fond of dressing so grim, preferring sunny colors and jewel tones, but my mother had encouraged me to dress appropriately for my last meeting with Madam Alana. And since the woman was always dressed severely in business attire, I'd pulled out the only thing I owned that could double as professional attire.

My funeral dress.

It was the only time I purposely wore head-to-toe tailored black. Though I imagined the platform-wedge cork sandals I wore with it softened the severity quite a bit, and also probably didn't go as well as a pair of stilettos would have. Something I personally didn't own.

As I stood there unspeaking, the man bent forward, bringing his face a tad closer. I swallowed nervously as he invaded my space, his broad shoulders blocking my view of anything but him.

He inhaled deeply through his nose and his coffee-colored eyes rose to meet mine, sparkling with what I believed was surprise as he laughed.

I frowned and took another step backward until I hit the wall of the elevator.

"What?" I cleared my throat.

"You smell like a summer's day…"

Elation spread through my veins like wildfire, my cheeks flushing with heat. "How funny because my name is…"

"I wasn't done speaking," he interrupted coolly, and a little niggle of uncertainty pierced my happiness bubble.

I held my tongue and waited.

"You smell like a summer's day…" He dipped forward again and inhaled boldly. "If you were sitting on the beach smoking a joint." He grinned and stood straight again.

Technically, I had partaken in my hotel bathroom while I was getting ready. My anxiety had been off the charts as I prepped for the last meeting to determine if I'd be chosen as a candidate in the auction happening tomorrow night. And I really wanted to be added to the lineup.

I frowned and crossed my arms over my chest. "And that's a problem because…" I was so tired of the stigma around cannabis use recreationally and, more importantly, medically. The medicinal properties being my primary reason for regular use. I took advantage of my rights as a Californian to use as I desired. And it was also legal in Nevada, where we were now. Not to mention my opinions on the matter were intense due to what I did for a living, and the entire reason I wanted to be a part of the auction.

"Did I say it was a problem?" he challenged.

I glared. "Your tone insinuated there was something wrong with me smelling of weed. And frankly, I don't give a rat's ass what a highfalutin, dressed-to-the nines, *on a weekday*," I added as a burn that probably wouldn't hit the target, "feels about my scent. As a matter of fact, I take back what I said. You smell like shit." I took a couple steps closer, inhaling his magical scent once more in order to make a statement. "Horse shit, specifically." I pointed at his chest, my finger dangerously close to making contact.

The man's eyebrows rose toward his hairline. "Is that right? I believe you said I smelled fantastic. You can't take that back…"

Before I could respond with a pissy retort, the world around us shook.

Not the world, the elevator.

I screamed and grabbed for the man. His arms wrapped around my body, flattening me to his broad chest. I clung to the lapels of his pristine suit, digging my fingernails in as the elevator swayed and rocked, dropping down several feet at a shocking speed, before it rumbled, then came to a screeching halt, jolting us both.

He kept me pressed to him, one arm tightly wrapped around my back, the other in a vise-like grip around the bar attached to the walls.

"*Jesus Kristus!*" he swore in that sultry accent.

My knees shook as I stared up into his gorgeous face. Fear clogged my throat and my eyes started to tear.

He lifted his hand and cupped my cheek. "Don't cry. I'll keep you safe."

My nose tingled and the tip likely turned a bright pink as I opened and closed my mouth, wanting to speak, but nothing came out.

"You're white as a ghost." He rubbed his thumb along

my cheek tenderly.

My bottom lip trembled as a couple of pesky tears fell.

"It's going to be okay, *solskinn*," he whispered the last part in a language I didn't understand.

I nodded, keeping hold of him as though my very life depended on it. Maybe because it did.

"I'm going to press the emergency button," he said calmly.

I nodded, but didn't let him go.

He smiled sweetly and wrapped his hands around mine, lightly tugging them free of his clothing. "It's okay. I'm right here. I'm not going anywhere," he murmured and interlaced the fingers of one hand, while he reached out and pressed a big red button.

Alarms trilled around us, and I jumped closer to him, pressing my body to his side as I wrapped my arms around him completely and put my face exactly where I'd wanted to from the second he entered. His chest.

I sighed against the warm, safe space.

He didn't move, allowing me to soak in the comfort of his presence and body. Even after I'd been bitchy toward him.

"I'm sorry about before," I whispered against his skin.

He rubbed a hand up and down my spine. "It's okay. Everything is okay."

I gripped his waist and held on. The alarm quieted as a staticky voice split through the tension and fear building in the small space.

"This is the hotel maintenance. We have received your request for help. The power shorted and the elevator mechanics glitched. I assure you we are doing everything we can to free you as soon as possible. The elevator is locked in place as we assess the damage and determine the best way to extricate you from the car. It may take a little time, but help is on the way. We can see you in the cameras."

I untucked my face and glanced up to the corner where a

red light was blinking next to a small globe. Stupidly, I waved at the item, and the voice chuckled.

"This is no laughing matter," my stranger announced gruffly, still holding me tightly, for which I was grateful.

"We understand, sir. The fire department is a few minutes out. Please relax and stay calm. We'll free you shortly."

"Um…thank you!" I called out, my voice sounding shaky in the confined area.

I began to slowly extract myself from the comfort of the stranger's hold. I stepped back until I reached the rail. When I did, my nerves took over and my knees became jelly. I crouched until I was closer to the floor where I planted my ass rather ungraciously. My long, wavy blonde hair fell over my cheeks, shrouding me from the world. Still, I kept a hold on the rail above my head and closed my eyes.

Then I breathed.

In and out.

Slow and steady.

I felt a weight shift at my side, and a long, pair of midnight-covered legs stretched out across the floor.

Unexpectedly, a warm sensation covered my nape. "Hey there, are you going to pass out?" His voice carried nothing but concern as his hand rubbed at the tension in my neck.

I swallowed against the panic threading through every single one of my pores and nodded.

"My name is Jack Larsen. What's yours?"

After he'd made such a big deal about me smelling like summer and weed, I opened my mouth and lied. I wasn't about to give him any more verbal ammunition to wound me with. "Rebecca," I stated flatly.

His brows pinched together. "Are you okay, Rebecca?" he asked.

"Yeah, I'm going to be fine. As soon as we get the hell out of this elevator." I reached across the floor, noting that my purse must have fallen off my shoulder as it was lying on the ground, most of its contents having spilled out.

Horror hit when I noticed my birth control pills, a couple of tampons, a tube of lip gloss, a wad of used tissues, a compact, a one-hitter, and my backup pair of lace undies spread out like confetti across the floor.

I scrambled toward my things. Just as I was about to reach a loose tampon that had rolled farther away, next to my backup undies, a large masculine hand wrapped around both. I looked up in horror as Jack dangled the lacy white thong from a single finger.

His eyes turned a fiery sienna, dazzling me stupid as he crouched before me. He spun the lace around in a circle. "You know, people say the contents of a woman's purse are fascinating, and I'd have to agree with them, *solskinn*." He chuckled and that warm rumble tore through my chest, spreading like a soothing balm over my shattered nerves.

"Give me those." I went to grab them, but he pulled his arm back, evading my reach.

"I'm curious. Why would you have a saucy pair of panties in your bag?" He tapped his lips with his free hand. "Were you coming from a tawdry evening out? You know, I've heard what happens in Las Vegas stays in Las Vegas. Is this proof of such a thing?" He grinned wickedly.

I stood and snatched the undies from his hold lightning fast. "How rude! You don't touch a woman's panties."

He scoffed and crossed his arms, his lips twitching with mirth. "I beg to differ. I very much love touching a woman's underthings." He leaned closer, his face now a few inches from mine. "I think I'd rather enjoy touching your panties, while you were still wearing them...or perhaps, I'd prefer taking them off."

"You're delusional," I snapped, shocked at the surprising curl of heat coiling low in my pelvis as the image he presented filtered through my mind.

The elevator shook and once more I found myself

pressed up against Jack's solid frame.

"The feel of you in my arms is astonishingly welcome, and since you keep ending up there, I believe it must be fate."

"Fate?" I growled, my hands curling around his shoulders as I narrowed my gaze.

"What else could it be?" he asked.

"Coincidence?" I gasped as one of his arms slung low around my waist, pressing our bodies even closer. I could feel his breath against my cheek, sending goosebumps along my skin.

"You don't believe in fate?"

I shook my head noncommittally. I actually did believe in fate, but I did not, however, believe in coincidence. What was it about this man that had me lying through my teeth?

"Divine intervention then?" He continued smiling.

"They are far too busy dealing with all the shitty world leaders and making deals with karma to be involved in a little elevator malfunction."

"They?"

I rolled my eyes. "Let me guess… You believe God is male?"

He shrugged. "Most likely."

"Ugh. God is technically not female nor male. God is an entity. All powerful. All knowing. *They*," I enunciated, "are nonbinary if you must assign a gender specification."

Jack laughed so hard and for so long, I found myself wanting to hit someone.

Not someone.

Sexy, accented, beautifully dressed, annoyingly gorgeous, magnificent-smelling Jack Larsen. And I never wanted anything to result in violence.

Why did all the yummy ones have to be so irritating?

I moved away from him and picked up the remaining items that had fallen out of my bag.

"Hello in there. We're about to force open the doors.

Stand back," came a scratchy feminine voice through the speaker.

Jack and I plastered ourselves to the back wall and watched as a slice of metal appeared near the top of the split in the doors. Then a loud noise boomed, and the door ripped open a few inches.

Idiotically, I reached for Jack's hand. He held mine firmly, giving me the support I needed. Unexpectedly, my vision became blurry and little stars appeared at the edges. My heart pounded a million miles an hour in my chest, and I felt as though I couldn't catch my breath.

Several pairs of yellow-gloved hands yanked the doors open. But what we saw when they opened was a female fire fighter crouching and several pairs of legs with no upper halves.

No, that couldn't be right.

I blinked several times as my vision wavered in and out, my breath coming in gasps.

"Rebecca, Rebecca," someone called my cat's name. Was my cat here? All I could see were hazy forms.

My body was lifted and a bright light pierced my eyes.

People were talking around me but it sounded like garbled nonsense. All but one voice cut through the sludge coating my ears.

"Open your eyes, *solskinn*. Let me see those pretty blues." Jack's face was all I could see. His spicy, earthy scent invading my nose and calming me down.

"Jack…" I croaked.

"There you go." He helped me up to a seated position and rubbed a hand up and down my back in long strokes as my vision came back. "Just breathe, Rebecca." He called me by my cat's name again.

Oh, that's right, because he was an ass who'd made fun of my smell and the backup panties I always kept on hand. A woman never knew when she would need a clean pair. My mother had forced that life hack down my throat since I was a teenager, and more times than not, it had been a great help. Especially when having a tawdry night out, as Jack put it.

Though I didn't think of hookups that way. If a person wanted to be intimate with someone, so be it. I despised how some of the population demonized women for having sexual freedom. Men could go screw ten girls a month and that was often considered a slow month for the single guy. A girl had so much as one partner every few weeks and she was seen as a ho. Not cool. Double standards sucked.

Why am I thinking of this now?

Jack helped me to my feet. "Give me your phone number," he demanded as he pulled out his cell phone.

"Why?" I pressed my fingers to my forehead as a paramedic led me to a comfy chair.

"I want to check on you later. Make sure you're okay."

"Why?" I asked again.

"Humor me," he deadpanned.

I rattled off a phone number I'd had memorized my entire life. Though it wasn't my own. It was the same I gave sketchy dudes while being hit on in a bar or club.

"I'll be calling," he said as the paramedic flashed a pen light into my eyes.

"I'll be holding my breath," I snorted, and he blessedly took his leave, disappearing into another elevator.

Jack Larsen was weird.

Usually, weird was my jam. But after the harrowing experience we'd just gone through together, where I was all kinds of awkward and fumbled around like a dumbass, and he was rude, I was glad to be rid of his presence.

Besides, I was here to marry a rich businessman, and Jack Larsen was not him.

Episode 5

Swindled By a Little Girl

RHODES

"Dad, ugh. Hold my backpack," Emily griped for the hundredth time that day.

I ground down on my teeth as I stopped in the middle of the Las Vegas airport, where I was already pushing her carry-on and my own.

She held out her arm, her backpack dangling from her hand. "It's getting stuck in my hair." Her shoulders were slumped, a scowl firmly in place on her face, per usual.

"You can handle your own backpack, Em. We still need to get your suitcase, even though I told you to pack light for this leg of our trip."

She rolled her eyes. "Mom never goes anywhere without at least two suitcases. And she looks perfect. I want to be just like her." She curled her lip into what I liked to call her Elvis snarl. She brought out the snarl every time she wanted to wound me. I allowed it, mostly because her anger with me was in fact my fault. I was the one who'd divorced her mother and made her life miserable. According to her. And Emily took every chance she could to shove that fact in my face.

I inhaled fully and allowed the breath to slowly seep out of my nostrils. I reached out and took her backpack and tossed it on top of her carry-on. "There. Happy?"

"Whatever." She crossed her arms over her chest and pushed past me, walking ahead.

Lord give me the strength to get through the summer with my teenager.

I had it all planned out. First, we'd start in Las Vegas where I would show her the Strip and take her on a helicopter tour over the Grand Canyon. I saw it for the first time with my parents when I was maybe ten. It was one of the most memorable family trips we'd had. My brother was still alive then and things were different.

Simpler.

Happier.

After we lost him, everything changed.

"Dad, what the heck? You're staring into space again. I'll meet you at baggage claim." Emily sighed dramatically, turned around with a flip of her long blonde hair, and continued on, leaving me behind. My instinct was to chase her down, but she was almost 14 years old, and had been traveling since being in the womb. With the careers her mother and I kept, she knew airports better than playgrounds.

At least we'd have company during the first part of our stay, I reminded myself. We were meeting up with Alana and Christophe Toussaint, people who Emily happened to like. And I wanted Emily to be around a woman like Alana. She was always kind, poised, and incredibly put together. She had a way about her that Emily had always gravitated toward like a duck to water. Probably because her own female example spent most of her time unclothed and partying, living the life of a lingerie supermodel.

Portia was the best and worst decision I'd ever made. If I hadn't married her, I wouldn't have Emily. The downside, however, was that Portia wasn't the faithful type and had made that painfully clear in year one of our marriage when she cheated on me multiple times. I kept taking her back, believed her tales of woe. I suffered through five years of an unhappy marriage in the hope I could keep Emily from having to grow up in two separate households. I would listen to Portia's sob stories about wanting to stay a family. Hear all her excuses about how she accidently ended up on some man's cock while I was taking care of our toddler and running an architectural empire, and I'd cave.

All of it was lies. It had always been lies and half-truths with Portia, and I feared she'd been rubbing off on our daughter as of late. Hopefully a little one-on-one time with her old man would bring things into perspective.

Besides, the Toussaints were good people, and Emily needed to be around mature adults who were successful. They were longtime friends of mine and the first clients I'd designed a home for after I opened my business. The same business that went from working out of a small, 900-square foot space in downtown Los Angeles while I pinched pennies into a billion-dollar business, including the skyscraper that I designed and owned alongside many other profitable architectural ventures.

I was also planning on meeting up with the owner of my most recent hotel build, Joel Castellanos. The Alexandra had been a passion project for both of us, and now that it was fully operational, I wanted to show it to Emily. Not that my thirteen-year-old daughter would be impressed with anything I created. Very few things brought a smile to her face, but I hoped this summer together could bring us back to a healthy and happy father/child relationship.

Just as I turned around, I slammed directly into someone. A flurry of dark hair and soft skin pressed against me. While I tried to catch my balance, the person who hit me started to fall. My legs crashed into one of the suitcases as I wrapped my arms around the small body, flattening her to my chest as we both went down.

My hip hit the shiny airport floor painfully and I rolled to my back breaking the fall of the small woman who landed right on top of me.

"Oomph!" she breathed, her dark hair a curtain over my face as her forehead conked mine. "Shit!" she yelped.

All I could see were a pair of dazzling, warm-brown eyes as I blinked several times to gather my composure. Our breath mingled together, sawing in and out—hers smelling of mint, mine of coffee. We both took in air as though we'd been hit by a truck. My heart beat double time and my hip screamed and throbbed painfully where I'd landed on it.

"Good God. Are you okay?" I asked while I tightened the arm that was wrapped low around her small waist, before I tunneled my fingers through the thick, wavy hair at the back of her head. "Miss, you alright?" I stared into her dreamy gaze as she shook her head. "No? You're not okay?"

She frowned and put her hand to her forehead, the other one firmly planted on my chest over my heart. Her small frame was straddling my much larger one, her knees on either side of my hips. I used my core to push up into a seated position as she looked at me awkwardly, her mouth slightly opened.

The girl was beyond beautiful.

And when I say *girl*, I meant it. She couldn't have been more than early twenties, but her face was so uniquely shaped, I wanted to stare at her for eons. Press my lips to her perfect mouth and taste that minty scent directly from the source.

What the fuck? I had no idea where those thoughts came from. I was old enough to be this woman's father. Probably.

I cupped her high, rounded cheek and dipped my face closer so I could stare into her mesmerizing eyes to determine if she was indeed okay. At least that's what I told myself.

"Hey there, sweetheart. Do you need medical attention?"

I ran my thumb over the swell of her cheekbone. Her eyes were wide set with long, black lashes framing them. She reminded me of a fawn, all docile and sweet innocence. Her skin was the color of a toasted walnut that paired magnificently with her eyes and the thick, rich brown hair that tumbled all over her shoulders and back. Her lips were that of a cherub, perfectly pink and bare, no lipstick or gloss to be seen.

The question I asked seemed to snap her out of whatever spell she'd been under. I watched her brows furrow with confusion.

"Um, I'm sorry, mister, I didn't mean to run into you like that. I-I wasn't paying attention, I'm…" She pushed against my chest to stand, seemed to fumble, and then tucked her hands behind her back as I stood. I reached my hands out, curling them around her small hips to help steady her. She looked at the mess around us and then up at the people who had stopped to gawk.

"You guys okay?" an airport employee asked, carrying a mop and pushing a bucket on wheels.

"Fine, right?" I focused on the young woman who nodded avidly. I turned around to the employee. "We're good. Thank you," I said with a smile.

When I turned back around, the woman was already halfway down the corridor heading toward baggage claim.

"Hey! Wait up!" I grabbed the small suitcases and the backpack and rolled them as I ran to follow her.

Either she didn't hear me, or she pretended not to. Still, I was in great shape. I may have been almost twenty years this woman's senior, but I was fit as a fiddle and worked out regularly. Catching up was not a problem, even while dragging two suitcases and a backpack.

I nudged her in the arm as I reached her. She acted as though she'd been punched in the shoulder with how fast she jumped to the side to avoid my touch.

"Oh, it's you." Her voice was raspy, sounding almost fearful.

"Yeah, me. You know, the guy you just mowed down." I chuckled. "I asked you a question back there," I reiterated.

"You did?" She seemed to play dumb.

"You know I did. I wanted to make sure you were okay."

"Oh. Perfectly fine. Just a bump on the um, forehead." She reached up and rubbed at hers. "You okay?"

"I'm shocked you care, seeing how fast you disappeared." I chuckled, amused at this woman's odd behavior.

She crossed her arms over her chest and rubbed them together while glancing at me from the side of her eyes. "Mmm-hmm well, you know, that was embarrassing."

"Accidents happen. No harm, no foul." I smiled.

"Is that a sports saying?" she asked, but her gaze kept tracking the people and businesses around us.

"Not really," I answered feeling as old as dirt. "Are you looking for someone?"

She frowned, bit into her bottom lip, and kept looking around. "No. Are you following me?" she blurted.

"We're headed the same way. Baggage, ground transportation?" I lifted my chin toward the sign that we were about to walk under.

"Oh, yeah. Right. Cool."

"Do you know where you're going?" I set down one of the cases and grabbed her arm. "Are you sure you're okay? That conk to the head was sharp, but I didn't think it was that bad. You seem like you're lost or looking for someone."

She shook her head. "Don't worry about me. I'm fine. Really. Flying makes me nervous," she randomly stated.

I scanned her up and down, noting that she wasn't carrying anything with her.

Strange.

"No suitcase or purse. Where you headed?" I asked, even more curious about this young woman.

Her entire face pinched together at my question, but her gaze continued to roam. Maybe she was *hiding* from someone.

"Why are you asking so many questions?" she snapped. "Look, I said I was sorry. Please leave me alone or I'll call for, uh...*security*." Her eyes widened as she looked me dead in the face and lied about calling for security. Then she bolted around me and speed-walked away.

"Weird." I let out a frustrated breath then followed the signs for baggage claim.

Emily was standing by the appropriate carousel, cell phone pressed to her ear.

"Gawd, it's already the worst trip in the entire world and we haven't even left the airport. Why can't I come to the Maldives where you're shooting? I'll be good. Stay out of the way. I promise!" I heard my daughter plead with who I assumed was her mother. What was worse was that Portia didn't want Emily with her. Since our divorce, it was rare that she'd take Emily on any trip. Half the time she skipped her weekends with her daughter and those were court mandated every other week if she was in town. But Portia always found a reason to be "out of town" when it was her turn to have Emily.

"But Mom, Pablo likes me, right? Wait, you're not with Pablo anymore? But I thought you were getting married..."

I rolled my eyes. Portia was *always* about to marry someone she dated, but if she did, that would mean she would stop getting those ridiculously large alimony checks she didn't deserve, right alongside the child support checks she blew on herself. Besides, the boy toys she played with were young, dumb, and full of cum. They didn't want to get married. They wanted to bang a supermodel, get seen by the paparazzi on her arm, get some press, then move on to the next best thing. Usually a much younger, more successful woman, or a modeling/acting gig. Whichever came first.

The carousel started up and the bags slowly made their

appearance.

"Honey, keep an eye out for your suitcase while I see if our driver is outside." The Alexandra was sending a car. They always did for VIPs.

I stepped out of the airport and reached inside my jacket pocket to pull out my cell phone to check the reservation, but it wasn't there. I patted down my chest and shoved my hand into both inner pockets of my suit jacket.

Both my wallet and my cell phone were gone. Just disappeared.

Could I have dropped them in the fall earlier? Maybe if I retraced my steps, I'd find them.

"Fuck!" I checked all of my pockets again, finding absolutely nothing.

There was no way that during the fall, my wallet *and* my phone could have slipped out of the inside, very deep, jacket pockets. Something that had never happened before.

And then I remembered how strangely the young woman acted after she'd run into me, then tried to escape without notice. How she took a while lying on me, her hands pressed to my chest.

"Fucking hell," I laughed bitterly.

I'd been swindled by a little girl.

That beautiful, tiny young woman was a pickpocket.

Episode 6

The Kindness of a Stranger

MAIA

The airport bathroom stunk like shit. Two of the toilets were clogged again. I held my breath as I pulled out the wallet and phone I'd pilfered from the hot Zaddy I'd purposely run into at gate 14. I hadn't meant to trip, and was surprised when he caught me, protecting me from hitting the floor. Though the fall wasn't what had me shaking in my knockoff Doc Martens.

It was his eyes.

The steely gray pierced through me as if he could see straight to my soul. It'd unnerved me. Made me want to stop and question my choices. Except my choices were eat or not eat. Pay the rent on the tiny studio I rented above Sam's garage or potentially go back to living on the streets.

My landlord was cool though. He'd give me more time to pay up if I needed it. Sam was a man who had fallen on hard times more often than not in his past. His motorcycle club had given him what he called a second chance. An opportunity to make something of himself and find his purpose. Sam wanted the same for me. The man had become like a big, gruff, scary older brother with knuckles of steel and the softest, mushiest heart on the planet.

Sam had saved me all those years ago and continued to do so by being the number one family I chose. Though Alana was a close second. The memory of when Alana and I met four years ago skated across my memory.

The airport was hopping as usual. Travelers coming off planes, holding the hands of screaming children, dragging carry-ons over their shoulders and rolling down by their feet as they attempted to avoid the extra baggage fees by bringing all their crap onto the planes.

Thanksgiving was always a crush of activity, which made it perfect for pickpocketing. And I never stole more than what I truly believed a person could live without. Usually if I stole a wallet, I'd pilfer whatever cash they had and attempt one or two charges on their credit card before cutting it up. Most people wouldn't even notice a small charge on their credit statements. And I didn't charge material things or wants. When I stole from someone, it was because I needed something to survive. A warm coat to get me through the winter. New pair of shoes to protect my feet. Perhaps a hot meal that day. A bed to sleep in.

I wasn't without a conscience. It's just that after what I'd lived through and currently had to do to survive the streets, my priorities were different than the everyday person's. If they could afford to travel, they could afford a ten-dollar meal, or a thirty-dollar used winter coat from the thrift store. At least it's what I told myself day in and day out so that I didn't go down a dark path and numb my pain and suffering with drugs or alcohol.

I knew I could sell my body for cash. I'd been approached by more pimps than I cared to admit in my nineteen years, but after the abuse I'd lived through, the mere thought made my mouth fill with a sour taste and the need to vomit.

Slowly, I breathed through the sludge invading my thoughts and focused on the travelers. One beautiful woman stuck out like a beacon of light in an unrelenting sea of nothingness.

She was petite, definitely of Asian descent and had perfectly lined dark eyes that drew attention to her elegant features. The woman had long black hair that she'd slicked back into a severe ponytail, the length running down her spine like a silky ribbon. She wore a winter-white suit that had me wondering how she kept it from getting dirty. Her lips were painted a bright cherry red that demanded attention.

I took in my mark, wishing I could be like her. Live a life where I paraded through an airport looking like a million dollars, not a care in the world. What would that be like? To be so beautiful and poised that people were drawn to you like moths to a flame? I sure as hell was as I followed her through the airport determining what I could pilfer that might go unnoticed long enough for me to get the hell out of Dodge.

Then she entered the bathroom. Bingo. Bathrooms were a hotspot for a girl like me. A lot of people left their belongings right out in the open, across from where they used the toilet. People were so stupid sometimes. I couldn't imagine trusting perfect strangers with my things while I sat behind a flimsy door.

Wisely, my mark took her rolling luggage into the space with her. But that didn't mean everyone had. I spied a plain black suitcase in the corner of the room across from one of the stalls. As patrons washed their hands, I waited and watched until the ones who had been at the sinks left. Then I curled my hand around the suitcase and walked right out of the bathroom with it. I sure hoped it had electronic devices and jewelry instead of just clothing and regular toiletries. I could have used some deodorant though. I'd run out of the free one I'd gotten from the gospel mission downtown.

On quick feet, I pushed through the patrons until I made my way outside. I'd need to score something expensive if I was to hock enough stuff to pay for room and board the next couple days. The last thing I wanted was to stay at the shelter again. Not that it was horrible, but it was only one step above the streets, and if I didn't get there in time, all of the beds would be taken. I needed a hot shower and a place I could wash the few outfits I hauled around. I hadn't had a full night's rest in at least a week and it was showing in the way I was grifting. Usually when I visited the airport, I'd have a pocket full of cash. Except the two wallets I'd stolen had only contained a few bucks. Not enough to score me a day or more in a one-star hotel.

As I scanned the ground transportation pick-up line, I laid eyes on the woman in white. She stood with her phone in her hand, a cool pair of expensive sunglasses perched on her pert nose. That's when I noticed the diamond-encrusted watch on her wrist. It was loose enough I'd be able to flick that latch and have it off her and in my pocket in less than a few seconds.

My heart hammered against my ribcage and the guilt and shame rose through my chest as I approached.

I didn't want to steal from her.

But I had to.

A diamond watch equaled a bed and a hot shower probably for a whole week. Maybe two depending on whether or not it was a name brand. Which it had to be. The woman oozed money from her pristine suit and makeup all the way to her red-bottomed shoes, which I'd caught a glimpse of while she rolled her ankle and readjusted her footing where she stood waiting for a car. Probably a limo.

Just as I suspected, a white limo slowed in front of the woman. My timing would need to be perfect. Picking up speed, I rolled the stolen piece of luggage her way. When I got close, I bumped into her back with my shoulder. She spun to the side, and I was there, as planned, to grab hold of her wrist. With my finger, I flicked the latch and let gravity do its job, as she fell backward. Since I'd done this move a hundred times before, I braced her shoulders with my free arm and pocketed the watch at the same time with my other.

"Oh, shoot!" I yelped to make it look real as I hauled her back to her feet where she teetered on those high heels.

Her glasses slipped off her face, but she caught them with a catlike reflex in midair. "Merci," she spoke in a cultured French accent I hadn't expected. "I mean, thank you, dear," she reverted to English.

"Uh, sure, no problem. Take care." I turned around to make my escape, but was thwarted when a cool hand encircled my wrist.

"I'm sorry, but I do believe you have something that belongs to me." Her voice was direct and brooked no argument.

Fear prickled against the back of my neck and my hands went clammy. "Um, no, I think you must be mistaken." *I looked around aimlessly for effect.*

The woman's lips twitched into a smirk. "Dear one, I know when I've been stolen from. Had you not scratched my wrist when you unlatched the watch, you may have fooled me. Alas, I am not an easy target."

My entire body went ice cold, goosebumps skittering along my skin. Today was the day I'd get taken to jail. And based on the value of the watch I'd stolen, I'd be looking at a felony.

I was going to end up in prison. I'd never survive.

Panicked, I yanked the watch out of my pocket and shoved it in front of her face. "Please, ma'am. Take it back. I'm sorry. I just needed a place to stay tonight and a watch like this goes for a lot. Please don't call the cops," I pleaded, tears filling my eyes and falling down my cheeks.

She took the watch, returned it to her wrist, and tilted her head. She assessed me—from the uneven, shaggy lengths of my dirty hair to my beat-up sneakers with a hole where my big toe was pushing through. They were too small, but they were all I had.

"Get in the car." She gestured to the limo.

I looked around and thought about running for it. Leaving the suitcase and bolting as fast as my skinny legs could take me.

"If you run, I'll just have my driver chase you. He's an expert at retrieving things."

A huge, muscular white guy with a barrel chest and a sour expression stood right behind me. He looked very capable of being able to do any manner of physical things, especially catching a hungry pickpocket with very little muscle mass to speak of.

I got into the limo and scrambled to the side. The driver put my pilfered luggage in the trunk along with the woman's things.

She entered smoothly and her driver shut the door. Her onyx-colored gaze set upon me, and I felt like a bug under a microscope about to be dissected.

"What is your name?" she asked.

"Are you taking me to the cops?" I asked, ignoring her question.

She shook her head. "No. I'm taking you to the hotel where I have my offices."

"Why?" I croaked, wondering what it meant that she was taking me to her workplace. Which happened to be a hotel.

"Because you said you needed a place to stay tonight. I'm in the position to provide you with one." She smiled primly.

"I don't understand. Why would you help me when I just tried to steal from you?" I frowned.

The woman adjusted the watch I'd tried to steal and smiled almost sweetly. "Let's just say I've been in your position before. The kindness of a stranger can go a long way. Now what is your name?"

"Maia." I cleared my throat. "Maia Fields."

"Nice to meet you, Maia. You can call me Madam Alana."

The slamming of the door on the toilet stall next to me snapped me out of the reverie. I stared down at the wallet I'd taken off Mr. Salt & Pepper.

Rhodes Davenport was his name.

Address on his ID stated Los Angeles, California. Must be here on business or pleasure. Though I never understood why anyone wanted to come to Las Vegas for pleasure. It was a shit hole. A place where people lost their houses and college funds for their kids, all in the hopes of winning big. There was a saying in Vegas: The house always wins. And it did. It was fact, and yet people came to Sin City by the droves, desperate to change their lives for the better.

Never happened, but they kept coming.

I scanned the rest of the info on the card. He was thirty-eight years old, six feet even, and two hundred and twenty pounds. He had several credit cards I didn't care about, including a fancy-ass black American Express. Those meant the guy I'd grifted from was obscenely wealthy. Only people that had bookoo bucks had one of those. It was like finding a unicorn. I could easily rob this man for thousands and he'd likely not even notice. Then I thought back to the bratty-ass daughter with him. She'd been a piece of work. Demanding he carry her bags, talking to him in that bitchy tone I noticed spoiled teens often used.

The fact that he even cared should have meant something to her.

And then I'd swooped in and had taken his wallet and phone. Goddamn. It suddenly made me feel like shit. He'd been super sweet to me too. He'd worried I'd been hurt when I was the one who'd created the entire incident in order to steal from him. I looked in the long space that held cash. It was loaded with green bills. A few hundreds, a couple fifties, and a wad of twenties. I pocketed the cash and left the rest.

I'd give it back. The phone, too, even though it would have scored me a couple hundred with my contact.

I fought with myself internally as I watched Rhodes from a distance, speaking with his daughter at the baggage carousel and then walking outside.

If I was going to let my conscience lead, I needed to move now. I approached the teenager who'd just gotten off the phone.

"Hey, um, I ran into your dad earlier and he dropped these." I handed her the phone and wallet.

"Ugh, he's so dumb. How could he lose his wallet and phone at the same time?" Her expression twisted into an ugly one that did nothing for her natural beauty.

"Stranger things have happened. Besides, he was making sure I was okay. He blocked my fall and ended up slamming into the concrete. If you'd been with him, you might have seen it. He was a real hero. Prevented me from getting hurt," I added for some insane reason, talking him up to his kid.

Why was I defending my mark?

I was losing it. Must have been. It was the only explanation.

"A hero? My Dad? Pffftttt. Hardly. He never does anything that isn't work related. Unless he's trying to annoy me." She sighed dramatically and wrapped a long curl of blonde hair around her finger.

"Maybe he just wants to connect with you?" I asked flippantly.

What. The. Fuck.

I was getting too involved. I needed to shut this down ASAP.

"Well, anyway, please give him my best," I blathered and turned around, crashing right into the man himself.

"Christ!" he cursed as I stomped fully on his foot while his hands curled around my shoulders, holding me in place.

I tried to push around him, but he held on tight.

"You, again! Where the hell is my wallet, you little thief!" he barked.

"Dad, it's right here. You dropped your phone and your wallet." His daughter yanked me out of his hold. "Relax. Jeez. She was just returning them."

"Oh." He held his hands in the air palms up in supplication, and I slid to the side. "I'm sorry, I didn't know."

He also didn't know I'd taken all his cash—not a small amount—so I needed to skedaddle quickly.

"No harm, no foul, right?" I repeated the weird phrase he'd said to me earlier. I pointed to the carousel that only had a few bags left on it. "I think your bags made it out," I noted.

When both of them turned around to check, I bolted.

"Hey, come back!" he called out, his voice spreading like an echo through the large open space and drifting away the farther I ran.

That shit had been too close.

Why the hell did I go back to return what I'd stolen?

Maybe Madam Alana was right. I was developing a conscience after years of grifting. It was time I made a big change. She'd been asking me to be a candidate for The Marriage Auction for years. I think the time had come.

I pulled out my personal phone from a small hidden pack around my waist and dialed her number. She answered on the first ring.

"Maia, are you okay, dear?"

"I'll do it. Put me in the auction this time around." I gulped as the idea of marrying someone made me break out into a cold sweat.

"You're sure?" she clarified.

"No, but it's the best option I have."

Episode 7

Be Careful What You Wish For

JULIANNE

"If you don't put me in the next auction, Alana, I'll go to Angus," I threatened through the phone line.

"You wouldn't dare. Your mother would roll over in her grave, *chéri*. May she rest in peace," Alana's familiar cultured voice warned.

I inhaled sharply at the mention of my mother, that wound still too fresh only three months after the crash. "They've gone too far," I whispered.

"Just give it time, *ma petite fleur,*" *my little blossom,* she cooed. Usually when I spoke to Alana, she'd give me the best advice and counsel me on how to maneuver a difficult situation, especially in the business world, but this was different.

This was personal.

"You are not listening! She's destroyed *everything*. My brother, my position in the company…*Gio*?" I gulped down the emotion twisting my gut every time I thought of the one man I could never have. My brother's ex-best friend and current business partner, Giovanni "Gio" Falco. So much had changed since our parents had died in that plane, Giovanni's parents flying with them and also perishing. But that wasn't what broke us. That was all her—Bianca.

"I will admit to being surprised at the sudden announcement of Brenden and Bianca's nuptials in light of her having been Giovanni's fiancé only a short time before. That, my dear, says a lot more about her character than it ever would about Gio."

"And my brother? He stole his best friend's fiancée right out from under his nose! Gio's crushed, Alana. Annihilated. He hasn't been to the office in months. I've done the best I could, but when my brother brought me into that meeting and asked me to step down as Vice President of FM Enterprises so that his new wife, Bianca, could step into my shoes, I lost it."

"*Chéri.*" Her words were tinged with sorrow.

If anyone could understand what I was going through, it was Alana. She was my godmother, after all. More importantly, one of my mother's closest friends and confidants throughout the many years they'd known one another.

"My entire life is wrapped up in the company, Alana. It is my birthright. Ever since I was a little girl, it's all I wanted to do. Work the family business, right alongside my parents and their best friends. It's what I went to college for. What I devoted every hour of my life to since I graduated six years ago. I built up the clients to what they are today, and my parents knew that."

"I know. And I can understand your anger with them not leaving you a percentage of the company," Alana agreed.

"Brenden and Gio were supposed to take over in a few years as CEO and CFO when our parents retired. I was their VP. *Me.* The person who trained her entire life for the role. And then hurricane Bianca rolls in and poof! My brother fucks over his best friend. Giovanni hasn't been seen anywhere. All four of our parents are dead. And my brother is married to a viper. A heartless, cutthroat bitch who everyone thinks is an angel." I pressed my thumb and forefinger to my temples as I paced my high-rise apartment in Manhattan, located walking distance from our corporate headquarters.

"What is your plan, Julianne? Enter into the auction for what purpose?" Alana asked, intrigue threaded through her tone.

I stopped pacing and grinned. I could hear in her voice that she was going to help me. Alana was nothing if not dependable. Plus, she was the most impressive business-woman I knew. Once she understood the position I was in, she would do as I asked. I just needed to tread lightly.

"You know my entire portfolio of investments is locked in FM Enterprises. Most of my money. I'm not about to sell my interest, *my birthright*, to a stranger. That's not what my parents would have wanted. But since Brenden and Gio are technically the co-owners per our parents' will, I need to find a way to get back on top."

"And how do you propose to do that, *chéri*?" Alana asked.

"First step is to hook me a bidder for millions of dollars. I'll use that money to start up a competing business. One that—if things go as planned—FM Enterprises can buy into later or absorb into our larger umbrella."

"And how would things go as planned?"

"Eventually, I'll get Brenden to see who Bianca really is and what she's done to our family. My hope is that one day he will figure out Bianca is nothing but a backstabbing, conniving, heartless wretch who needs to be kicked to the curb, not worshipped on a pedestal like some Greek goddess. And then he'll come crawling back to me for help."

"You could sell the estate," she countered.

"I can't believe you'd suggest such a thing." I choked on my reply. Alana knew what my parents' home meant to our family. It was where we'd lived and loved. Where Brenden and I grew up. Where our parents came up with the very idea to start FM Enterprises. Together. Two sets of best friends going into business. Falco and Myers. Putting their money together and creating magic. I'd never sell it. Not in a million years. One day I wanted to bring my own child home from the hospital to that house. I couldn't fathom losing the one place in all the world I felt safe.

It was my home, even though I hadn't been there since the funeral reception.

"Jules, I know you miss your parents." Her voice lowered to one fueled by grief. "I do too. But do you truly believe starting a war with your brother instead of reasoning with him is the best action?"

"Alana, he's left me no choice. We fought. I ripped into him for what he did to Gio. And then I told him how horrible Bianca was to me. How she was going to ruin everything we'd built. He f-fired me. Told me his lawyers would be in touch regarding buying out my shares. I told him to fuck off and I'd see him in court." I swallowed down the hurt as Brenden's scathing words saturated my memory.

"Bianca is twice the woman you could ever hope to be. Get out of my company and get out of my life. You're not wanted here, Julianne."

A tear fell down my cheek and I wiped it away, right alongside every last one of my dreams for the future. I had to pave a new path. One of my own choosing. And I needed to be smart. Stealthy.

"I'm so sorry. Do you want me to reach out to him?" she offered, as I'd suspected she might.

"No! He can't know what I'm doing," I growled.

"Why? Are you embarrassed?" Alana struck gold.

"That I'm asking my godmother to put me in one of her clandestine auctions so that I can score a rich husband? I'll let you think on that for a second," I scoffed.

"You know the answer to that question, *chéri*. Do not play coy with me," she chastised, and instantly I felt my cheeks flush with shame. Alana was not the enemy. That position was reserved for my asshole brother. Without Alana, I might not have existed at all.

"Julianne, I need to know that you genuinely want this if I'm to even consider your involvement. Once you sign, there's no going back. You will be married to a man sight unseen for three years. That man could up and whisk you away to Timbuktu. When you're the candidate, you go where the bidder demands."

"Then I'll run my new business from Timbuktu. I'm resourceful," I fired back.

Besides, part of my larger plan was to take every last client I'd brought in to FM Enterprises and bring them over to my new business. If I crippled my family's bottom line, Brenden would have no choice but to grovel at my feet. I could easily do both of those things from anywhere. All I needed was an Internet connection and a phone.

"And why do you need the money? I know your parents not only left you their estate but investments, stocks, bonds, life insurance…"

"I'm contesting the will. Everything is on pause. That means I get nothing from their estate until we've gone through the legal proceedings."

"*Chéri*, I wish you'd discussed this with me prior to acting. Fighting a legal battle with your own brother? This is not how healthy familial relationships are made."

My heart sank because she was right. Alana was always right. And yet I knew I had to do something in order to work this thorn that was Bianca out of our lives forever. And that would take time and money. The first of which I now had seeing as I wouldn't be working in the office. The second I'd get from the auction to implement my plan.

"Julianne, there's more to the contract than just a simple 'I do.' You'll also be expected to willingly share your body. All marriages must be *consummated* within two weeks of the wedding. The ceremony must take place, and the marriage certificate signed by an officiant no more than thirty days after the contract is signed. Do you understand what I'm saying? You will not fully be your own person any longer. You will be one half of a couple. A married couple."

I didn't exactly love the idea of becoming intimate with a stranger, but it's not like I was scared of the idea. I'd had plenty of casual hookups. Sex was sex. I had a healthy libido. It was something everyone needed to take the edge off. At least in my experience. Aside from my first sexual encounter, which I'd locked away in a vault within my mind and would not be spending time thinking about.

"And what does Giovanni think about all of this?" she asked, speaking of the devil, the one person I'd been praying she wouldn't bring up.

My nostrils flared at the thought of Gio, and I fisted my hands, desperate to hold back my anger.

"How should I know? I told you, he hasn't been seen since everything went down. The night he found Bianca fucking my brother, you know, the day before he was supposed to marry the wicked witch of the West, he walked away and never came back. No one's heard from him. I tried his penthouse in New York, even got the manager to do a wellness check. He wasn't there. His assistant is the only one who knows anything about him and she's not sharing. Apparently, he threatened to remove her from her position if she did."

"*Mon Dieu*," *My God*, Alana fretted.

"Yeah. I'm all alone."

All alone.

I closed my eyes and shivered as the realization hit me as fast as a car going fifty miles per hour. Everything I'd ever known was gone. All that I worked for these twenty-nine years, gone the moment my parent's charter plane crashed into the side of a mountain overlooking the Swiss Alps.

And then there was Gio. I couldn't allow myself to think

about him or our past. I'd spent years getting over what happened between me and my brother's ex-best friend. Besides Alana and my therapist, I'd never told a single soul. And I never would. He didn't remember it anyway.

"You're never alone, *chéri*. You will always have me," Alana vowed with a confidence I believed.

And I did have her. She'd been a kind, intelligent, and compassionate presence in my life. I didn't see her regularly or often, but she'd always been available when I called. And she'd visited our family throughout the years when her schedule permitted. Alana even attended my high school graduation party and then again when I graduated with my bachelor's. She also sent me two dozen roses and a pair of diamond earrings when I secured my MBA from Columbia University. Alana was like extended family who lived abroad. You didn't see them all the time, but you loved them from afar and gloried in the time you had with them when you had it.

"Then prove it. Put me in the next auction. Help me secure my future. You did it for my mother all those years ago. Until she died, she was the happiest woman in the world. She'd lived her dream life until it was cut short at the young age of fifty-two. Help me find my happily ever after, Alana. Please."

"Julianne…"

"*Please*," I begged, desperation coating my plea.

"I'll do it." Alana sighed deeply.

I let out the breath I was holding. Three years of being married to a wealthy man would be nothing. I'd spent more years as an undergrad striving for a perfect GPA. I could be a doting wife while I built my new empire and got my revenge on my brother.

"On one condition." Her response was ominous.

"And that would be?"

"A private auction. Held immediately following my scheduled event in two weeks' time. There will be no more than five bidders. All personally chosen by me. And you will agree to marry whoever is the highest bidder, *chéri*. Sight unseen, just like everyone else. Alas, as your godmother and a dear friend to your parents, I have a vested interest in your happiness and well-being. Therefore, I will choose wisely."

"Fine," I agreed instantly. "I trust you to put my wishes and desires at the forefront of your process."

"Be careful what you wish for, *ma petite fleur*. You just may get it."

Episode 8

Save My Seat

GIOVANNI

Grief was a fickle thing. One minute, I would be completely fine, going about my day-to-day activities as I would any other time. Then I'd catch a scent on the breeze, see a happy couple smiling in a frame on my bookcase, and I would be reminded of what I'd lost. When that moment hit, it was like I'd been gut-punched. My stomach would tighten, abdominals flexing against the invisible intruder. The rest of my body would realize something was amiss and would react accordingly. A sudden ache would throb against my temples. Deep, unending fatigue would coalesce in my veins, a sorrow-filled cocktail of sadness and emptiness.

Everything just felt *heavy.*

Before my parents left this earth just under three months ago, I would have said I had the perfect family. A stunning fiancée I was head over heels in love with. A best friend I could count on for anything. Extended members of my familial circle, a successful empire, and more money than I could ever spend in one lifetime.

Now, I had nothing.

All of it, gone.

I'd thought losing my parents in that plane crash was the worst thing that could have ever happened to me.

Wrong.

The final blow had been finding my best friend in the entire world fucking my fiancée the night of our rehearsal dinner. A dinner that was already grief-stricken because our parents—mine and my best friend's—weren't in attendance after perishing together.

That was the day I knew that none of it mattered. All I'd worked for was gone. The years I'd spent building unshakable trust in a person *obliterated*. Brenden was not only my partner in business, he'd also been a man I thought of as a brother. We'd been through school, family gatherings, birthdays, holidays, and heartbreak together.

All for what?

Then there was Bianca. When we met, I'd been convinced she was a unicorn. An ethereal creature who'd entered my life on a rainbow of color. Beautiful, intelligent, sexy as sin, and great in bed. From the first day I'd been taken by her charms. Befuddled into believing I was her everything. The voodoo that woman pulled over me was unmatched by any cutthroat businessperson I'd faced before. She chopped up my heart with a machete and never looked back.

The wound Brenden and Bianca created in my soul might never close. It went that deep. Festering and puss filled. I prodded at it often. Tortured myself with thoughts of what might have been if my parents hadn't died. Would she and Brenden have betrayed me otherwise? How long had they been seeing one another behind closed doors with me none the wiser?

All of these questions, however, didn't mean shit. Especially once the two eloped shortly after Bianca was supposed to marry me. I'd given that woman eighteen months of my life. Asked her to be my wife on our first anniversary. We were to be wed six months later. But the night before...

I slammed my hand down on the desk before me, forcing myself to push the nasty thoughts aside. As I rubbed at my throbbing temples, a soft knock rattled against the door before Muriel, my assistant, popped her gray-haired head in.

"Mr. Falco, I'm sorry to interrupt, but I've got an urgent message for you from a woman named Alana Toussaint."

I frowned hearing the name. Alana was a family friend of Lewis and Rachel Myers, Brenden and Julianne's parents who'd died right alongside my parents. *Best friends for life,* they'd always said. Even in the end that held true. Unfortunately, the same didn't hold for the relationships their children had built.

"What's the message, Muriel?"

"It was kind of cryptic actually. She simply said to check your email, and upon receiving it to enter a code that she's texting to your phone. Claims it's information you and only you need to see." She shrugged.

I sighed, my bones feeling weighed down as I slumped back into my leather chair.

"Thank you. I'll take a look." I waved Muriel off and she slipped out of my home office at the lake house, where I'd been holding court and hiding for the better part of two months.

Sometimes I'd sit in the library, reading through tome after tome until I'd lose myself in another world. It was easier than facing reality. Other times I'd set myself up in the small kitchen nook while my chef prepped meals. Having people around who I trusted to keep my whereabouts a secret was imperative. My staff was also amazing at coexisting without endless unnecessary small talk. I wanted to be around people—I was a human who needed the presence of others—but not the kind that was overwhelmingly in my face. Just gentle sharing of space was what I expected, and my assistant, my chef, my personal trainer, and housekeeper understood that need. Besides, the house on Saranac Lake in upstate New

York, was massive and had a guest house with several rooms for the people I've allowed into my circle of grief.

I didn't know who I was anymore, and I needed the time and space to figure it out. Everything I'd known and understood to my core about where my life was headed and who would travel that path by my side had been shaken. Destroyed by the worst possible betrayal I could have ever imagined.

Not in a million years would I have believed that Brenden could be capable of such deception. And after the loss of our parents?

The fury, hurt, and disgust reared its ugly head, distracting me once more from the world around me. Until I heard a soft ping come from my cell phone.

I picked it up and glanced at the message. It was from Alana and simply stated JULIANNE.

Why the hell would she put Julianne's name as a password?

Julianne was Brenden's younger sister. A woman I admired and respected. She was an incredibly savvy business-woman who knew the real estate sector inside and out. Her gifts with human resources and bringing in multimillion-dollar clientele were second to none. Not to mention she was funny. Almost cute with her zany, slapstick-style humor. Julianne also happened to be drop-dead gorgeous. Natural red hair that fell in thick waves around her porcelain-white skin. The freckles, though, stole my breath. Ever since I was a teenager, I'd had a crush on my best friend's little sister, but she was the epitome of off-limits.

Brenden had made it clear that his sister was not a romantic option. He'd drawn a hard line, and I wasn't to cross it. I think Brenden and I were about fifteen and Julianne thirteen when I really started to see her differently. Brenden started noticing the longing stares I'd give Jules. How I'd tease her endlessly about her freckles even though I wanted nothing more than to play connect the dots across them with my lips. Pay homage to every sprinkle and dot across her pert nose. Run my fingers through that mass of silky, fiery strands.

Julianne represented the one thing I could never have. And because I was a genuine guy, a true best friend to Brenden, I'd pushed my interest aside. Fell in and out of relationships with women over the years like any young man. Until Bianca.

Bianca had swooped into my life and taken it over. I'd been smitten with her. I would have done just about anything to see her happy and now that was Brenden's job. He'd stolen her right out from under me.

My blood boiled as I glared at the message on my phone, considering just calling Alana and getting to the bottom of whatever it was she wanted to share. And yet something told me to open the email first. Evaluate the information and then make the call.

I opened my laptop, signed into my email, and waited while the damn thing presented the hundreds of messages I'd ignored over the past couple months while I was lost to my grief.

The top email was from Alana Toussaint. I clicked on it and read the paragraph.

Giovanni,

I'm deeply sorry to intrude on your time away. I understand and share in the great loss you've experienced. However, a situation has come to my attention I knew you'd want to be apprised of. As you know, I run The Marriage Auction. A candidate has entered who I cannot turn away for reasons that are my own. I will be hosting a private, five-bidder auction in two weeks' time. Please review the attached candidate information.

Shall I save you a seat as one of the bidders?
Alana Toussaint

Was she delusional? The woman and her husband had been invited to my wedding to Bianca, for crying out loud. How dare she drive a knife into my heart by suggesting I'd want to bid on a new bride. And so quickly after what she knew had been a horrifying betrayal?

"The nerve," I sneered as I clicked on the attachment.

A pop-up box demanding a password appeared on the screen. I ground down on my teeth as I typed JULIANNE in all caps the same way it was displayed in her message.

Instantly a headshot of Julianne Myers covered my entire screen with the words *New Candidate Entered Into Private Auction* typed above her head.

The fuck?

I snatched my phone up from where I set it on the desk, scrolled through my contacts, and dialed her number. She answered on the first ring.

"*Bonjour,* Gio," Alana greeted in that melodic French lilt.

"What the fuck are you trying to pull sending me this?" I snapped.

"Ah, I can hear in the tone of your voice you have reviewed my email, *oui?*"

"Yeah, I got your fucking message. What kind of shit is this?"

"I'm afraid what you see is what you get, *chéri.* I couldn't turn her away."

"You're her godmother, for Christ's sake. You own the auction. Of course you can turn her ass away. You just say no! Or in a language perhaps you understand better, *putain non!*" *Fuck no!* I said in French to make my point crystal clear.

"You are angry," she surmised.

"Yeah, I'm furious. What were you thinking?" I barked.

"Darling, I understand your frustration as it is shared by two. However, Julianne is her own person with her own mind. And she's made hers up."

I opened my mouth, closed it, opened it again, and

growled. "*Alana*," I grated and took a full, deep breath in to calm my wrath. "You cannot agree to this. She's pulling something."

"This I know. Our Julianne is a spitfire. She's also very convincing," Alana explained gently.

"Pull her ass out!" I demanded.

"*Je suis désolé mon cher.*" *I'm sorry, dear.* "It is done. Julianne will be sold to the highest bidder in two weeks' time. I have saved you a very coveted seat. When the waitlist of suitors saw *ma petite fleur,* my little blossom, they went into a frenzy. Many know exactly who Julianne is and the reputation she will bring as a wife. I'll leave you to your thoughts. It was good talking to you. Ta-ta for now. *Au revoir.*" *Goodbye,* she finished and then promptly hung up.

I sat very still, Julianne's beloved face plastered across my laptop screen.

My Julianne.

The childhood partner in crime I'd climbed trees with alongside her brother.

The friend I'd shared my fears and woes with.

The girl I'd experienced my first kiss with, out on the docks at the very lake house I was hiding in.

The eighteen-year-old I'd deflowered on the best night of my life. One I later had pretended not to remember.

I'd shoved that experience so deep into Pandora's box over the past eleven years, I was surprised when shame rose to the surface along with the sweet memory of our single night together.

Julianne was going to allow herself to be purchased in The Marriage Auction. Be bid on by strangers. My mouth dried out and bile rose up my throat.

"Over my dead fucking body," I swore to myself.

I hit the response button on the email and typed out a three-word reply.

Save my seat.

Episode 9

Coincidence or Fate

MEMPHIS

I tossed and turned all night, thoughts of Naomi keeping me awake.

Her gorgeous smile.

The way her eyes sparkled like black diamonds when she laughed.

How she constantly crossed and recrossed her long-as-hell beautiful legs.

Our kiss.

That kiss had been one for the memory books. I replayed it so many times I eventually had to take matters into my own hand and tug one out. It's the only reason I even caught a solid hour of sleep.

I had no business carrying on with a woman like that when I was about to put myself up for auction to the highest bidder. And yet I couldn't find it within me to feel too broken up about it. I couldn't believe I'd kissed her like that. What a player move.

I'd had the best date of my life. If one could call it that. I guess a better term would be the best non-date I'd ever had.

Damn, Naomi was everything, absolutely *everything* I'd ever wanted in a woman romantically. She was funny. Cool as a cucumber when she needed to be. Smokin' hot. A body that could make a grown ass man beg on his knees to worship. And smart. So fucking smart. She had a quick wit that I couldn't match but loved verbally sparring with all the same.

If the circumstances had been different, I'd be calling her the second I opened my eyes. Not letting the grass grow under my feet, as my granny would put it. Not that I'd gotten her number. I'd known better. If she'd given me the ability to reach her, I might have taken her up on it. Cancelled all that I'd committed to and ruined everything I'd been working toward. And for what? The hint of a possibility at a romantic future together? It wasn't enough.

I needed a big payday. My family needed it even more. Much of my family's future success depended on my ability to help offset college fees. Sure, my little sister had applied for scholarships and had secured a few thousand here and there. But I wanted the best possible start for her. My mother and father had worked themselves to the bone to give us kids a good chance at a strong, prosperous future but it was nowhere near enough monetarily.

Now, I myself had never been a 4.0 type of student. But what I'd lacked in grades I made up for through skill and talent on the field. All that crashed and burned when I got hurt. Technically I only had a few more college credits to get in order to be a college graduate, and could start as low man on the roster in some corporate office that I'd hate, but it wouldn't make me happy. It wouldn't pay the tuition for Paris who'd been accepted into Harvard of all fuckin' places.

And boy, was I proud of her for making that dream come true. My sister had set her sights on Harvard before she'd even graduated the eighth grade. She'd been committed to the idea of going to that particular school and no other would do. She was even willing to go into hundreds of thousands of dollars' worth of school debt in order to live that dream. My parents were talking about taking a second mortgage on their small home to help.

Me and Sydney and Paris had had a meeting about that suggestion and immediately tossed the idea right out the window. Between the twenty thousand Paris had been able to get in scholarship monies from different organizations and the ten thousand she was able to get in government grants, she was still about twenty-five thousand shy of the fifty-three thousand per year tuition. And that did not include monthly living expenses, books, food, incidentals, and more. Sydney was going to pony up a couple thousand a month for rent, food, and a bus pass, but Paris was still going to have to get a job. Even then she'd still be looking at going into tens of thousands of dollars' worth of debt per year. And that was just for undergrad. My baby sis wanted to be an attorney.

Odessa, my twenty-year-old sister, was currently up to her eyeballs in debt from nursing school and worked a million hours a week as a Certified Nursing Assistant while continuing school and living at home. It was ridiculous.

The system we had in America was jacked. If you wanted to make something of yourself, you had to go into decades' worth of debt to achieve it. How did that make any sense?

My plan had been to go pro. Pay for all my siblings' school needs so they could be something without the weight of debt hanging around their necks. And it was within my reach, too. Or it had been. Now I was putting up my body for sale in a different way, but with the same hopes for a high payout.

Three million would be put to great use, that was for sure. I could pay Paris's and Odessa's school tuition and room and board. Pay off the remainder of my parents' house. Sock away a good chunk for their retirement. And set up a couple high-earning college plans for Holland and Cheyenne who were still in high school. The rest I'd invest in myself. Figure out what the hell I wanted to do as an ex-baller whose only talent lay on the field.

Football was all I knew.

Hell, maybe being a kept man living under a rich-as-fuck wife's thumb could teach me a few things about the business world. Lord knows I had zero experience in the corporate sector. Either way, first step was to secure myself a wife.

Groaning, I pulled myself to a seated position on the bed, sloughing off the covers with a deep sigh I felt to my core. Thoughts of what Naomi might be feeling this morning invaded my subconscious.

I shook my head and rubbed at my tight-cropped hair, scratching my dome. "Memphis, you have no business thinking about Naomi. Nothing good will come of it," I reminded myself as I stood and stretched my arms above my head.

First things first: coffee. Then I'd hit the shower.

With more effort than should have been needed, I pushed all thoughts of last night and the most captivating woman I'd ever met to the farthest reaches of my mind, intent on focusing all my energy on what was happening today.

Today was Day 1 of the auction process.

I'd been through this part once before. Madam Alana would have each candidate review the contract for the final time, sign across the dotted line, and then be taken to the Candidates' Room where I'd meet the others.

A pang of sadness prodded at my chest. The last time I was in that position I'd made friends. Lifelong friends. Faith, Ruby, Savannah, even ball-bustin' Dakota, though she'd never admit it. I still had Jade, which helped. Though she wasn't putting herself in the auction, instead learning the art of the auction as Alana's protégé, I still would miss her company on the other side. Then again, maybe I wouldn't be the only man in the bunch this time. That could be cool.

"Yeah, Memphis, focus on the positive," I spoke out loud to my empty hotel room as I made my way to the shower.

I scrubbed every inch of my skin, allowing the heat and steam of the hot water to work the tension out of my shoulders. When I was done, I exited a new man.

Brilliant what a hot shower could do for the psyche.

I stared at my large frame in the mirror's reflection. I was built. Took impeccable care of myself even after the injury. I'd treat whoever chose me like a true queen. Ever since I was a little boy I wanted to be married and have a big-ass family just like my own. I worshipped the very ground my father walked on. A vet and later a man who drove giant semi-trucks, ensuring people got the food or products they needed to have a good life. At least that was how he put it. He even took me on the road with him once. It was hard, often boring work. Sitting behind the wheel for hours on end, trying to occupy your own mind. But my father never complained. Not a single day in his life. He thought if he was making a living that provided for his family, he was doing what he was supposed to. And it would have set him up for life had he not gotten in that accident. His semi jackknifing across the interstate and plowing into concrete girders during a freak snow storm the likes the South hadn't seen in decades.

He lost all he'd worked for in that accident. His ability to walk normally. To drive a truck again. His full pension, because he was just shy of hitting the vested limit when the accident happened. Almost lost his life too. Sometimes I see that look in his eye where the darkness comes in, rearing its ugly head and whispering nasty things into his ear. Things like his family would have been better off if he'd died because we'd have gotten a life insurance policy.

I heard him say those words to my mother in the kitchen late one night when I was supposed to be in bed. It was only the one time and the words had ripped me to shreds. Did the same to my momma too because she smacked his ass silly.

Right in the face. Pointed that finger at him and made him swear he would never leave her on purpose. Reminded him that they'd taken vows to be with one another through sickness and in health and by Lord he was not going to take the easy way out. Then she broke into tears and apologized for losing her mind and laying a hand on him. He just shook his head and did something I didn't think he was capable of. I watched my father drop his head, wrap his arms around my mother, and cry into her chest, just like we did when we were hurt or needed our momma's love.

My father wasn't a crier. He could get a wet eye now and again, such as when he held one of my sisters when they'd been born, but on average, he was the very foundation our family counted on to keep us strong. He was the Jiminy Cricket encouraging us to do good, dream big, and be our best selves.

I admired the man more than anyone on this Earth. And I hoped in doing what I was about to do, that he'd eventually be proud. If I could help my family monetarily, pave the way for my sisters' successes, I too would feel worthy of his respect and praise.

When I lost the chance to go pro, I became adrift in an open sea of endless options. None of which I could grasp for myself. I didn't know what I wanted to do as a job. Wasn't even sure what I would be best qualified for. I was a twenty-four-year-old man who'd played football all his life, who was close to having a college degree in political science, and yet no prospects whatsoever for work. All I knew was that I needed to do something.

My family was counting on me.

I would not let them down a second time.

"I will be chosen tonight," I promised my reflection. "Whatever it takes, Memphis. You got this. Put it all out on the playing field and score that goal, get the golden trophy."

Or in this case, I was the *trophy*, and my ultimate prize

would be at least three million dollars and a rich wife.

I got dressed in a dark-navy suit with a crisp white button-down shirt that I thought complemented my features well. Naomi sure hadn't been able to keep her hands to herself.

Memories of her wrapping her pretty hands around my thigh trying to compare our quads was something I wouldn't forget any time soon.

Once I was finished getting ready, I tucked my wallet into my pocket along with my room key and headed to the bank of elevators at the end of the hall. I hit the button and waited for it to open.

I lost my breath, my entire body going solid once the double doors opened to the one person I wanted to see more than anyone, but also didn't want to see because of what I was about to do.

Naomi Shaw.

She looked up, her sexy mouth dropping open as those mesmerizing eyes sparkled.

"Well, I'll be damned. What a coincidence." She grinned coyly. Her body was wrapped in another body-hugging, absolutely stunning dress. This one a pristine white that offset her fawn-colored skin magically.

"Naw, I don't believe in coincidences." I stepped into the car, bringing my body closer to hers.

"No?" She swallowed visibly, taking a step back.

I shook my head and took another step forward, caging her against the back wall. I shouldn't have but I wasn't entirely in my right mind, my instincts raging with the desire to get closer. She pressed her small hands to my chest, the same way she had last night before she'd wrapped them around my neck—only this time it was to keep me at a distance.

"No, pretty lady, I don't believe in coincidences. I believe in fate. And that bitch has the worst timing ever."

Episode 10

Let Destiny Be the Driver

NAOMI

I couldn't believe my eyes when the man of my dreams entered the elevator.

I'd literally been dreaming of him all night. Our non-date yesterday had been the stuff of a fluffy, made-for-TV movie. And it all came crashing down when he'd admitted that he was waiting to meet his soon-to-be wife. Even though we'd continued our time together, cracking jokes and getting to know one another, it was all very innocent. Until of course that blistering, life-altering kiss. I'd never had a more bittersweet kiss because essentially it was a stolen moment never to be repeated. At least that's what I told myself every time I thought about Memphis while I got ready this morning.

And there he was. Looking magnificent in a midnight-colored suit and a pristine white dress shirt that made his dark skin glow in contrast.

"Well, I'll be damned. What a coincidence." I grinned, trying to play it cool.

"Naw, I don't believe in coincidences." He had plenty of

room to stand but chose to invade my personal space by stepping closer.

"No?" I swallowed and took a step back.

He stepped forward, coming so near that I instantly put both of my hands to his broad, muscular, brick-like chest. It was a valiant effort to keep him at a distance—something he was not having. My heartbeat sped up and my knees shook, but I wouldn't let him see the hurricane of emotions invading my mind and body.

"No, pretty lady, I don't believe in coincidences. I believe in fate. And that bitch has the worst timing ever," he grumbled, sounding put out.

"Oh, you think it's fate that you entered my elevator car this morning?" I asked, buying time so I could think of how to best respond.

My body wanted to wrap around this hunk of a man and give into the sexual chemistry coasting between us. Though my brain and heart knew better. There was a third person not invited to this party, and I would not be the reason a sister was brought low.

His nostrils flared, his breathing audible as he pressed even closer. I swear he became a fire-breathing dragon who'd cornered his prey and was about to feast. And I wanted that...*badly*. But I wouldn't give in.

I pushed more firmly against his chest. "What does your fiancée think about you talking to me about fate? I'd bet she'd be pretty pissed off if she knew her man was standing so close to another woman and looking at said woman as though he wanted to eat her whole and lick the bones clean." I showed my teeth on a hiss.

Memphis inhaled sharply, his wild gaze softening as he took a step back, and then another, and again until he was resting his body against the far wall.

I nodded curtly. "Smart move." I crossed my arms over one another. "So, when are you meeting up with the lucky lady?" I changed the subject to his woman. It was best for us both to remember that she existed and wasn't a figment of our imagination.

His jaw firmed and his lips compressed together. "Soon," he bit out, which was an interesting response from someone who would be seeing who I had to assume was the love of his life, the person he planned to commit his future to. I mean, he was marrying her after all.

The elevator dinged at the floor I needed. I made to leave but in the last moment I put my hand to the doors preventing them from closing and focused on the man who I had to let walk away.

"You know, Memphis, maybe instead of believing in fate, you should think about what your destiny entails."

"How do you mean?" His voice was a low rumble I wanted to listen to for eons.

"Well, I believe your destiny is what you make it. You drive where your destiny leads and there are many different paths you can take. There's choice in it. All the hills and valleys of your life are of your own making. I guess it's a matter of thinking. Do you want to drive toward your destiny or fall into your fate? One way or another, the choice is yours. I wish you all the blessings in your future marriage. Take care of yourself. You're one of the good ones." I winked and backed away, allowing the doors to close on a future that wasn't meant for me.

"Ms. Shaw?" a feminine voice spoke from behind me.

I turned around and was greeted by a young woman of Asian descent. She wore a perfectly tailored black suit jacket and short pleated skirt that showed off a nice pair of legs. She had her hair slicked back into a small bun at the nape of her neck, making her appearance a bit more severe.

She held her hand out. "I'm Jade Lee, Madam Alana's protégé. We have been expecting you."

I shook her cool hand and then followed her down a

corridor to a set of double doors. She opened one side and gestured for me to precede her.

Madam Alana was sitting at a glass desk wearing an eggplant-colored suit with a slim line of black satin edging the lapel. The purple tone was magic against her skin tone. She too had pitch-black hair but hers was parted straight down the center, the long lengths pressed behind her ears and lying in a flat sheet down her back. What I wouldn't give to have such ease with my hair. I, however, preferred the bigger-is-better approach and let my curls flow where they wanted to. Of course, I kept them in line with heaps of expensive hair product, but the fine results couldn't be denied.

I reached my hand over the desk, greeting the woman with a handshake.

"Pleased to meet you, Ms. Shaw. Please take a seat." Alana gestured to one of the empty chairs. When I'd chosen one, Jade sat in the other one, an electronic device in her lap.

I glanced at the woman and then at the Madam.

Madam Alana smiled coyly. "Jade is tutoring under me in order to learn the business. We are growing at an astronomical pace. There seems to be an increasing need for marriages of convenience these days."

"It's definitely not easy to meet the right person." I thought of my chance encounter with Memphis once more. If only…

"Let's get right to business, shall we?" She interlaced her fingers and rested her hands on her desk.

I nodded.

"You've been completely vetted and all background checks cleared as I suspected they would. Though I am rather surprised to see you show up at this auction and want in at the last minute. May I ask what drove you to come to Las Vegas and join my event?"

"Honestly, I've been kicked by another man I'd let in. Used up and spat out." I gritted my teeth.

"I can't imagine someone of your caliber would be left in the lurch," Madam Alana tutted.

"Here's the thing. I haven't told anyone I've dated recently how wealthy I am. Just that I work in the business of designing jewelry. Most men assume it is something I do as a side hustle. I simply never correct them."

"And this approach failed," Alana surmised accurately.

"Brutally. Painfully." I shook my head and sighed, the memories of my many failed attempts at finding a true partner destroyed repeatedly.

"I see. I'm sorry to hear of your unfortunate experiences. I can assure you that if you choose a husband tonight, you will have a man devoted to you and you alone. He will be your husband in all things. Travel with you as desired. Be faithful only to you. But I cannot promise love. That is something that you will have to nurture with the man you choose. If it is meant to be, it will be. Do you understand?"

I thought of Memphis and how I knew from one night together that I could fall so deeply in love with him that I'd never see the sun again. Hell, I'd live in the darkness to have a man like that call me his own.

"I need a partner. A man who I can bounce ideas off of. A person who works out and knows the value of keeping healthy. An active person who enjoys the outdoors. Someone protective and a little alpha in nature to help keep the creepers off me when I'm in public. I need to be his priority, but I won't take that for granted. I will listen to his interests and support his needs. I will be faithful and kind."

"And would you be interested in getting to know his family?" Alana surprised me with such a question though it made sense. If two strangers were to combine their lives as one, their families would be involved. My family would be an absolute nightmare to whomever I chose.

"I would be happy to engage with my future husband's family. I usually am well-liked by my significant other's family members. Unfortunately, the person I choose will not have the same experience. You know about my father." I lowered my face and stared intently into the Madam's eyes.

"I do. He is beloved by the players within his circle."

"Mmm-hmm," I chuffed. "There is a fine line between love and hate. Usually that line meets right in the center at fear."

The Madam's lips pressed together, but she kept perfectly poised. I expected nothing less. This was a woman who walked in every circle. I'd done my research on Alana Toussaint. Everyone seemed to know of her, but no one would say a single word about what she did. It took me digging into my friend Joel Castellanos's sudden marriage to a woman no one knew in order to learn about The Marriage Auction. And he'd been drunk when he'd provided the information, handing me a slim black card with her name and a phone number on the back. It had been very hush-hush and had intrigued me to no end.

"Do you think you have a candidate who would suit my expectations?" I asked.

Alana sat back in her chair and smirked. "I do."

I waited a full ten seconds while Alana stared me down. "I'm all ears," I stated.

Jade snickered and I turned my head sharply, gaze narrowed.

Her cheeks reddened. "I apologize," Jade said and then looked at Alana who cocked a single brow.

Madam Alana was everything I wanted to be in business. She gave very little away in her expressions and vocal intonation. A master at communication who always had the upper hand. Jade would learn a lot from a magnate like her.

"Darling, I do not matchmake, per se. I research and find willing candidates of marriageable age and circumstance. Every person is different. Each agree to the terms as set forth in the contracts I sent you a couple months ago. Did you read them?"

I had. They were lengthy and far more detailed than I'd expected. Even though the buyer was bidding and paying a hefty fee, the contracts protected the candidates as first priority. I actually found this appealing because it meant there were guidelines both were expected to follow.

"I found no flaws in the parameters set forth in both contracts," I agreed.

"Then you also read that every bidder has the same opportunity. It wouldn't be fair for me to give any of you a leg up on your competition." It was a statement, not a question. It needed no response because it was a fact.

Damn, she was a savvy businesswoman.

"I see. Then what does this phase of the auction entail?" I asked, feeling a bit eager.

"You will attend the event at the hour specified detailed in the invitation Ms. Lee sent you via email. The audience space will darken and each of you will have a lighted paddle displaying a number. The candidates will be brought out one at a time for bidding. When you want to bid on a particular candidate, you may press the button on the paddle and hold it aloft. I will call it out."

"So very similar to an art auction."

Madam Alana smiled, her face lighting up so beautifully I was taken aback by her splendor.

"I like the visual of my candidates being precious art." Something shifted behind her eyes as though she was reliving a memory of her own.

"And I don't have to bid on anyone if I'm not interested," I clarified. I thought I was ready for marriage but after meeting Memphis, I wasn't so sure. Maybe I could find the man of my dreams, though that wouldn't be possible if I chose a husband tonight.

"The choice is always yours." She eased her chair back and stood. "I must tend to my candidates. I hope to see you at the auction tonight."

I stood up and shook her hand and then Jade's.

"Ms. Shaw?" Alana called out when I reached the door. "May your destiny lead you down the right path."

My mouth went dry, and I clung to the door handle, my palms becoming clammy. It was a sign. Maybe even divine intervention. She couldn't know the conversation I'd had with Memphis in the elevator only a short time ago.

"My destiny?" I gulped, the hairs on my arms standing at attention while a flurry of mixed feelings soared through me.

"Yes, *chéri*. I always let destiny be in the driver's seat."

I nodded and left her office. I got into the elevator and waited silently. I forgot to push the button, not paying attention, my mind still working through the conversation I'd just had.

The door opened and there was Memphis, standing about ten feet away holding a ring box. It was open, and he was staring down at a diamond solitaire, the smile on his face so large it was as though he'd won the lottery. It was the image of a man who knew exactly what he wanted.

And it wasn't me.

I shoved myself to the side and out of sight and smashed the "close door" button. He must not have been paying attention, so focused on the ring he'd bought for his woman. I was able to narrowly escape another interaction.

The shock of seeing him in that private moment absolutely settled my mind firmly in one direction.

I was attending that auction, and I would buy myself the perfect husband.

I deserved nothing less.

Episode 11

Buds and Booze

SUMMER

Once the paramedics had assessed me and determined I'd had a small anxiety attack due to the fear when the elevator glitched, they'd left with the suggestion that I get some rest and relaxation. I didn't have time for that as I was now late for my meeting with Madam Alana. We were currently on the fifteenth floor and there was no way I was ready to get back into an elevator to go up a few floors. I found the stairs and trudged up the five flights, feeling incredibly winded from taking them in heels, not to mention I was still rather shaky from what I felt had been a harrowing brush with death. It was probably more of a normal occurrence for those that took elevators regularly, but I was still shaking in my cork platform wedges.

I made it through the exit at the twentieth floor and walked over to the reception desk where I was greeted by two stunningly beautiful Asian women.

"Oh, *chéri*, you must have had a terrible fright." The older female approached, one of her hands on my arm as she looked at me with compassion and concern.

"Madam Alana?" I guessed.

She responded with a soft smile and a nod. "Please come, come. Have a seat in my office so you can rest, and we'll chat."

The woman led me by my elbow as though she was supporting me lest I might suddenly fall. I appreciated the gesture because I was still a bit wobbly. She led me to a large office that had floor-to-ceiling windows that overlooked the Strip. Her view was breathtaking. I could see the desert beyond and the sun creating interesting shadows along the ground from the high-rise casinos.

I was brought to a small seating area where I sat on a white leather couch.

"Jade, please pour Ms. Belanger a glass of water. Or would you prefer something stronger?" Madam Alana asked.

I shook my head. "Water is fine. Thank you." I eased back against the comforting leather and closed my eyes, taking a few deep breaths and then letting them out slowly.

"Relax, take all the time you need," she encouraged.

Her voice was so soothing with a French lilt to it that I instantly did as she said. I kicked off my shoes and curled my knees and bare feet up and to the side, letting the entire scary experience leave me one breath at a time.

"Ms. Belanger?" the woman named Jade called, and I opened my eyes to find her holding a glass of water in front of me.

"Thank you." I sipped the cool water and slowly started to come back to myself. Being a woman who lived regularly with anxiety and depression, I had a few coping tools of my own, but being able to just sit and breathe was often the best method for bringing me out of a spiral.

My therapist had taught me to focus on my five senses. The first being sight. Look for something in your general vicinity; it could be anything. In this case, it was the bouquet of flowers that sat on the low glass coffee table.

The flowers were the palest pink roses mixed with bright yellow yarrow flowers that had a long blooming period, usually from June through September. I then inhaled fully, using my second sense, smell, to take in the lush scent of the roses. They were lovely, and the floral notes were subtle but pleasant. Next was touch. I tuned into the chill of the glass I held and focused on how the cool temperature contrasted against the warmth coming from the windows. I tried to ignore sound, because the fear I'd experienced elevated even the slightest noise, making my own breath seem overly loud. Last was taste. I swore we'd been so close that I could practically taste Jack's cologne on the tip of my tongue.

Even though the man was frustrating, he did help me through a frightening experience. Perhaps I should have given him my real phone number? It wasn't likely that he'd call anyway, but when he did, he'd get a rude awakening. I smiled to myself. Part of me liked the visual of such a suave, attractive man calling the local pizzeria in my hometown of Eureka, California, and being told that "Rebecca" did not work there.

"Feeling better, Summer?" Madam Alana asked.

I took another sip of the icy water and sighed. "Yes, thank you. I will admit to being pretty scared."

The Madam waved her hand. "As would anyone, *chéri*. Are you feeling well enough to discuss the auction?"

I sat up straight and put my glass down on the coaster so it wouldn't leave a wet ring on the pristinely clean glass. Someone must wipe that down every single day for it to look that nice.

"Summer?" Alana's voice brought me back from my squirrel moment. Often when I'd had an anxiety-induced attack or episode, my mind would drift to random things. It was annoying, but also part of who I was.

I shook my head to clear my thoughts. "Yes, sorry. I'm

very eager to be entered into the auction," I announced my intention, something she already knew, which was why we were meeting in the first place.

"You've read through the terms and conditions?" she clarified.

I nodded. "I have. Nothing seemed out of place or unacceptable." I knew both of those things because my parents had poured over every detail of the paperwork. They then had one of our family lawyers do the same. The lawyer found the entire situation rather disturbing, because signing your life away for three years for a lump sum of money wasn't the normal path couples took toward holy matrimony. However, I wasn't a normal woman, and my parents were the absolute opposite of it.

They were born and bred hippies who lived in the Emerald Triangle of Humboldt County. We ran one of the nation's largest cannabis farms. My father was a botanist handling the sciences behind our many strains while I was the family horticulturist. I made sure things grew. Every farm in our county called me to evaluate their plants and discuss their needs. Regardless of the potential for competition, I always helped. There was room in the cannabis sector for everyone. Now my mom, well, she was a practicing witch. Basically, a magical fairy in her own way. She was in touch with nature and the universe in all its many forms. Everything she handled turned to gold, or in our case, green.

We were a family of growers, and so far, we'd been the best at it. The problem wasn't our product, it was the fact that we were so big, one of us needed to truly take the business to the next level. Since my parents were already in their sixties and my sister wanted no part of the business side, I needed to be the one to do it. Except I didn't know anything about running a business. We'd always hired those people to do the office work, but we were at the point where we probably needed to go public or hire someone who could take the company further. Whatever that looked like, we needed help.

"I will admit to having been surprised when reviewing your file. If I may be bold and up front with you?"

"Please. I'm an open book. Ask anything you want to know," I encouraged.

"After reviewing your background checks and history, I note you are already a multimillionaire."

I nodded. "Yep. Business is booming."

The Madam cleared her throat and crossed her toned legs, placing her hands to her knees looking incredibly prim and proper while I had my bare feet up on her white leather couch. I instantly realized my mistake and shoved my legs back down and reached for my shoes with my toes, to no avail.

"Then I'm to assume you don't need the money from the auction?"

I shook my head. "Nope. I have tons of money. My family is set in that regard."

Her sculpted brows narrowed. "Then may I ask what is the reason you want to be entered if not for the money? You're uniquely beautiful, so I can't imagine it's a problem for you to find a prospective mate."

"Pshhhhh. Don't let the cover of the book fool you. I'm super awkward when it comes to attractive men. There was a man in the elevator... Whoo, boy. Hot as the California Valley in the middle of July. I was all kinds of dorky. Fumbling around. I dropped my purse that had a pair of undies in it. That was embarrassing. Meeting men has never been a problem for me. It's my flighty and carefree nature and clumsiness that often puts a man off."

"Oh?" she asked, suggesting with her tone that I continue.

I shrugged. "Sure. I spend a lot of time with my parents. They're really cool, and I like being around them. I also love my community. We're very family-oriented."

"Family-oriented?" Her gaze flitted to her assistant who sat quietly next to us. They looked at one another, something passing between them I wasn't privy to.

"Are you interested in having children?" Alana asked.

A wave of happiness immediately flooded my system. "Gosh, I would *love* a whole bunch of kids. I can just imagine teaching some little ones how to plant and grow their own food. The pride in eating something you've grown yourself. Teaching them the business my parents started from a small acre on their own private land, that has grown into hundreds of acres over the years. Kids are awesome," I agreed.

"What are you looking for in a bidder, if I may ask?" Alana changed the trajectory of her questions.

"Truthfully, my mom and I discussed this concept, and we figured that bidders are probably successful businessmen in one way or another, right?" I asked, wanting to ensure I was on the right track. Otherwise, it would all be moot.

"Yes, that is an accurate assumption, however the businesses vary drastically from artists, famous composers, entertainment investors, real estate tycoons, and the like."

"Exactly what I'm looking for. I need a man who would be interested in teaching me how to be a better business-woman. A man who has been successful running one already would know the ins and outs. I figured three years with someone like that would be a one-on-one, hands-on approach to learning everything."

"And could you see yourself committing to this person for more than three years?" she asked.

"If the connection is there, rock on!" I blurted, getting more and more excited about the idea. "That would be best case scenario for sure. Oh man, my parents would be thrilled. As it is, this was their unorthodox idea for me to find a mate and business partner. They worry about me being alone and having a lousy sex life."

Madam Alana's eyebrows rose into her hairline. "Your

parents are worried about your sexual relations?"

I grinned. "Yeah. We have a very open relationship. We talk about everything. No subject is off-limits or too personal. My mother is deeply worried I'm not getting an appropriate number of orgasms to offset my hormones and other important chemical levels within my body. Getting married and being intimate with my bidder means I'll be getting properly laid, God willing, which was another reason my parents thought this was a good idea. Honestly, I agree with them. Finding a man to take home from a bar is all kinds of uncomfortable most of the time."

"I see how that could be difficult," Alana agreed. "To clarify, you want a businessman who is willing to teach you how to lead, or at the very least allow you the opportunity to shadow him in a business environment?"

I nodded avidly.

"And you're looking for regular sexual intercourse," she stated smoothly, not a hint of emotion in her expression, though it almost sounded a little racy when she said it with that melodic accent.

"Mmm-hmmm. You've got it."

Madam Alana smiled and eased back into her chair. "This is a very interesting reason to be putting oneself up for auction."

"If you say so. I'm used to being the quirky girl in pretty much any situation, but my parents taught me that I shouldn't change for anyone. That I was good enough just being me."

"They are one hundred percent correct, *chéri*. Don't make yourself less so others can feel like more."

I laughed. "That's an excellent way to put it. I'm going to remember that."

Alana dipped her head. "If you are certain, I will put you in the auction. I know of a couple men right off the top of my head who may be very interested in a woman like you. One just recently requested a woman who has a great family and wants kids. He's truly looking for a love match."

"Is he hot? I mean, not that it matters, but it does a little if I'm going to be having sex with him for the next three to fifty years."

"The man she's thinking of could be a fashion model but has a rugged edge and an accent," Jade said, speaking for the first time.

Madam Alana's lips twitched. "Jade is correct. He even requested I give him a hint during the auction."

"Okay, so he's hot. Is he a businessman?" I asked, feeling excitement thread through my solar plexus.

"He's the CEO of one of the most successful alcoholic beverage companies in the world," Madam Alana confirmed.

"Girl, hook a sister up! Buds and booze! It's a perfect match!" I started to dance in my chair, getting even more enthusiastic about the idea now that I'd chatted with these two ladies about it.

"I too couldn't imagine a better pairing." Alana pressed a red-tipped nail to her chin, her gaze out the window as though deep in thought. "Perhaps I will break the rules tomorrow and give the bidder a sign."

I sat up and put my hands together in a prayer position. "Please do. My future depends on it."

Alana suddenly stood up. "Well, I have much to consider. Please follow Jade to the conference room and she'll have you sign everything. Then be here tomorrow morning at eight a.m. sharp. All the candidates go through the makeover process the day of the auction."

"A makeover! How fun. Do you mean someone is going to do my hair and makeup and put me in a swanky outfit?"

Madam Alana smiled in a way that you would at an overactive child. "Yes, Summer. It's a long process, but the results are always appreciated by the bidders."

"I am soooooo down with this plan. If all I have to do is show up, and someone else gets to make me look worthy of three million dollars, I'll be living my best life." I stood up and dashed over to Alana, pulling her into a hug.

She stiffened at first, then relaxed a bit and patted my back. I turned from her and then did the same to Jade who stayed perfectly still. "Thank you for your help!" I gushed, then went over to the couch to grab my shoes. I looped them around a finger letting them dangle. "You guys are awesome. Thank you for the talk and for including me. I'm super pumped about the auction tomorrow. I can't wait to call and tell my parents that I'm in."

I walked to the door and grabbed the handle, turning around to look at the two gorgeous women. "Thanks, ladies. This has been amazing." I lifted my hand and gave them the international rock symbol with my index finger, pinky and thumb sticking up and my middle fingers tucked in.

"Buds and booze for the win!"

Episode 12

Slim to None

JACK

I woke to the sunlight streaming through the windows. I'd forgotten to pull the blinds and curtains, but I was eager to start the day.

Tonight was the auction.

I could hardly wait to attend, but I was also rather nervous about making a selection. My hope was that my appeal to Madam Alana yesterday to give me a sign had worked. The woman was a tough negotiator, to be certain, but I also could tell she had a big heart. The fact that she checked on her candidates regularly and had attended both of Erik and Savannah's weddings proved her loyalty and commitment to her pairings. Now I just hoped I'd done enough to convince her of my need for assistance in choosing the right bride.

Checking the clock, I found it was only just after six a.m. Which meant it was three in the afternoon for my best friend, Erik, back in Norway. I snatched the phone sitting on the charger and dialed his number.

"Jack. How's Nevada treating you?" Erik answered on the

second ring.

"It's definitely warm, but I'm faring well. How is Savannah? Getting excited about your trip to Turks & Caicos for the late honeymoon?"

Erik chuckled. "That she is, my friend. Though she keeps packing all of these long sleeves and pants and all I want to see her pack are bathing suits."

"Going to try for a baby right out the gate, mate?" I chuckled at my little rhyme.

"Goodness, no. Savannah wants to learn more about the beer business. Once we get back from our honeymoon in two weeks, we'll spend a few months in the office getting her more comfortable being in Norway. Then right before Dakota and Sutton have their twins, Savannah wants to head back to Montana. She can finish her undergrad and be there for her nieces," he explained.

I was excited for Dakota and Sutton Goodall. I knew they hadn't expected to get pregnant right after their wedding, but life throws you curveballs, as the Americans often said. They seemed to be doing fine now that they'd gotten the situation with her father taken care of, not to mention the terrifying arsonist/attempted murderer that was Savannah's ex who was now facing a life sentence in prison. Both Savannah and Erik had suffered gunshot wounds but had healed over the months since and finally married back in Norway just a few days ago.

"Well, I went and spoke to Alana yesterday," I said.

"Oh yeah? What about?" he asked.

"The fact that she didn't provide any of us with portfolios on the candidates up for auction. I explained how ridiculous it was to spend millions on a marriage contract when I knew nothing of my prospective bride other than what she looks like." I huffed, allowing my friend to hear my frustration firsthand.

Erik snorted. "And how did that conversation go for you?"

"About as well as expected, I'm afraid." I sighed. "How did you know Savannah was the one?" I toyed with the comforter and stared out the window.

"Before I saw her, I felt nothing inside. Completely numb. There was no joy left within me. After losing Troy in the accident…" His voice trailed off for a moment and I could hear him take a ragged breath. Suddenly his voice lowered to a calmer, quieter pitch. "I'm okay, *elskede*. Don't worry. I'm talking to Jack about the auction. Finish packing. I'll be fine." He lightly chuckled. I'm assuming he was interrupted by the one and only person he called his "beloved" or "*elskede*" in Norwegian, which was Savannah, his wife.

Oh, how I wanted a woman who was devoted to me and who worried about how I was handling a difficult topic. That was the whole reason I was here in Las Vegas. To find what my best friend had. The right woman for him. And Savannah was perfect. It was funny that I thought that way now. When I found out about her, I'd been determined to break them up. At the time, the entire thing had sounded fishy. My friend, who'd been lost to his grief for a couple years, suddenly came home all smiles with a fiancée in tow. Then, when I looked her up, I'd found all the debt her family had incurred on their land and had assumed she was a gold digger taking advantage of a broken man. Boy, had I been wrong. Still, I was glad I'd snuck my nose in their business because it brought Savannah and Erik closer together. It also gave me the idea to enter the auction myself.

I'd dated many women over the past few years, trying to find that spark that told me it could be forever. Those relationships never lasted more than a few dates, making me seem like a player, which was the furthest thing from the truth. There were different reasons why each of those relationships didn't work out. Many didn't want children or were focused entirely on their careers and had no immediate plans to procreate. Others seemed interested in me for what I could bring them monetarily, or just wanted a single night between the sheets.

I dreamed of having a loving wife who I could worship and a house full of children. I didn't want to wait until I was well into my thirties to create a family like so many in my country did. I'd lived my entire childhood bouncing from place to place in the Norwegian Child Welfare Services known commonly as Barnevernet. I lived my early years falling in and out of love with a new mother figure. Most were nice, but every time I'd connect to one of my guardians, I'd be moved for one reason or another. Until the last home I was sent which was an institution for boys. I'd been around ten years of age then. That was when I was placed in a school where I met Erik Johansen.

His family became my extended family. Irene, his mother, became the only woman in my life who I knew loved me for me. Not because she was being paid to do it. And she was always available with a kind word, a hot meal to fill my belly, a big hug, and my own bed when I stayed over, which was often.

Henrik and Irene showed me what true love looked like and how a family could be. I wanted that desperately. And the first step to having it was finding a wife.

If Erik could be saved by a redhead from Montana with the kindest eyes and the sweetest soul, why couldn't I?

My brain instantly circled back to the elevator yesterday with that sassy, blonde, blue-eyed woman named Rebecca. She was something else. Pretty eyes and a knockout body. When she'd clung to me for safety, I'd imagined a thousand different inappropriate ways I would have liked her to hold me and vice versa. Unfortunately, Rebecca in the end hadn't seemed interested, even if the sparks between us had burned white hot and the sexual chemistry off the charts.

Which reminded me, I needed to call and check on her

today. Though was it appropriate to do so when I planned to bid on another woman tonight? Who knew? I sure as hell didn't. But I was worried about her. She'd had a bit of a scare and had seemed out of sorts when I left her yesterday. Maybe I should have stayed even after she told me to go?

"Sorry, Jack." Erik broke me out of my musings over Rebecca. "I don't know exactly how to explain it other than I just knew she was the one for me when I looked into her eyes. My heart pounded, my hands became clammy, and I swear there was a halo of light around her body."

"Probably the stage lighting," I presumed.

"Maybe. I don't know. It was just her," he finished.

"Well, I asked Madam Alana to give me a sign in the auction tomorrow, and I'm hoping since you and the others in your auction went smashingly, I too can find the ideal woman."

"Did she agree to give you a heads up?" he scoffed.

"Not exactly." I groaned. "I still have faith that she might."

"I wouldn't hold my breath. She's a strict businesswoman and fairness for all is part of what makes her so reputable. I would discourage you from pushing her in any way. She doesn't need you in the bidding. She has plenty of people. So many that I understand she turns bidders away and has a waiting list a mile long. I'm crossing my fingers for you, Jack."

"Thank you. I appreciate you taking the time to chat when I know you're in a rush to get Savannah off to the islands. But I have another request."

"Oh? Go ahead and shoot," he stated gruffly.

"*Shoot*? You've been hanging around Sutton Goodall for too long," I teased.

"That is the truth. I pick up so many of their colloquialisms. Americans have the best slang," he agreed.

"Be that as it may, I wanted to see about taking some time off. If I pick a bride tonight, I'm going to want to spend uninterrupted time with her. I've already put our Chief Operating Officer in charge this week, but if all goes well tonight, I may not want to come back to the office for the next month until the wedding. I'll be available online, of course, but it's important to me to meet my bride's family and see how she lives her life wherever that may be."

"I forgot about the wedding ceremony terms. You have a month, if memory serves. Then again, you could do what Sutton did and marry her in Las Vegas," he suggested.

The idea of getting married in Las Vegas didn't appeal to me. Especially after having been the best man at Erik's wedding this past week. It had been a small but beautiful affair and had felt like a coming together of families. If I wanted to create a true bond and work toward a future longer than three years with whomever I picked, it should probably start with a solid connection of our friends and family. Something a wedding ceremony would do naturally.

"Hmm... Something to think about," I responded.

"Look, Jack, you know what the company needs almost better than I do. If you say Markus Pedersen can handle running the ship for the next couple of weeks, take as much time as you need. As I said, I'll be back in the office after our honeymoon."

"Technically, he's been running everything for the past week with no issues. Thank you, Erik. I appreciate your support."

"You always have it, brother. I'm looking forward to meeting whomever you choose. Savannah is beside herself with the idea of getting a new sister-in-law."

"Just keep it quiet. I don't want Henrik and Irene to find out or I'll have them breathing down my neck. They want both of us married off and having babies right away. Your parents are incredible, but they are tired of not having grandchildren." I chuckled.

"Don't I know it. I swear Mother talks about when she'll

be a grandmother so often you'd think we were already pregnant. I keep telling her we want time together as husband and wife before we bring little ones into our lives."

I envisioned myself with a child on my lap and my chest tightened. I'd have loved nothing more than to get married and have a child right away. A living, breathing human being who was guaranteed to love me unconditionally? It was more than I could dream of.

One day.

I kept telling myself it would happen someday in the future, when the time was right and when the woman for me came along. Who knew? Maybe I'd meet her tonight.

"Stick to your plan. You and Savannah deserve some time together. Especially after everything you've both suffered the past few months."

"Both Savannah and I are fine. I'm not going back into the depths of depression like during those years after the accident, so you can stop worrying. I've got so much to live for now. The future is positively glowing with opportunity and good memories to be had."

I smiled and finally forced myself to get out of bed. "Good to hear. I'm going to make some coffee and get ready for the day. Send my love to Savannah, Henrik, and Irene."

"Will do. I'll catch up with you in a few days, but I'll text you to let you know where we are," he said.

"Excellent. Have a wonderful time in the Caribbean."

"Good luck! Text me if you find the woman of your dreams tonight. Savannah won't let me sleep if we don't know one way or another." He chuckled.

I laughed out loud imagining how Savannah would pester her husband until she got the answers she wanted. The woman could be ruthless if she chose. Something I was sure she learned from her big sister Dakota.

"Goodness. You both are ridiculous." I gave a long, drawn-out sigh. "Fine. I will let you know what happens.

Bye."

We both hung up and I set about getting coffee, taking a shower, grooming everything, and then ordering breakfast in. By the time I finished my routine and breakfast was delivered, it was nine in the morning. After I checked my work emails, I scrolled through my phone looking for the number I'd entered yesterday for Rebecca.

The phone rang once before an automated voice answered.

"You have reached the number for Eureka's Pizza. Our hours are from eleven a.m. to ten p.m. Monday through Saturday. We are closed on Sunday. Please call back during normal business hours. Have a great day."

I stared at the phone, double checked the number, and shook my head before bursting into a laughter so intense my belly ached with the effort I'd exerted.

"The most beautiful woman I've ever seen, who had a panic attack in an elevator, carried sexy panties in her purse, and smelled like sunshine and marijuana, has blown me off." I couldn't believe it.

It had never happened to me before. Usually when I asked for a female's contact information they would fall all over themselves to give it. Apparently not this woman.

I grinned as I stared out the window at the Las Vegas landscape. "A fake number. *Bravo, solskinn.*" *Bravo, sunshine*, I whispered in my native language at my reflection in the glass.

Too bad tonight was the auction.

The odds of us seeing one another again were slim to none.

Episode 13
Age Is Only a Number

RHODES

I knocked on the door to the penthouse apartment of the luxury resort Alana and Christophe used when they were in Las Vegas. As I understood it, they'd leased the home from the resort owner indefinitely. I'd never seen them live anywhere else in Nevada, other than the same hotel where she kept her office space. It was an odd setup. Most of the year they lived in their home in France. I also knew they owned a home in Hawaii because I'd designed it, and they were thinking of purchasing land in Montana of all places. That idea fit Christophe perfectly, as he adored American culture, but not Alana. She was far too poised and pristine for me to imagine her tromping through the countryside or up on top of a horse. I simply couldn't picture it.

Emily gave a long sigh as she stared at her phone, her head always down, face glued to the device.

The door opened and Alana stood there looking as beautiful as ever in a pair of gray slacks and a white silk blouse. Her makeup and hair were meticulous, the red of her lips a pretty contrast against her skin tone, while her hair framed her face on both sides and fell like shiny black ribbons down over her chest.

"Rhodes, Emily!" Her arms extended and Emily dashed into her embrace.

"Auntie!" Emily gushed, clinging to the petite woman.

"*Ma douce.*" *My sweet* she spoke the French nickname she'd been calling my daughter her entire life. "Let me get a good look at you." She put her hands to Emily's shoulders and held her at arm's length. "Just as I suspected, more stunning than the last time we were together."

Emily blushed as a beaming smile spread across her face. Something she rarely did with me anymore. I gave my daughter compliments all the time, but somehow, they always fell flat.

"Is that my niece I hear?" Christophe called from deeper inside.

"Uncle C!" Emily hollered, let Alana go and bolted into their apartment on the hunt for Christophe. He'd likely be in the kitchen.

Alana tilted her head to the side and my shoulders drooped. "Hey Alana," I said, the weight of my life loosening the tension at the sight of someone I cared for.

She put her hands to my biceps, leaned forward and air kissed one side of my cheek and then the other before pulling back and assessing me. Her gaze was shrewd and all-knowing.

"Teenagers are complicated, no?" She smirked.

I let out the sigh that I'd been holding in since I got off the plane.

I'd been pickpocketed by that gorgeous young woman, who ultimately stole all my cash, but returned everything else. But my hip throbbed from the fall, and I couldn't get the woman's warm brown eyes out of my head. Then the second we'd gotten in the car and started our journey to the resort, Emily had started in with her complaints.

"Las Vegas is ugly."
"The weather is too hot."
"The desert is sooooo boring."
"When are we going home?"

It was getting more difficult to deal with a contrary, unhappy teen day in and day out. She needed a female figure to look up to. And her mother wasn't exactly the best example of the kind of woman I   hoped to see Emily grow up to be.

I looked into Alana's sympathetic eyes and nodded. "Yeah," I muttered in answer to her question.

She chuckled lightly and I swore it sounded like music. "Come. Christo has prepared a feast."

I rubbed my stomach. "I have thought of nothing else." Lie. Technically I'd thought a lot about the woman who ran into me and stole my cash.

I shook off the thoughts as I entered the kitchen where Christophe was holding a wooden spoon up in front of Emily. My daughter sipped from the ladle and made a groaning, appreciative sound.

"Good, *non?*"

"So yummy, Uncle C. You cook the best food," Emily offered, reminding me that there was a sweet girl hiding behind that combative teen angst.

"*Merci, chéri.* Why don't you set the table as I finish up here," he instructed.

She jumped to help, already knowing where everything was as we visited Alana and Christophe a few times a year. Whenever Alana had her quarterly auctions, Emily and I would pop in from Los Angeles. The flight was short, and they were great company. Really the only extended family we had, besides her mother, and my parents, who were living their best retired life down in Florida.

I greeted Christophe and then eased into a bar stool where I finally started to relax.

Alana poured three glasses of red wine and a sparkling

cider for Emily in her own wine glass, something I knew Emily would appreciate since she wanted to be twenty-five like yesterday, instead of the thirteen-year-old she currently was.

I accepted one of the glasses and watched as Alana set one down on the counter next to where Christophe was pan frying pork chops. She placed her hand against his back in an encouraging manner while she peeked over his shoulder at the sauteed peppers and onions he was also cooking. He smiled and then quickly bent down and kissed the crown of her head.

I watched them move around the other, a well-practiced melody they'd perfected over the thirty years they had been together. I had hoped to have that with Portia, Em's mother, but it wasn't in the cards. I also didn't see a romantic relationship happening any time in my near future, as I rarely made it out on dates anymore, preferring the solace of my work over the uncertainty of dating.

"Last we spoke, you mentioned something about looking into land in Montana and having me build you a home there. What could possibly have stoked your interest in Montana?" I asked.

"We have made new friendships there. People we connected to and look forward to spending more time with." Christophe answered.

"Oh? Tell me more."

Over dinner they told me a wild story that could be made into an action-packed blockbuster movie for how incredibly unbelievable it all sounded. And all of it surrounded a pair of down-on-their-luck sisters who'd been in her last auction.

"So, you're now close to Dakota and Savannah who were candidates, the bidders, and their extended families?" I asked while shoveling in a delicious bite of porkchop with a dollop of homemade applesauce on top. "You haven't befriended clientele in that manner in a long time," I added.

Alana nodded. "True. I have felt a change come over me

as of late. A need to connect to others outside of my Christo," she said while looking at her husband with pure adoration.

He reached out a hand to hers and squeezed. "My wife is broadening her horizons. She is learning that she doesn't have to let all of these people leave her life for good once she's befriended them during the auction process. And one of them is pregnant with twin girls, and you know how my Alana loves to dote on the little ones as we were never blessed with any of our own."

"Well, I love you like a second mother, Auntie Alana," Emily announced. "You've always been one of my favorite people on the planet. You're so cool, and beautiful, and you dress awesome," my daughter breathed with awe.

Alana reached out and cupped my daughter's cheek. "And I love you, *ma douce*," Alana cooed.

Emily preened under Alana's praise. Goodness, how I wanted her to have that every day.

"We're just getting to the point in our lives where we want to spend more time with friends, who are the family we choose, rather than working nonstop." Christophe answered.

"Are you talking retirement? Do artists do that?" I frowned, not sure how that worked.

Christophe chuckled and shook his head. "*Non.* An artist rarely retires, but we do stop taking commissions and planning regular gallery exhibitions. Alana, however, has hired a protégé."

"You mean you're going to retire from the auction business?" I gasped and focused on Alana.

Her lips twitched but she didn't respond right away. "Perhaps one day. We shall see. Depends on what the future will bring."

"Well, if Uncle C decided to stop creating new artwork for Auntie to sell in her auction, then it would make sense that she wouldn't be working much, right?" Emily surmised incorrectly. We'd never told Emily what type of auction Alana ran. She assumed based on Christophe being an artist that she sold art. We simply never corrected her, and I didn't plan to.

I tossed my cloth napkin on the table after I wiped my mouth. "Well, I'll be damned. I never thought I'd see the day when Alana Toussaint wasn't burning the midnight oil, trying to connect bidders and clientele to one another," I said cryptically.

Alana laughed. "One must always keep their options open, darling. Especially when it comes to living the life you want."

* * * *

Later that evening, Emily was crashed out in the living room watching a movie when Christophe waved me over to the balcony. I held up a finger, gesturing that I'd be out in a minute, then went to my sport coat to grab the two cigars I'd brought for this evening.

I opened the balcony door and found Christophe and Alana seated in a small lounge chair for two. I took up residence in the lone armchair next to them and handed my friend a cigar. He instantly brought the stogie to his nose and inhaled.

"*Magnifique!*" he said and then held it aloft so Alana could sniff it.

She dutifully and daintily complied. "It's lovely," she agreed, and sidled up close to her husband's side.

Christophe had already prepared the table before us with the straight cutter to clip the tip and an ashtray and butane lighter. Traditionally, when I would visit, we'd have dinner and then smoke cigars together, usually with an after-dinner drink. Since the wine was delicious, the three of us had stuck to drinking the vino.

"I believe it's your birth year, 1964. The Padron Anniversary series. Claims to be one of the best out of Nicaragua."

"Oh, a treat! *Merci, mon ami.*" *Thank you, my friend.* Christophe rubbed his hands together.

We both clipped the tips and set the rolled bits of heaven ablaze. Instantly my mouth was hit with floral and fruity notes that were quite pleasant. "Do you taste the fruit and flowers?" I asked.

Christophe nodded jovially, taking long, slow puffs, holding the rich smoke within his mouth and then releasing it.

For a bit we said nothing, just spent time smoking our cigars, enjoying the quiet comfort of good friends, and a stellar view of Las Vegas and the dark desert beyond.

"Rhodes, I would like for you to attend the auction tomorrow." Alana announced seemingly out of nowhere.

I groaned and stretched out my legs, crossing my feet at the ankles. "Alana, we've talked about this many times in the past. I don't think choosing a wife by sight alone is the right path for me."

She sat up and placed her hands on her knees. "Then what is the right path? You've been divorced and alone for eight years. Emily's mother is nowhere to be found, constantly jumping in and out of bed with one man or another and leaving her daughter behind. Emily craves continuity and stability, *mon cher*. She is floundering."

"I agree, I am the one constant in her life and it's not enough. Unfortunately, I can't seem to get Portia to care about her daughter's needs in the slightest," I grumbled.

Alana nodded. "Exactly my point. Choose a wife tomorrow, and that woman would be committed to you and your daughter. Also, you'd have help through these emotionally difficult times. Another person to fill that lonely void within your own life. And maybe having a woman around would do some good for Emily," Alana suggested.

I rubbed at my face with my free hand, the cigar burning away in my left. "Maybe, hell, I don't know, Alana. Marriage was hard. Dating alone is a nightmare. I've tried a couple times over the years, and it never works out. Don't even get me started about how some women responded when they found out I have a child," I huffed. "They bolted so fast their stiletto heels left black streak marks on the concrete in their wake."

Alana made a tsking sound. "My candidates are all fully committed."

"For three years. That gives me until when Emily is sixteen, almost seventeen. Then what? Another woman leaves her life?" I shook my head. "Nah. I couldn't do it to her."

"You wouldn't be doing anything *to her.* You'd be bringing in a woman who adds value to your lives for a period of no less than three years. Just because the contracted term is three years, it doesn't mean the person you chose couldn't be convinced to stay."

"And staying with Portia five years worked oh so well," I scowled.

Alana's lips snapped together, and she glared. "There are very few people I wish ill will toward, and that woman is one of them," she bit out frostily.

I burst into laughter, sat back, and puffed on my delicious stogie. "I know you mean well, Alana, but I just don't see it happening for me. At least not until Emily is an adult and headed off to college."

"You'd be forty-three by that time. Do you truly want to put your life and needs on hold for five more years? You've already done that for the last eight, and the five before with Portia weren't any better. When do you get to find your happily ever after, hmm?" Her tone was soft and nurturing, much like a sister might respond if I'd had one.

I shrugged and shook my head then stared up at the twinkling stars in the sky above. "I don't know. Sometimes I believe I'm not meant to find true love. Take today, for example. I had a run in with a young woman at the airport. It was the first time in forever that I'd had a physical attraction to a woman. She ran straight into me. Knocked me on my ass in more ways than one."

"Oh?" Alana perked up.

I laughed. "Yeah, and it turns out the woman was a pickpocket."

Alana tilted her head to the side. "A pickpocket at the airport? Explain this person to me," she commanded abruptly.

"Dark hair, super light brown skin or maybe she was tanned. Large brown eyes. Cute, petite, curvy and too young."

Alana waved her hand in the air. "You think everyone is too young because you act old. Did she seem to be over eighteen, twenty perhaps?"

"Of course. I wouldn't be attracted to a child, you know that." I scrunched up my face and made a gagging expression. "She was definitely in her twenties."

"Then the problem is?" She continued.

"First of all, the woman stole from me. Second of all, she had to be at least fifteen years younger than me."

Alana shrugged. "Age is only a number. Love, chemistry, nor attraction, give two figs what someone's age is."

Christophe snorted through his own chuckle. "I am more than eight years older than my wife as you know, and we have been happy for thirty years. A few more years wouldn't change that."

"Tell me more," Alana interrupted.

So, I told her everything that happened.

"Sounds like Maia," Alana whispered under her breath and smacked Christophe's leg with exuberance. "You must come to the auction! I beg of you."

I groaned again, showing Alana my frustration at her constant request that I attend one of her auctions. "If I attend this one time, will you promise to never, ever, ask me to come to one again?"

Alana smiled slowly without showing her teeth. A devilish cat-that-ate-the-canary type of smile if I'd ever seen one. She knew something and wasn't sharing.

"Of course, *mon cher*. I promise to never ask again." She sipped on her wine nonchalantly.

"Why do I feel like I've just signed my death warrant?" I asked Christophe.

He grinned. "Have a little faith, Rhodes. Who knows, you might find exactly who you've been looking for at the auction tomorrow."

"I doubt it." I puffed on my cigar and stared out at the view.

The only person I wanted to see again was a sexy, sticky-fingered brunette, who was long gone by now.

Episode 14

It's Showtime

MAIA

"Sign here, and here," Alana's new assistant instructed. I focused on the pearlescent paint she had on her nails. It shimmered like the scales of a fish under the bright office lights.

I scribbled something illegible where she pointed. No one would be able to prove that was my signature. I signed everything differently so no two were alike.

Jade pursed her lips in a manner that reminded me of Alana herself, but not quite as polished. Upon my arrival, she'd scrutinized my worn jeans and beat-up Doc Martens with disdain. Something the Madam never did. She always treated me with respect and kindness. I'd even dressed to impress by wearing my prettiest top, too. It was purple and had a little ruffle at the hem. My biker friend/landlord had bought it for me as a birthday gift this past year when I turned twenty-three. I'd wear it most often when interviewing for jobs that paid in cash. Since this was kind of a job interview, at least that was the way I chose to think about it, I'd dressed to impress.

"How do you know the Madam?" Jade asked in that cool, richy-rich tone that was almost off-putting, but not quite rude.

"What did she tell you?" I always answered a question I didn't want to answer with a question. People easily got confused, changed the subject, or they'd answer and then I could shift the conversation to something else.

"Not very much, I'm afraid."

That confirmed what I thought.

Madam Alana and I had an odd relationship. I often saw her as a fairy-godmother type. Over the years she'd often slipped me gift cards for restaurants or grocery stores to ensure I was eating properly. One time she gave me a prepaid cell phone and told me to come visit her when the credits were gone so she could add more to it. Her rationale was that a young woman like me should never be without a phone for safety reasons. And it made a lot of sense, so I made sure to add credits whenever I was low. I also texted with her every week or two. It was nice having someone beyond Sam, my best friend/landlord, who cared about my well-being.

I shrugged and let the silence between Jade and me grow. Another trick from the street. Silence, especially while standing or looking at a person directly in the face, freaked people out.

Jade seemed immune to that trick, staring me down like a pro in a blinking competition.

Surprisingly, I caved first. "Where is the Madam?" I asked.

"She's in a meeting but will be out shortly." Jade crossed her arms over her chest and tilted her head. "Are you related to her?" she asked, seemingly out of nowhere.

I frowned. "Do I look like I'm related to her?" I countered.

Jade's gaze ran up and down my form. "Not really."

"There you go," I responded noncommittally.

"You're an enigma…"

"So are you," I interrupted. "This is the first I'm seeing you and I've known Alana for a long time. Never seen you before." I dragged my gaze up and down her form. "Though you look like you shop at the same stores. What? Did you guys get a buy-one, get-one deal?" I smiled innocently even though I knew my observation hit the target when she winced.

Jade glared. "I'm the Madam's protégé."

I had no clue what a protégé was or did, so I nodded.

The door to the conference room opened and a gaggle of people entered. I jumped out of the leather chair and immediately took up a position in the back of the room to assess what was taking place. Jade grabbed the paperwork on the table, putting it neatly into a stack.

Madam Alana entered at the back of the pack, her lips twitched into a barely there smile before she dipped her head in greeting at me and then approached Jade.

"Did everything go well with Maia?" she asked.

"Yeah, but we didn't have time to review the male bidders' images so she could X one out if she wanted," she replied.

"Maia, darling, did you want to see the bidders and choose one you'd like to remove from bidding? Every candidate gets to review the images of the people attending and mark one off based on sight alone." She explained in front of the entire group.

I shook my head. "Why would I want to limit my options?"

She smiled fully which I found odd. "As I suspected," she praised, and I felt my spine unfurl as I stood taller.

"Thank you, Jade. Go ahead and get these sent over to the attorney and I'll brief the candidates before we take them to get their makeovers."

"Of course." Jade nodded and left the room.

Alana took the seat at one end of the table. She gestured with a hand to the chair next to her. I moseyed over and eased into the seat, ensuring I had a good view of the exit in the event I needed to bolt for any reason. Another street fact—always be aware of all exits. One never knew when they'd have to bail from a difficult situation.

"Welcome, everyone." Madam Alana sat up in her chair. "Today will be very busy. After our chat here, you will be taken to one of the ballrooms to get made over. Makeovers include, but are not limited to facials, pedicures, waxing, makeup, hair, and, of course, attire."

One of the women beamed at the idea of a makeover. She was blonde with big blue eyes that oozed joy and happiness. She looked like a living, breathing rainbow. Her clothing was a wild mix of patterns and swirling colors. Her wrists had so many beaded bracelets they made noise when she moved her hands. Long dangling earrings fell from her ears like dripping icicles.

"I can see Summer is entertained by the prospect of being made over." Alana looked at the rainbow woman I was evaluating.

"Girl, I'm hella excited," she spoke, a big, toothy white smile spread across her glossy pink lips. "It's like a spa day!" Summer gushed.

A ridiculously beautiful redhead rolled her eyes. "No, it's not," she tutted. "Alana, why am I here? I'm not in the regular auction anyway." One of her perfectly shaped eyebrows cocked in what could only have been disdain.

First of all, the redhead didn't say "Madam" which I understood to be a no-no in mixed company. I perched on the edge of my seat, put my elbows to the table, and looked from Alana back to the redhead. I was eager to see a battle play out.

"Julianne." Madam Alana's tone was icy cold.

Daaaannnnggggg, this was going to be good.

"Yes, Godmother." She batted her eyelashes.

Godmother! Oh, shit.

I watched as Julianne crossed her arms over one another

in that arrogant manner wealthy people tended to fall back on. The redhead exuded old money with her perfect hair, makeup, clothing, and poise. She also wore a pantsuit that had to have been tailored to fit her. If she wasn't sitting in this room filled with candidates, I would have thought the woman was a bidder, not a participant.

Why was the Madam auctioning off her own goddaughter?

My mouth dropped open and I straight up stared at the two women, my head jockeying from one glare to the next. Every single last person in the room held their breath in anticipation of what the Madam would do and say.

"Not that I need to explain myself, *ma petite fleur,*" she said in French. I had no idea what she called her, but it didn't sound mean. "As I have instructed everyone here, my standards are exacting. The bidders will be paying no fewer than three million dollars for the benefit of your hand in marriage. I prefer to have my candidates look and feel their absolute best. You may have had more advantages in life, but you will undergo the same process as everyone else here. That is the last I will speak on it. If you do not wish to follow my guidelines and expectations, the exit is right there." Alana lifted her chin toward the large double doors.

Julianne snarled and sat back in her chair. "Fine. I apologize. Please continue." She ultimately gave in.

Point for Alana.

"Now, I want you to look around at the people in this room. You each have one thing in common. These will be the only people who understand what you have committed to and will undergo over the next three years. I suggest you make friends with one another throughout the day."

Madam Alana spent the next hour reminding us of our commitment. I knew the details by heart as I had a photographic memory.

-You must marry your bidder within one month of a signed contract.

-You must consummate the marriage within two weeks of said marriage.

-You must go and live where the bidder wanted you to go. This could be anywhere.

-You must not run away from your bidder, or your money is forfeit.

-You must make a concerted effort to please your bidder, including regular sexual relations.

-You must accompany the bidder to events and functions as they desired.

-If you wanted out within the first year, you were to return all of the money.

-If the bidder wanted out within the first year, they forfeited their deposit only.

In exchange for all of that, I would get the following:

-No fewer than three million dollars.

-Three years of marriage.

-A fully vetted bidder with no criminal record and the promise they will do no harm to the candidate.

-A roof over my head, food in my belly, clothes in the closet.

-Protection from Madam Alana and her lawyers.

-Regular checkups and in-person visits by Madam Alana to ensure the candidate's safety.

Finally, Alana stood up and clapped her hands. "Let's get made over."

* * * *

The makeover process was whack. I had never been poked and prodded so much in my entire life. My face was on fire. The space between my eyebrows felt like a throbbing, open wound. Apparently, I had a case of "unibrow," according to the waxing professional. And don't even get me started on what they wanted to do to my *hoo-ha*, which I straight refused.

Jade had been called over to mediate when I wouldn't allow them to remove more hair than just the sides of my bikini line. I declined removing my underwear too. They could fuck right off. No one was touching me there again without my permission.

No one.

Jade calmly asked me my preference, without a judgy expression, and promptly told the waxing gal to touch only what I permitted.

"Her body, her choice," she stated simply, and that endeared Jade to me.

"Thank you," I whispered, clutching the robe to my body as I slipped off the table.

Jade put her hand to my elbow and lightly led me out of the waxing room where I could still hear the other candidates crying out in pain, one after another. She leaned her head toward me. "If anyone tries to touch you inappropriately or do anything that makes you feel unsafe, you call us. No questions asked. Our candidates' safety and well-being are our highest priorities"

I snorted. "I thought money was."

"You don't know the Madam that well," Jade surmised accurately.

I'd had lunch and dinner with Alana many times in the past. Throughout the years, I'd learned her quarterly schedule and would pop up when I needed a meal or a really good place to stay. Sometimes it was just because I was lonely, and I liked having someone to spend time with who didn't want something from me.

The Madam was cool. Even though she was the one helping me, I always got the feeling that doing so helped her in some way. It was a weird yet symbiotic relationship. We rarely got deep into our pasts, but I definitely shared more with her than anyone else besides Sam. He knew it all. He was only ten years older than me but had also lived a hard life, so he wasn't surprised by much.

"The Madam has plenty of money. She does what she does because it's her calling. Not only did it help make her independently wealthy, but she also helps people out of difficult situations by offering them an alternative life. One that has financial security and, ultimately, freedom from whatever life they are leaving behind."

I nodded, imagining what I was going to do with all that money. I didn't give a shit about myself. I'd lived on the streets, worked the shittiest jobs in the world, and had survived things that most people couldn't even imagine. What I wanted was to save my mother, brother, and, most important, my baby sister. The three of them were still stuck under the thumb of the Devil himself and his demon spawn. I just hoped I wasn't too late.

Jade brought me over to a woman who immediately started fiddling with my hair. "How long has it been since you've had it cut, sugar?" the woman asked as she chewed noisily around a wad of green gum that smelled like sour apples. My mouth watered as I hadn't had anything to eat yet that day.

"Um, professionally? I honestly can't remember. I chopped about six inches off last year because it was getting in my way."

"Mmm-hmm. Well that explains it." The woman smacked her gum as she held up the varying lengths of my hair. "Don't you worry, sugar. I'm going to fix you right up and you'll be good as new!"

"Cool," I said, not knowing how I should act.

Over the next several hours, the candidates received face and hair treatments that transformed us into beautiful prospective brides and grooms. I was happy to see a couple men in the mix. One big Black guy named Memphis cracked jokes and kept everyone laughing and having a good time. I'd have been surprised if he didn't score himself a willing bidder.

And then of course there was Summer who literally spewed sunshine from her mouth every time she spoke. The woman was that happy. I didn't think I'd ever met someone who seemed so perfectly content in their own skin.

Julianne, the redheaded goddaughter, seemed bored, her face plastered to her phone the entire time, not interested in making conversation with anyone. I didn't care either way. I wasn't here to make friends. I was here to make a lot of money so I could get my family out of a horrible situation, even if my mother had forsaken me years ago. I still loved her and wanted her happy and most important, safe.

Once I'd put on the black lingerie my stylist had instructed me to wear, Madam Alana approached my privacy screen.

"Maia, I have picked out a dress that I feel best displays all your physical assets," she claimed.

I peeked around the screen and cringed at the tiny dress. "It's a mini-dress," I grumbled.

"*Chéri*, you are petite. One does not put a floor-length gown on a woman who is five foot three. The fabric would swallow you whole. Try this and we'll discuss," she tutted.

I snatched the dress from her fingers and slipped the damn thing over my head. The silky black fabric slid delicately over my curves, the hem falling to mid-thigh in a flirty ruffle. The halter style immediately pushed my boobs up to highlight my cleavage but showed very little.

"Snap, snap, my dear. We are preparing to leave," she called out.

I came around the screen and Madam Alana openly stared. She walked around me slowly and silently, one of her fingers curled under her chin.

"*Magnifique!*" she gasped.

I couldn't help the grin that spread across my face or the heat that flooded my cheeks "You think so?"

Madam Alana placed two fingers under my chin and

forced me to look up into her eyes. "He won't know what hit him," she said and then winked.

"He?" I asked. "You have someone in mind for me?" I breathed, desperate for any detail of what I'd be up against.

She shrugged one delicate shoulder. "That I'll never tell," she murmured, then handed me a pair of shiny black stilettos and walked to the front of the room. I grabbed my thrifted Doc Martens just in case and followed the Madam.

She smiled.

And for the first time I felt a bit excited.

"All right, my friends. It's showtime!"

Episode 15

Godmother Knows Best

JULIANNE

"Memphis Taylor, this is your final opportunity to walk out that door—no questions asked." Alana put a handheld recorder in front of the footballer.

Throughout the day, most of the candidates had opened up to each another, sharing bits and pieces of their lives. Memphis was an athlete who'd lost it all after an injury on the field. While Alana spoke with him, I checked him out. He looked dashing in the bespoke suit Alana had chosen for him. He was also massive, confident in his mannerisms, and very attractive. I was sure some debutante would snatch him up that evening.

"I understand," Memphis stated clearly, dipping his head toward the device.

"Are you willingly entering into The Marriage Auction? Do you agree to marry whoever offers the highest bid for your hand in an arranged marriage?" Alana continued. "The rules have been explained and you've signed the contract. Now I want your verbal agreement that this is what you want, that you understand what you have committed to, and that you are not being coerced in any way. Please confirm your name and your agreement."

"I, Memphis Taylor, understand the terms and agree as set forth in my contract. I am committed to marrying the woman who bids highest for my hand in marriage. I am not being coerced or forced in any way." He finished with a bright smile.

"This is ridiculous," I hissed under my breath as Alana approached me with an old-as-dirt handheld recorder.

"Darling, you've watched every last person here give me verbal confirmation. I expect no less from you. If you want to leave…"

"Yes, I know. The door is over there." I let out a long sigh. "Fine. My name is Julianne Myers. I willingly agree to marry the highest bidder in tonight's auction. I was neither coerced nor forced to enter The Marriage Auction. Happy?" I asked.

"*Oui.*" She clicked a button, turned around, and faced the entire group. "Let's breathe together," she instructed, taking the group through a yoga-style breathing method for a few minutes.

It actually did help calm my irritation. Usually when I was nervous on the inside, it manifested as frustration on the outside. Alana would know that and was being kind not to call my ass out on my bitchy behavior.

Jade entered the room, a frown marring her pretty features. "Madam, I must speak with you." She shifted from foot to foot.

"What is it, Jade?" Alana asked as she approached her mentee.

"Um, I made a grievous error. I accidentally made the start time the same for both auctions. Now all of the bidders are already here for Julianne's private event and the others are also here for the primary one."

"They're all here now? At the same time?" she clarified.

My heart started beating wildly behind my chest. Very soon I was going to be leaving here with a stranger. A man I was supposed to marry and share my body with, regardless of whether or not there was an attraction or even a remote connection. I clamped my jaw shut, forcing myself to stay quiet and not interrupt. This was Alana's world, and I would do well to remember that. She was helping me, not the other way around. And she wasn't even taking a commission on my auction—even though I tried to fight her on that choice. She planned to give me her cut on top of whatever I brought in. Somehow I'd find a way to give that money back. I mentally planned to talk to my godfather about it in the future.

"I'll handle it," Alana stated flatly.

"I'm really sorry. The hotel is preparing the primary auction room now. Many of the bidders are already in the meet-and-greet space having hors d'oeuvres and cocktails. What do I do?" Jade's voice shook.

Alana reached an arm out and put it over Jade's hands where she was fidgeting. "Go into the meeting space. Tell them we have some very exciting candidates, but we are experiencing an unfortunate delay. Encourage them to drink freely at the open bar and assure them the wait will be worth it when they see the lineup we have tonight."

Jade's shoulders dropped. "Thank you, Madam. I apologize. It will never happen again."

Alana smiled gently. "We learn through making mistakes, *chéri*. Now go. I'll take Julianne."

Jade nodded and bolted out of the room so fast you'd have thought fire was licking at her sky-high stilettos.

Alana spun around to face the group, a smile plastered across her face. She put her hands together in front of her chest in a prayer position. "As you likely heard, we are experiencing a scheduling snafu. Julianne, you will be auctioned first. As for the rest of you, I will have champagne brought in. Relax, freshen up, use the restroom, and mentally prepare yourself for your entire life to change tonight."

The rest of the candidates looked at me sideways, but I didn't care. I was very used to being the center of attention, good or bad. When you were the vice president of one of the most successful real estate firms around the globe, and also happened to be a woman under thirty, dirty or suspicious looks were par for the course.

"Come, *ma petite fleur.* Let's get you a husband," she cooed and offered me her hand.

I placed mine within her much smaller one and let her lead me out of the room and down a long hallway.

"So you're not going to give me any information or even the slightest hint as to what I'm going to be up against?" I asked, my tone expressing my concern.

She shook her head. "That is not how this works, Julianne. I've already done something outside of the box by hand choosing the five prospective bidders. Christophe was shocked."

I snort-laughed imagining my godfather being told that I wanted to enter the auction. "He's not disappointed in me, is he?"

Alana came to an abrupt halt. I teetered for a moment, the fabric of my long, slinky white dress fluttering around my ankles and sexy-as-sin strappy Manolo Blahniks. The dress was stunning and fit me beautifully. It had spaghetti straps and was made of light, silky material that clung to my curves but didn't dig in. The dress shimmered like diamonds but there was no beading or sequins anywhere to be seen. The way the material caught the light tricked the eye. It honestly could have been a sexy wedding dress, which felt rather appropriate seeing what I was about to do.

"Christo could never be disappointed in you, *chéri.* He is concerned about you, Brenden, and Giovanni. His heart is broken for all of you. However, he did try to encourage me to convince you to accept the money you need from us personally."

I shook my head avidly. "Hell, no! There is no way I'd accept millions of dollars as a gift from my godparents."

"A loan then?" Alana tried for the fifth time.

This very issue had been a point of contention between us leading up to this moment. One I very much wanted to nip in the bud. "No. I said no. I understand that you and Christophe mean well."

"We love you very much, Julianne. We are your family. When your mother and father bestowed upon Christo and I the gift of being your godparents, we took that responsibility seriously." Her dark gaze focused so intently on me that I swear she was touching my very soul with her affection.

"And I have known and felt your contribution and commitment to me my entire life. You allowing me into the auction when I know it's the absolute last thing you want also proves how very much you care. But, Alana, I can take care of myself. This thing with Brenden…" I inhaled sharply, not wanting the many issues I had with my brother to invade my thoughts and put me into a spiral of blubbering sobs and tears. "Eventually, it will all work out as it's supposed to."

"Do you truly believe that, Julianne? You are planning to go after him and the family business with everything you've got. I know how incredibly capable you are. In truth, I fear for what will happen between you two. Your parents would be destroyed by what has already occurred. Part of me is thankful that they are not here to see what has become of the three of you. Their loss should have brought all of you together."

"And instead, it ripped us apart. I know. I live it every single day. It's forever on my mind," I agreed. "But something has to change. I'm being pushed out of my birthright, and I need to find out why. That's the primary reason I'm contesting the will. The people who raised and loved me would not have left me out. I don't know what they were thinking. Maybe they were coerced. To be honest, there are too many questions and not enough answers. Lastly, I need to make sure everything I've built for myself isn't pushed aside or washed away by my brother's new wife, Hurricane Bianca."

Alana closed her eyes for a moment and finally nodded. I could see the physical change in her expression from concern to determination. "Then let's get you a husband for the highest amount possible."

I grinned. "Now that's the Alana I know and love," I teased.

We came up to a door and she stopped when she put her hand on the metal knob. "I'm going to go in first and greet the men. Then I'll call for you to enter, okay?"

I nodded. "Got it."

Alana cupped my cheek and stared deeply into my eyes. "You are loved, Julianne. Never forget that. You have people you can count on."

I put my hand over hers and nuzzled into her palm. "I know. Thank you for helping me."

She pressed her lips together and nodded. "Remember you asked to be in the auction. You also asked for me to choose the most ideal bidders according to my knowledge and experience. You might question one of my choices, but I assure you, Godmother knows best."

My mouth dropped open as her words filtered through my mind. "Wait, what does that mean?" I asked as she opened the door.

"You'll find out soon enough," she tutted in that cultured voice I adored, and yet her words felt foreboding.

"Alana," I tried again, but she disappeared into the room.

I paced back and forth for at least five full minutes before I heard my name called.

"You've got this, Julianne," I said to myself as I faced the door. "In the past, you've come up against men twice your size and meaner than snakes and still ended up on top.

Nothing and no one will stop you from achieving your goals."

I plastered a smile on my face, opened the door, and walked into my new life with my spine straight and my head held high.

There was a circular riser in the middle of the room with five men sitting in chairs about ten feet from the platform. Close enough to look, not close enough to touch.

"This is insanity!" I heard the deep rumble of a voice I knew all too well. Sometimes I'd heard it in my dreams, or when I was reliving a particularly intimate moment from my past while manually stimulating myself.

My head snapped up and our gazes met. His the color of a pristine blue sky to my unusual aqua shade. I turned my head toward where Alana stood behind a small podium. "What is the meaning of this?" I barked.

She smiled brightly. "Please take the riser, Julianne."

I did as she bade on autopilot, my gaze flicking to one of the last men on Earth I'd expect to be sitting in a chair at a private auction for my hand in marriage.

The man I'd lusted after my entire life.

My brother's ex-best friend, business partner, and the man I'd given my virginity to.

The one person who had always been off-limits.

Giovanni Falco.

"I don't need to go over Julianne's information as it was all in the brief I sent when you received your invitation. Let's start the bidding at three million dollars," Alana announced.

Immediately a man with a large cowboy hat raised his hand. He was ruggedly handsome and dipped his head in greeting, a hand tipping the brim of his hat the way a southern gentleman might.

My cheeks heated as the numbers rose.

"Five million…"

"Ten million…"

"Twelve."

My heart pounded so hard in my chest it was as if I'd run a marathon. I chanced a glance at Gio, and as I feared, he was beyond angry. His arms were crossed over his chest, his jawline firm and unmoving. His nostrils flared as he glared daggers each time a new bid was called.

Why was he even here?

He didn't want to marry me. He barely looked at me as anything other than his vice president and his best friend's little sister. After we'd crossed that intimate line on the best and most embarrassing night of my life, I'd kept myself scarce through college. Sure, we'd seen one another at family gatherings over the years, but I often brought a friend or a boyfriend in order to keep things between us completely copacetic and platonic. After years had passed, our relationship became strictly about business. He trusted me to bring in new, lucrative clients and help lead the business in the direction our parents set out for us.

Giovanni hadn't shown romantic interest in me since we were teens. He certainly hadn't made any advances after that night over a decade ago, and I didn't push it. There was no way I'd embarrass myself again, even if he was the most attractive man I knew. And a gifted lover, if memory served.

The bidding had slowed, the last number at twenty-four million from the handsome cowboy.

I winked at him, and I could have sworn his cheeks pinked up but the shadow from his hat made it difficult to see.

"Twenty-four million going once..." Madam Alana said. "Twice..."

"Thirty million." Giovanni stood, looking ridiculously handsome in his tailored Tom Ford suit. He turned away from me and faced the other men. "None of you will be leaving with this woman tonight. You can offer any amount of money, and I will beat it. Try me if you dare," he growled.

The cowboy looked at me, opened his mouth as if to counter the bid, and finally shook his head.

Alana had her hand at her throat, her dark eyes darting from me to Gio. "Do I have thirty-one million?" she croaked.

Not a single person spoke.

The silence was thunderous and filled with tension that pressed against every last one of my nerve endings. When Gio turned around and looked me straight in the eyes, I could hardly breathe. It was as if the very air had been sucked out of the room by his fury, determination, and resolve.

"Sold to Giovanni Falco for thirty million dollars."

Episode 16

Say Yes

GIOVANNI

I leaned against the wall waiting for the remaining four bidders to exit. Alana approached me, and I held up my hand. "I do not want to hear how she convinced you to put her in the auction," I snapped before turning to Julianne who was rubbing her arms as though she was cold. She seemed small and vulnerable. There were only two times I'd seen her look that way. One was at her parents' funeral. The other was the day after I took her innocence and pretended it never happened.

"What in the fuck were you thinking?" I barked, my focus on Julianne.

Her shoulders fell, but her eyes narrowed and shimmered with white-hot rage at my outburst.

"Why are you even here?" she fired back.

I spread my arms out wide, gesturing to the empty bidding room. "To make sure you didn't make the biggest mistake of your life!"

"It wasn't a mistake. And even if it was, it was mine to

make," she sneered.

"What on Earth would give you the idea to put yourself up for auction? You don't need money. You have means."

"Really?" She laughed dryly and crossed her arms. "You must not have gotten the memo. Brenden fired me as VP of FM Enterprises. Told me to pack my bags and never come back."

"What?" I pushed off the wall, anger fueling my every step.

"Excuse me." Alana clapped, the sharp sound echoing around the empty room. "I'm going to need you both to sign the final contract. Julianne, as previously discussed, the commission has been waived and added to your deposit. It will be entered into your account tonight. But only once the contract is signed. I must leave for the next auction. I'll touch base with you both after. Good luck, my darlings," she cooed and left the room.

"I'm not signing anything," I stated with conviction. "If it's money you want, I'll back you in whatever it is you need."

"I need the thirty million you bid." Julianne snapped. "And if you're not going to sign that contract," she pointed to the document Alana had placed on the podium, "I'm going to go hunt me down a cowboy who was willing to marry me for twenty-four million."

I watched as she hiked up the swaths of fabric around her legs, and headed toward the door.

Over my dead body would that cowboy put his hands on her.

When she moved close, I hooked her around the waist and plastered her against my much larger one. Julianne wasn't a petite woman by any means. Actually, most would consider her full-figured or plus-sized. To me, the more curves the merrier. The woman was drop-dead gorgeous. Large, full tits, a soft, nipped-in waist, hips that were made to be grabbed, and an ass that begged to be bitten. All I wanted to do was run my hands over every inch of those succulent curves. Which was when my mind reminded me that Julianne had always been off-limits.

"The fuck you are," I hissed, my breath making the fiery hair around her face shift slightly. "Just talk to me. Tell me what's going on."

Julianne sighed and dropped her head to my chest, all the piss and vinegar leaving her as she clung to me.

I soaked in the comfort of her familiar presence and the beauty of physically touching another human being. Since I'd walked away from my life, I hadn't hugged anyone, preferring to stay alone and shut out the world at the lake house.

"She's ruined everything. I have nothing." she whispered as tears filled her eyes and fell down those creamy, pearlescent cheeks.

I cupped the back of her neck with one hand and embraced her fully against my chest, wanting her to know I was there and she wasn't alone. Dipping my head, I rested it to the top of hers. "Who has?"

"Bianca!" she bitched, moving away from me suddenly.

"What did my ex do now?" I scowled. Even hearing her name was like a knife to my gut.

Jules huffed, then wiped at her eyes angrily. "Besides all that she did to you, she got my brother to fire me."

"He can't fire you," I stated flatly. "Not legally, nor without my written consent. Besides, you're an owner. I assume you received a quarter of their shares—as he did— after Lewis and Rachel passed, right? I'm my parents' only heir, so I was left all of theirs in the company."

She laughed haughtily as though I was missing out on some big joke as she paced the room. "God, you really have no clue what's been happening in your absence, do you?"

"Enlighten me." I crossed my arms and waited her out.

She approached an empty chair and slumped into it. "Hmm, let's see if I can bring you up to date since you disappeared off the face of the planet after the funeral."

"You know why I had to get away," I grated through my teeth. "I couldn't look my fiancée or my best friend in the eyes after what they'd done. Not after losing my parents too."

"Yeah, well, while you've been hiding wherever it is you went, your ex has been very busy. Not only did she get my brother to marry her in a quicker-than-quick wedding I wasn't invited to, but my parents' will was also read. Let me give you the Cliff Notes version. They didn't leave me any of their shares in the company."

"You're joking," I deadpanned, shock and disbelief threading through my tone.

She shook her head. "I wish I was. They left me their estate and half the money they had in their accounts and investments."

That was unbelievable and beyond what I could even imagine. The Myers had been devoted to both their children. And they knew that Julianne was responsible for most of the business's recent success and the boon in the high-paying clientele. The woman was a beast in the real estate industry.

"You've worked at FM Enterprises your entire working life. You love it more than anyone," I managed to croak.

Her bottom lip trembled as she nodded. "Which is why I'm contesting the will."

A bomb going off couldn't have been more of a surprise. "No," I gasped. "That will tie things up for years to come."

"I have no choice! Neither Brenden nor my folks left me any option. I still can't wrap my mind around why they would do this to me. My entire life is in that company." She sniffed, her eyes shimmering with tears that fell in perfect streaks down her cheeks. "Dammit all to hell!" She lifted her face to the ceiling as if to stem the flow, but it wasn't working.

There was no way I could let this continue. I approached and sat in the chair next to her, then reached out and put my hand to her knee in support. "We'll fix this. I'll help you."

"The thirty million you promised would help me," was her sassy reply.

I ran my hand through my hair and leaned an elbow on my knee so I could face her. "You know thirty million is a drop in the bucket for me. If you need that money, Jules, I'll give it to you." There was a tendril of unruly dark-red hair that had fallen in front of her left eye. I reached out and gently pushed it behind her ear, then caressed her face with the tips of my fingers as I let go.

She shivered at the featherlight touch to her jawline, and I felt that response below the belt. My cock started to harden behind my slacks and I shifted my legs to allow for more room. I calmly started thinking of cats, old ladies knitting, dirty socks, and whatever else I could conjure so that I wasn't focused on Julianne and how fantastic she looked in that white dress.

"I don't want or need a handout, Gio. I want a partner. I want fucking revenge against Bianca and Brenden. Don't you?"

I inhaled sharply. "I do, but it's not healthy."

"Says the man who's independently wealthy with more money than you could ever spend in a hundred lifetimes. FM Enterprises may be just one of many successful companies you now own, not to mention the generational wealth your family has accumulated, but this was my *livelihood*. My passion. My living, breathing dream job. And for all intents and purposes, it is my birthright. I don't know why my parents signed the business away to Brenden, but I'm going to find out."

What she wasn't saying was that she believed there was more going on than them leaving her out of the will. And after knowing her parents for the thirty-one years I'd been alive, I'd have to agree with her. "Besides the fact that it is incredibly strange that Lewis and Rachel didn't split the percentage they owned between you and your brother, what makes you think there's more to it?"

"Because they changed their will only a week before they went on the trip that ended their lives. Coincidence?" She tilted her head. "I think not."

My heart pounded a million beats a minute. "Wait, you think something *nefarious* went on with our parents' deaths?" I scoffed.

She shrugged. "Honestly, I don't know. All I do know is that my parents knew how much the company meant to me. It would have made more sense to leave the company shares to me instead of Brenden. I'm the one who loves it."

I nodded, then rubbed my fingers over the scruff at my jaw. It wasn't quite a beard or full mustache, more a fine shading of hair over both those areas. It was a look I'd perfected over the years. One Bianca had asked me to do away with. So when I left her, Brenden, and the business in the rearview mirror, I brought it back. Almost as if it was my own way of saying "fuck you" to her. Not that she'd care.

"So why the auction? What was the goal?" I asked, bringing it back to the matter at hand.

"Well, my plan was to get a boatload of money tonight. After, I would start a competing company. Then because I was fired without cause, I'd file a wrongful termination lawsuit as well as the legal proceedings to contest the will. Next, I planned to steal every last client I brought in and watch the entire company fall. Brenden would have to crawl on his hands and knees to get me back." She grinned wickedly.

"Because you would want to go back?" I clarified, trying to figure out why she would do so.

"I mean..." she let her words trail off before she spoke again. "You know, that's a good question. If I created my own successful business, why would I want to go back to working with my asshole brother and his gold-digging, nasty wife?" She made a sour expression that was rather adorable.

"Wouldn't it be more satisfying to not need him at all?" I added.

"Yeah, I guess. It's just...our parents built the company together. Four best friends. It's part of their legacy."

"So are you," I said. "Anything you do in life is also a reflection of the good they created. Never forget that, Jules."

She frowned. "What about you? Don't you want to get revenge on my brother and your ex?"

I clamped my mouth shut so tight my teeth clanked together while I fisted my hands. "It's uncouth and not the type of behavior my parents would have championed," I reasoned.

"Fuck that! Bianca cheated on you with your best friend the night before you were supposed to get married. Your best man, business partner, and lifelong friend fucked you over. Now they are both screwing me over. And to add insult to injury, they rushed a quickie wedding. All of it stinks to high heaven, and I'm not going to go away quietly. Bianca ruined everything."

"Brenden is no saint in this either," I growled, remembering the very moment I walked into that room and found him plowing into my fiancée from behind, her body bent over as she moaned like the hussy she was.

"Then help me stick it to them!" She pleaded with determination.

"By funding your new company?" I asked.

"Absolutely. And by marrying me. Tonight."

Marrying her.

My eyebrows rose up toward my hairline as shock rolled through me like a brutal heat wave. "You can't be serious, Jules. I came here this evening to save you from yourself. Not dig a deeper hole between our families."

She grinned wickedly. "Imagine how angry Brenden and Bianca will be when they find out that not only am I starting up a new company, but that you and I got married."

I couldn't help the small smile that appeared at the visual. "He would be enraged. Ever since we were kids, he made me swear you were not to be touched or he'd never so much as talk to me again."

"And what did he go and do behind your back? Fuck your fiancée and ruin your friendship. Now they're ruining my life. I think they both need a dose of their own medicine."

"Hmm..." I imagined the look on his face when he learned I'd married his baby sister. He'd lose his mind. The same way I had when he betrayed me.

Julianne abruptly stood and put her hand out for me to take. "What do you say, Gio? Will you marry me and fund my startup company and lawsuits while we seek the ultimate revenge on my brother and your ex?"

"Marriage?" I whispered, my response filled with uncertainty. "How would that even work?"

Julianne tilted her head and looked at me as though I'd grown horns. "When a man and a woman want to share their lives, they stand in front of an officiant and—"

I waved my hand for her to stop. "Don't be a brat."

"I make no promises," she taunted with a smile.

My nostrils flared as her sweet strawberries-and-cream scent filled my nose, making my pants tight once more.

"When I get married, Julianne, I want it to be real. That means sharing our secrets, our highs and lows. It means sharing a life and...*a bed.*" I watched her eyes light with excitement but tried to ignore it. "I won't enter into a sexless marriage with you or a loveless marriage like I was headed into with Bianca."

Suddenly, Jules licked her lips, hiked up her dress, and promptly straddled my lap.

"Oomph!" I let out a surprised breath when her lush, round ass hit my thighs. Before I could speak, she cupped my cheeks, lowered her head, and kissed me. Hard.

I went completely still, until the heat of her body, and the plump, delicious press of her lips to mine, wove through my mind informing me of what was happening. I moaned as I wrapped my arms around her body tightly and kissed her back, glorying in her minty taste.

She teased the seam of my lips with her nimble tongue and I opened instantly. Our tongues tangled and danced, flicking delicately one moment and sinking deep the next. Before I knew what was happening, one of my hands was cupping her breast, the other gripping her ass as she wantonly ground against my erection.

I ripped my mouth away. "Jesus!" I let out a harsh breath and rested my face against the tops of her heaving, beautiful tits.

Julianne ran her fingers through my hair, scraping her nails down my scalp. I arched toward her and the blissful sensation as I lifted my face and traced every last one of her gorgeous features with my eyes.

She smiled from her perch in my lap. "I never said there'd be no sex, Gio. And based on Mr. Happy I feel prodding my ass, I don't see desire being a problem between us. And I already care for you. I've loved you my entire life."

Love. A fickle, meaningless word if not said with the right intention and breadth of meaning behind it.

"Yeah, as extended family." I removed the hand from her breast and placed both to her hips. They were so plush I couldn't help kneading the curves there.

"I have never looked at you as family. Remember back when we were kids? You were my first kiss. A girl doesn't kiss her extended family, Gio. Then Brenden caught us and made a big deal of me being 'off limits' and you backed off right away. I just assumed you didn't truly like me that way. At the time, it actually hurt my feelings."

"Really?" I asked, hope and shock threading through the single word.

"Yeah, really. I was into you big time." She smiled and then stood, pushing off my lap and putting some much-needed space between us.

"I-I don't know what to say," I blustered, not having any idea how to respond after everything she'd shared.

"Say you'll work with me on getting revenge against Brenden and Bianca." Her gaze was pleading as she held out her hand. "Say yes to marrying me."

Episode 17

One of the Good Ones

MEMPHIS

Jade led the group of candidates to the auction room and showed us where to line up behind the stage. I'd done this before, but had never made it onto the actual stage, having left my spot to help Jade when she ran off the last time we were here. Now she was working for Madam Alana and seemed to enjoy it. The woman was definitely in her element. She walked down the line of people, checking in with them and ensuring their comfort. I watched as she tutted over each woman and man until she got to me.

"Second time's a charm, eh?" Her lips twitched in amusement as she reached out to readjust my tie into position.

I grinned. "Let's hope."

"I know I've said it before, but what you did for me— leaving the auction and helping me through my meltdown— was incredibly kind. No other man has ever been that chivalrous."

"Well that's a damn shame, Jade. You deserve a man who will treat you well and support you through all of life's challenges." I reached out and grabbed her hand and gave it a little squeeze.

"You deserve all of that too, you know. You're one of the good ones, Memphis. Never forget that. And if the woman who purchases you tonight doesn't treat you as such, we are here for you. Madam Alana has made it very clear that her candidates come first, no matter what."

I chuckled. "I heard that, sister. Definitely. She drilled it into our heads when we signed on the dotted lines. And I appreciate it, I do. Though I certainly can handle myself. I'm going to make the most of this experience. Let's just hope the woman who chooses me tonight has a great personality and a whole lotta fire within her."

Jade grinned. "I think you're going to be very surprised this evening. There's one woman in particular who I think will absolutely adore you."

"Oh yeah?" I nudged her shoulder. "Is she fine?"

"Stunning. Elegant. Smart and very wealthy." She lifted her chin in a knowing manner she'd likely picked up from Alana because it was smooth as butter and just as rich.

"All right." I rubbed my hands together, anticipation and adrenaline swirling in my gut. "And you think this queen is going to bid on me?"

She offered a coy smile. "Let's put it this way, you are exactly what she asked for during her interview. I'd be shocked if she didn't take you home tonight."

I chuckled. "Excellent. I can't wait to get this show on the road." I rolled my shoulders and shook off the excess energy.

"Speaking of... Tonight we're doing men first. You're up, my friend. Follow me to the front of the line."

I did as she requested. As I passed by Summer, she lifted her hand in the "rock on" symbol. "You've got this, buddy! Go get 'em, tiger," she said.

The petite woman named Maia gave me a solemn wave as though I was heading to the guillotine. She was an interesting one. Didn't say much through the entire process, giving nothing of herself. It was as if she wanted to fade into the background. It made me wonder where Madam Alana had found her.

Before I knew it, my name was called through the PA system and Jade held back the black velvet curtain. The lights blinded me momentarily as I pushed through.

"Welcome, Memphis. Please take your position." Alana spoke from where she stood off to the side in front of a podium.

"Memphis Taylor is from Atlanta, Georgia. He played college football and loves fitness, as you can see." A couple women in the audience made a few woot sounds which had me grinning. "Memphis comes from a large family and loves the outdoors, working out, and watching football. He is six foot three and twenty-four years old."

"First, we'd like to ascertain the bidders' interest in this young man. Please pick up your remotes and choose Yes-No-Maybe before we continue."

I turned around to see the results, my palms sweating as my nerves replaced the earlier excitement. This was the make-or-break moment. The first step in being chosen by someone tonight. If I was, then my plans for a successful, financially secure future for me and my family would be set into motion.

Yes – 7

No – 5

Maybe – 8

"Hell, yeah!" I whooped, so caught up in the moment I forgot where I was. Some members of the audience laughed at my outburst while Alana's lips twitched, showing she wasn't upset with me.

Out of the twenty women bidding, fifteen of them were interested in me. An injured college dropout who had no clue what to do with his future. Not that I'd be sharing that information anytime soon. I fully planned on wooing my wife and being everything she needed during the three years of our marriage.

I just had to convince my family that getting engaged out of the blue to a woman they'd never met wasn't suspicious. My mother would be concerned I was moving too fast. My father, would be thrilled beyond reason that I'd found someone. He'd always told me he knew the second he met my mother that she was the one for him. But my granny... Now, she would be the hardest to convince. She knew me better than anyone. I'd always been close to her, especially since my father had worked long hours driving while I grew up.

My mother was always there for us kids, but she had her hands full with the six of us. Dividing her time between my sisters, her job, and my sports schedule was difficult. My granny, however, had taken a shine to me from the second I was born. I'd gravitated toward her. She was wise, took no shit from anyone, and had three sons of her own. She knew how to connect without smothering. Getting her to believe I was marrying for love was going to be hard as hell, but I'd find a way.

"Memphis, please exit the stage and return in your robe for the second half of tonight's auction," Madam Alana instructed.

I smiled, waved at the crowd, and then spun around on my heel as though I was doing a complicated dance move. More chuckles could be heard from the audience as I suavely sauntered offstage.

* * * *

NAOMI

I sat with my mouth hanging open, my heart pounding, and my mind reeling as my dream man walked onto the stage. I could not believe it. Lady luck was finally moving in my favor.

Memphis motherfucking Taylor, in all his Black, hand-some glory, stood tall and proud, looking even more dashing than he did when we'd run into one another in the elevator just this morning.

All last night I'd bemoaned the fact that I'd not gone after him. We'd had the best date of my entire life. I hadn't met a man I'd connected to so completely before him. And after that goodbye kiss...I was a goner. But, I wasn't that kind of girl. I didn't steal another woman's man right out from under her nose.

Now I realized what was really happening.

The clever man. He'd never said his fiancée's name. Never mentioned how'd they'd met or why he was in town a day earlier than her. He'd only said that he would be meeting his wife the next evening.

And now I knew.

A million thoughts scrambled my brain as I stared at him. He wore a tailored suit that showed off his muscular arms and thick thighs. It was a dove-gray color that offset his com-plexion magnificently.

"Damn, I'll be taking that man home tonight," a scantily clad white woman to my left said to a bidder sitting next to her. "Look at that fine hunk of a man. Mm-hmm. I'm going to climb him like a tree the second I win the bid. And Daddy will be so angry when he finds out I'm engaged to someone without status too," she snickered.

I snarled, grinding my teeth. There was no way in Hell I was going to be outbid on this man by a giggling, spoiled brat. It was probably his money she was spending. I, too, had been born and raised with a silver spoon in my mouth, but I'd actually worked to earn what I had. Was independently wealthy outside of the family trust.

Memphis Taylor would be mine.

This was the exact sign I needed. Memphis and I had connected in a way that I hadn't experienced ever. It was as if our souls sighed when we'd kissed last night. I wouldn't let something so beautiful between us slip away a third time.

And I simply couldn't wait to see his face when I walked into the room to sign off on the final bid. He'd be shocked silly.

I smirked to myself as Madam Alana asked for the bidders to use their remote to show their interest. I clicked "Yes" so fast my thumb smarted against the painful amount of pressure I used to make my selection. Unfortunately, there were fifteen of us interested.

I tapped my foot as Madam Alana asked him to exit the stage and come back for the second round. I had no idea what the second round entailed. After he left, I watched each candidate come out and go through the same process of giving the bidders an opportunity to show their interest. The longer it took to get back to Memphis, the more irritated I became.

Listening to this woman next to me go on and on about what she was going to do in the bedroom with Memphis once she got her hooks into him made me want to pull on her blonde hair and rip her extensions right off her head. Instead, I minded my manners, sipped on my second martini, and tried my damnedest to wait patiently for *my man* to return—but it took Herculean effort.

Finally, the second half of the event started, and Alana called his name. He strutted through the dark curtains like a man on a mission. He was barefoot and dressed in a navy-blue satin robe tied at the waist.

I perched on the edge of my seat, my auction paddle ready to go.

"Memphis, darling, please remove your robe," Madam Alana cooed in that sultry, elegant French lilt of hers.

He smiled wide, undid the tie, and let the satin fall to the floor.

My mouth went completely dry as his massive, well-built

muscular frame appeared. He was cut...*everywhere*. He had toned pecs that were squared off and led down to a six, or was that an eight-pack, stomach. His dark skin glistened, making every dip and curve shine under the spotlights. He looked like the sun god Ra with his hands on his trim waist, his form seeming unbreakable, as we all looked our fill.

I gripped my paddle so hard my hand ached as I licked my lips. Damn, how I wanted to run my tongue all over his fine body. Press my nose to his neck and inhale his very essence directly from the source.

I used my paddle to fan my suddenly heated face. Hot damn! That man would make a nun wet between the thighs. Every inch of him was utter perfection.

"I'm going to pass out! He's gorgeous," the blonde gasped.

"Wow. You are not kidding. And look at that bulge," her friend whispered loud enough for pretty much everyone to hear.

I scowled but stupidly looked at the bulge. The sassy bitches were not wrong. He was absolutely packing some serious heat down below. I clenched my legs together as arousal flooded my system.

"I'll start the bidding at three million," Madam Alana announced.

Before I could even move, the blonde waved her lit paddle.

I narrowed my gaze at her as another woman closer to the stage waved hers and upped the bid to four million.

I was stunned as paddles went flying. Still, I didn't care. I not only was extremely wealthy, I had family money going back generations. There was no number too high. Especially since I believed Memphis and I had shared something truly special.

When the bids slowed to eight and a half million, and Memphis had turned his body around giving a nice view of his rounded, toned ass which he flexed so his cheeks bounced deliciously behind his boxer briefs, I finally raised my paddle.

"Ten million dollars," I stated coolly, raising the bid another million and a half.

Madam Alana smiled for the first time and winked in my direction. That small display showing her approval in my choice this evening made me grin happily. Not that I needed her encouragement. She didn't know what had occurred between Memphis and me before now. Still, having what I thought was her blessing at my choice didn't hurt in the least. She knew what I wanted and that wink expressed her agreement that I'd chosen wisely.

"Bitch!" the blonde grumbled.

I turned my head toward her as Madam Alana said, "Ten million going once..."

"Sorry, ladies, you simply never had a chance. He's far too much man for the likes of either of you," I tutted and waved my hand nonchalantly.

The blonde glared and sucked down a full glass of champagne, practically choking on it as she did so.

I laughed heartily at her frustration as she promptly stood. "Well, you can have him."

"Ten million going twice," Alana continued.

"I surely will. In every way possible." I lifted my martini up in salute. "Better luck next time."

"Sold, to bidder number four for ten million dollars."

Episode 18

May the Best Man Win

SUMMER

Madam Alana met the rest of the candidates at the stage after returning from the private auction she held for her goddaughter, Julianne. That had to be awkward as all get out. But then again, the connection I had with my family was strange to most people. Maybe Julianne being put up for auction was no big deal. I mean, my mother suggested The Marriage Auction to me. I'm not even sure how she heard about it or got me an interview. Regardless, I was here, dressed like an expensive fashion model, feeling like a million bucks. Or I should say, three million bucks.

I snickered to myself at the internal joke. Maia, the petite little brunette who stood next to me, frowned.

"What? Are you freaked out?" I asked her.

"Um, yeah?" She gave me big eyes. "How are you not?" The girl shuffled from foot to foot as if the high heels she wore pinched her toes. Either that or she was about to bolt.

I shrugged. "The stars, the moon, and the universe have all aligned. My mother called me earlier and told me today was the day my life would change."

"And *that* doesn't freak you out? What do you mean your mother told you? She some kind of psychic?" Maia asked, saying more words than she'd spoken all day.

I shook my head. "Nah, that's my sister, Autumn. She also called and told me she saw a tall, dark, handsome man with an accent in my near future. Which she was right about because I met one yesterday in the elevator."

Maia twisted her lips and cocked her head to the side. "And you believe this mumbo jumbo? The stars aligned. You will meet a handsome man, blah blah."

"I'm happy with whatever the universe puts in my path. If it's meant for me, I'm going to accept it, enjoy the present as much as possible, and be hopeful about tomorrow. What will be, will be, ya know?"

Maia made a huffing noise. "No, I don't know. The universe surely hasn't provided me with jack shit. As a matter of fact, fuck the universe. They can suck a bag of—" Her words fell away abruptly.

"Ladies, you look beautiful." Madam Alana approached smoothly, gliding across the carpet in her sky-high heels without problem. I was doing okay in mine. I'd worn stilettos before, just not recently. As soon as I could take those puppies off though, bare feet it was. I could already imagine the relief I'd feel.

"Thank you for the makeover. I actually feel beautiful," I gushed, planting my hands to my hips and showing off the red velvet gown that made me look like a blonde version of Jessica Rabbit.

Maia's gown was bold and short, but the small woman totally pulled it off.

"Yeah, thanks," Maia grumbled and looked down at her feet. She wore a pair of black patent leather stilettos with blazing red bottoms that gave her a solid three to four more inches in height. At five eight, I was above average in height for a woman, but in heels, I felt ten feet tall and powerful, ready to take on the world.

Madam Alana reached out and cupped Maia's cheeks with both hands. "Are you certain you are ready for this step? You've been hesitant for a while."

"It's time. I need the money. You know how it is." The young girl stared into Madam Alana's coal-black gaze.

"I do. And I'm proud of you. I will not let anything untoward happen. Not on my watch. I protect my candidates. I am but a call away and have many means to access the people I care about rather quickly. *Oui?*" Her tone was not only confident but final. Madam Alana had the girl's back. Had all of our backs. I was happy for Maia. She seemed like she needed someone to care for her. I didn't know her situation, but I hoped perhaps to be friends with her in the future.

Maia nodded quickly and averted her gaze almost as if she was uncomfortable with the scrutiny.

"You look perfect, *chéri*. Keep your chin up." Alana tapped under her jaw.

"And you, Ms. Belanger, are the belle of the ball." Her gaze took in my gown from top to toe. "You are definitely wearing that dress, it is not wearing you." She winked.

"I know, right?" The velvet tied in a bow around my neck, accentuated my breasts, dipped in at my waist, hugged my hips, and flared out when it hit my knees. I turned from side to side and then showed her my bare back where the dress was open all the way down to the top of my bum. My body looked amazing.

Madam Alana smiled. "Be sure to turn around like that on stage," she encouraged.

"You got it. Did, um..." I bit into my bottom lip. "Did you think any more about giving a sign to that bidder you thought might pair well with me?" I brought my fingers together and twisted them anxiously.

"Well, I decided that was up to you, my dear. If you'd like

me to share a bit of what you are looking for in a bidder, I can do so when I introduce you. However, stating so might limit those who may have originally been interested."

"Bah!" I waved my hand in front of us. "I don't care if it's only one man who bids on me, as long as it's someone who is open to tutoring me in business."

"And if that person is interested in finding a woman they can keep and build a family with?" She repeated a bit of our conversation from yesterday.

"As I told you before. I love kids. They are not a deterrent for me. Sure, I'd like to wait a little while so I can get ahead in the business, but I am open to kids. And regarding the long-term marriage possibility, I'm totally here for it. Either way, I'm excited about tonight." I rubbed my hands together.

"Indeed." Alana tapped her blood-red lips. "It's a welcome change. You are incredibly unique and rather refreshing, Summer. I look forward to seeing how your pairing works out."

"Madam Alana," Jade called from the top of a set of stairs leading up to the stage. "It's time."

The Madam squeezed my shoulder as she walked by.

I waited as each person approached the stage while humming "Hotel California" by The Eagles in my head. By the time my name was called, I was ready to go.

I excitedly made my way up the stairs and smiled as the curtains opened.

"Our next candidate tonight is Summer Belanger."

* * * *

JACK

I stared stupidly as the knockout blonde I'd met in the elevator breezed across the stage looking absolutely breath-taking. She stopped when she got to the center.

Summer Belanger.

"She told me her name was Rebecca," I growled under my breath then promptly tugged at my necktie which felt more like a noose than an accessory. I couldn't believe she'd lied to me when asking something as simple as her name. Then again, she'd also given me the wrong phone number, so I shouldn't be surprised. And there she was looking like a dream, strutting across the floor as if she owned the place.

"Summer is five foot eight, has blue eyes, and is…wealthy." A shared gasp and rumbling murmurs picked up throughout the bidders around me. Madam Alana pressed her lips together coyly. "Summer has not entered into the auction tonight because of the money she will receive. She has entered because she wants a husband who is willing to mentor her in the art of running a successful business."

My heart beat a million miles an hour as Alana shared intriguing facts about the woman I hadn't been able to stop thinking about.

"Summer is self-made, has a very involved family unit, and is not opposed to a long-term marriage or having children in the future," Alana continued.

My entire body quickly overheated as I stared at Summer and really heard the words that Alana was saying.

Involved family unit.

Not opposed to a long-term marriage.

Willing to have children.

These were the exact things I'd requested in my own interview. And all Rebecca—I mean Summer—wanted in return was a man to help mentor her in business? It was unbelievable. Beyond incredible. It's almost as if…

Suddenly, Madam Alana reached up and tugged on her right ear.

Holy Moses. That was my sign.

My mouth went dry, the rest of Alana's words disappearing along with all other noises in the room. I focused on nothing but the woman on stage. She was the one who Alana believed I'd be happiest with. The same woman I'd met in the elevator and had felt such an intense connection to. The one I'd been trying to force out of my mind since we met.

It was as if the universe opened its mighty hands and dumped her straight into my path.

I watched as Summer turned around and placed her hands on her hips before looking over her shoulder with a sultry smirk. Her entire bare back was on display, from the big red velvet bow tied around her neck, all the way down her delicate-looking spine to the roundness of her arse.

Physically the woman was stunning. Personality-wise, quirky, awkward, with a heaping dose of adorable. I think our time in the elevator barely scratched the surface of what the future could hold for us. Because we would definitely have a future together.

No matter what it took, or what I had to bid, Summer Belanger would be mine.

I grabbed my remote and punched the Yes button as fast as I could. Then I fidgeted in my seat as the numbers tallied.

Madam Alana turned to the large screen at the back of the stage.

Yes – 5

No – 30

Maybe – 15

"These are encouraging numbers. Summer, darling, please exit the stage and we'll see you back for the second portion of the evening's festivities," Alana said.

Summer moved to leave the stage and her heel got caught in the fabric. Her arms pinwheeled in the air as she wobbled on unsteady feet like my late friend Troy's baby did when he first started walking. Eventually she got her balance, yanked the fabric from her shoe, rolled her eyes, and shrugged at the audience.

Several bellows of laughter could be heard echoing

through the room.

"She is cute as a button. I'm going to bid on her," a blond man I didn't know nudged my shoulder from where he sat beside me.

"You'll have to fight me for her, brother," I announced coolly.

"Then may the best man win."

"I will," I stated flatly, staring him down as I would any true opponent.

He dipped his head, politely ending our little chat before turning to the side and leaving me to my thoughts.

All of them were about Summer.

I chuckled and shook my head. I'd given her the nickname *"solskinn"* when we'd met yesterday, because she exuded such a bright light. Now I found out her name was Summer. The endearment I'd called her meant *sunshine* in my language. Another startlingly clear sign that this woman was meant to be my bride.

After what felt like eternity, Summer appeared back on stage. She wore a red satin robe that came to mid-thigh and tied at her waist. Her hair was still piled up in a mix of intricate swoops and curls on top of her head. For a moment I wished it was down so I could see those long locks flow over her shoulders. Then I remembered I was the only one here who had seen her a little more wild and free. I was deliriously happy my competition wouldn't ever get the chance to see her that way.

"Welcome back, Summer. Please remove your robe, *chéri*," Alana announced.

Summer untied the bow, shimmied a shoulder until it was bare, and then repeated the process on the other side, still clutching the satin to her chest. She was absolutely putting on a show with exaggerated facial expressions and moving her body in a manner which I'm sure she believed was seductive, but came off entirely comedic, rather than sexy. The woman was positively charming as she gave her best mini-strip tease of the single item.

Then she let the fabric fall and my mouth dropped open. I knew she had a knockout body, but standing in a strapless red bra that her breasts were practically bulging out of and a tiny scrap of red satin that had a t-strap that went straight up her arse in the back, leaving absolutely nothing to the imagination? Priceless.

Before I knew it, I was standing and yelling, "Three million dollars."

Madam Alana chuckled lightly. "It seems we have the first bid. Please don't forget to use your paddle so that my team can record who is proposing an amount and when. *Merci*," she finished.

I grabbed my paddle right as the guy sitting at the table next to me held his aloft. "Three and a half million," he offered.

I snarled, my nostrils flaring. "Four million." I clicked my paddle on.

"Four and a half million," the man countered.

Irritation poured through my veins as another bid came through from somewhere on the opposite side of the room.

"Five million! She looks as sweet as apple pie," a man with a cowboy hat yelled in a booming voice.

I watched in horror as Summer's cheeks heated, turning rosy pink as she grinned at the compliment.

Absolutely not. No way. I was not leaving this event tonight without a bride on my arm, and that person would be Summer Belanger.

"Six million!" I waved my paddle angrily, skipping the halfway point monetarily in the hopes I could nudge these suitors to leave well enough alone.

"Six and a half million," the man next to me growled, and craned his neck from side to side.

"You really want to tangle with me?" I scoffed in his

direction. "I'm Jack Larsen, the CEO of Johansen Brewing. You know, the largest supplier of beer in the world. Ring any bells?" Usually all I had to do was share my position and the company I worked for and people backed off.

The man's eyes widened, and he lifted his hand to rub at his jaw. "Still any man's game. I don't care who you are," he boasted weakly.

I took a moment to assess the male before me. His suit was adequate but nothing of the caliber mine was. His hair was swept off his forehead neatly, but the sweat beading at his hairline and the way he was constantly fidgeting was telling. I suspected the bravado he was spouting may not be backed financially. My best guess was that he probably wasn't planning to offer much more.

"I can go all night." I crossed my arms with my paddle lit in front of me, staring him down, and hollered, "Eight million." I skipped right over another million and a half to let him know I was serious.

The man scowled as he grated, "Fine. You can have her."

"Excellent. I was planning on it."

"Going once…going twice…sold to Number 5 for eight million dollars," Madam Alana stated. "Please exit the stage, Summer." My bride-to-be crouched to grab her robe and slipped it on.

"Can't wait to meet you, Number 5!" she called out and waved.

I couldn't help but laugh. No matter what happened from here, at least I knew I was not only marrying a gorgeous woman who seemed to want what I did, but she would also fill my life with laughter. There wasn't a price high enough one could put on that.

I stood up, buttoned my coat, and left the bidding room. I was met by one of Alana's employees.

"Come this way, Mr. Larsen. We'll have you sign the final marriage agreement which includes your bidding details and payments over the next three years, the 20% commission for our services, and the $250,000 deposit that must go into the candidate's account tonight after she agrees to the same terms as you."

I could hardly wait to see her face when she found out who'd bid on her.

"Excellent. Bring me to my bride."

Episode 19

What Have I Done?

RHODES

"Is it almost over?" I asked Christophe as I adjusted my tie for the third time, then undid it and ripped the blasted thing over my head. I tossed it onto the small circular table where my auction paddle sat next to my drink.

We'd just seen several men and women auctioned off to the highest bidder. And if I was being perfectly honest, the entire process was fascinating. I could tell that Madam Alana was proud of her company. She exuded extreme confidence at the podium along with a heaping dose of her charm. She didn't make the process feel tawdry or debauched, even when the candidates were showing off their bodies. It felt rather similar to a private fashion event, like the kind I used to attend when my ex-wife would walk in a runway show for a particular designer.

"I'm surprised you haven't bid on anyone, *mon ami.* I thought for sure you would raise the paddle for Summer. She seems like your type." Christophe sipped his wine, one leg crossed nonchalantly over the other.

"Why? Because she's blonde?" I scoffed.

Christophe grinned and shrugged. "*Oui.*"

I shook my head. "Let me just say the only blonde I want in my house is my daughter. Portia put me off blonde women in a romantic capacity, for… Well, let's just say forever."

Christophe chuckled. "This makes sense. She could put any man off an entire group of women." His lips twisted into a sour expression.

"Too true." I snickered and then eased back into my chair feeling a tad lighter, the gin and tonic I drank easing the tension in my shoulders.

"We have our last candidate of the night. It is my great pleasure to welcome Maia Fields," Alana announced.

I was about to pull out my phone to check on Emily back at the resort when I glanced up at the stage and couldn't believe my eyes.

"My pickpocket!" I gasped.

"Maia Fields is twenty-three, a native of Colorado, and loves being outdoors. She is a petite five foot three. It is my experience that the best things in life come in small packages." Alana's red lips pressed together in a knowing smirk.

"Small enough to spin on my cock," said a rotund man who nudged his friend's shoulder while rubbing his hands together. "We call those types of little things *spinners*," he continued, licking his lips as he did so.

Before I knew it, the smarmy fellow lifted his paddle into the air. "Three million for the sugar baby," he called out.

"Sugar baby," I sneered under my breath. *How rude.* How dare he talk down about a woman in such a way when he was sitting there bidding on a bride without having to make any effort to woo her. Probably because he would never have been able to get a woman like that. The back of his balding head had a poorly done combover and he was sweating profusely, his wide, curved nose red and ruddy from the booze he likely partook of too often for his own good. His suit was expensive but ill-fitting.

"Have some respect," Christophe hissed while tapping the man on the shoulder, earning his attention.

"For what? A pint-sized whore?" he returned with laughter.

Christophe's head jerked back as though punched, and his facial expression shifted to disgust.

"Oh, I see we already have interest in Maia. As this is the last candidate of the night, and we already have a bidder, let's skip ahead. I have three million from bidder Number 19."

"Three and a half million," another bidder called out, and I sighed in relief.

My joy was short-lived as the jerkish man countered, "Four million!" He waved his lit paddle, then leaned over to his friend. "I'm going to hog-tie her, hang her from a hook in my bedroom, and play with her little body until she begs me to stop." He grinned wickedly, a malicious haze overtaking his already unfortunate features.

"Are you just going to let him get away with this?" I pointed my hand toward the disgusting person. Christophe's wife owned the auction. Couldn't he do something?

"My wife vetted him completely. She has checks and balances in place. Perhaps it's just locker room talk." Christophe's jaw was as firm as granite, his teeth clenched as he spoke slowly. I could tell he didn't truly believe his own words and it was weighing down on him.

"Pssshttt! Obviously a nasty one snuck through." I lifted my foot, considering shoving it into the back of the man's skull the next time he said something inappropriate. I was never one to result to violence, but this guy was fucking gross.

The bidding was now at five million in favor of the nasty bastard.

I stared into the warm brown eyes of the woman I hadn't

been able to stop thinking about since I'd opened my eyes and found her sitting on top of me at the airport after we crashed into one another. She was unearthly beautiful with a perfect little curvy shape, but her eyes were sad. Stunningly so. Much like what I saw in the mirror when I looked at my own reflection each morning. There was a shared unhappiness there, one I recognized all too well. Sometimes I thought it was loneliness, other times I believed it was my own karma staring back at me.

Why was Maia sad? Had she lost someone like I had all those years ago? Did her last man cheat on her more times than the years they were together? Did life continue to screw her over in ways most people could never understand? I'd bet I could relate.

Just because someone had money didn't mean they had it all. Frankly, I knew more rich people who were unhappy than people who lived paycheck to paycheck. The latter individuals knew that money wasn't the source of happiness. The former continued to try and force it to be, as if they could get more and more and eventually reach the highest level of bliss possible, only to find the top was lonely as fuck. It didn't mean jack if you didn't have anyone to share it with. At least that had been my experience.

"Five million going once…" Alana announced.

Maia heard that number and smiled for the first time.

That smile broke me in two. Shattered my resistance into dust. Everything I thought I knew was obliterated. My cock hardened behind my pants, my heart pounded like a drum within my chest, and I lost all common sense.

I lifted my hand in the air, the weight of the paddle feeling like a sword, as if I was going into battle. I flicked the button to fire it up, a beacon of light in a dark, unrelenting sea of bidders.

No other would get that smile pointed at them but me.

Maia would be mine.

* * * *

MAIA

"Seven million." A new voice that sounded slightly familiar entered the bidding war suddenly.

My mouth dropped open, and I swear my eyeballs practically bugged out of my head. Some man out there wanted me to be his wife for *seven million dollars*. Me, a tiny little pickpocket. That was more money than I could have ever dreamed of having. The entire process was absolutely unreal and blew my mind every time the bid increased.

I'd entered the auction in the hopes I'd be picked for the base minimum of three million. That kind of money was all I would need to get my mother and siblings away from that horrifying man and his abomination of a son. Seven million would be more than life altering. It was world-changing for someone like me and my family.

Alana smiled wider than I'd ever seen in the many years I'd known her. Whoever this bidder was, she recognized him and was blatantly thrilled he'd entered the battle.

"You just want to take her away from me," one of the voices that had been bidding griped loud enough for everyone to hear, but the lights on the stage were too bright for me to see anything other than shadows in the audience. I squinted and could vaguely see a large shape with his arm out pointing at something or someone who may have been seated, but I wasn't sure.

"Maybe I don't like the way you refer to women as toys." the new bidder fired back angrily.

That voice.

I'd definitely heard it before, but I couldn't put my finger on it…Wait. What did he say? Treating women like toys?

A different voice invaded my mind like a nightmare come

to life.

"You're my little toy, Maia. Whenever I want. However, I want. No one is going to save you. Now hush up and do what big brother says..."

Bile rose up my throat and immediately my skin broke out in goosebumps as fear slithered up my spine like a snake, wrapping its coils around me and squeezing every ounce of breath I had left in my lungs.

I let out a harsh cough, sucking in huge bouts of air as I fisted my hands until my knuckles turned white. I would be no man's *toy*. Alana had sworn up and down that I didn't have to do anything that could harm me. I'd been treated like a plaything for someone to get their jollies off before.

I squeezed my eyes shut and instantly shut down the darkness encroaching from the memories as they tried to invade. The darkness was always there, digging its claws and prodding at my mind to find a weak spot to slip through and take over. It took everything I had to shove those experiences back into the safety deposit box where I kept them concealed. I'd locked them away within the deepest reaches of the vault that was my mind, never wanting them to see the light of day.

Not ever again.

I wasn't that person anymore. No longer was I a terrified teenager with no choices. If the man who was to be my husband scared me, I wouldn't sign the final contract. I still had one easy out, and I'd take it if I had to.

"Gentlemen, we do not air our grievances during the auction. One or both of you may be removed if this continues," Alana stated, her authority over the room clear. She waited what felt like a full thirty seconds for the entire room to go silent before she smiled cooly. "Excellent. Let's continue. I have seven million to bidder Number 38 going once..."

I held my breath.

"Going twice…"

I thought I might pass out right there on the stage.

"Sold to Mr. Davenport for seven million dollars. Maia, love, please exit the stage. There will be a member of my staff waiting to bring you to the signing room."

My feet were glued to the shiny black floor. The rest of me as heavy as two tons as I stood there trembling, not able to believe what just happened.

I'd been sold to a man for seven million dollars.

I was going to be rich.

I was going to get married.

I was going to be some random wealthy man's wife.

Davenport. The name bounced around in my head as I blinked against the glaring lights. I knew that name. I'd seen it on the driver's license of the man I pickpocketed just yesterday. The hot *"Zaddy"* I'd used as my personal fantasy man when I got myself off in the shower just this morning.

There was no way the same man was here.

What if he was? What if he just bought me to get the money I stole back? Oh my god—what if I was going to walk off this stage and into a room filled with cops? I'd never be able to help my family if I was taken to jail.

He could hurt Maisie, too.

Sweat beaded on my hairline and under my arms as I panted, unable to get air into my lungs fast enough. A face I recognized, one that was safe, entered my line of vision.

"You okay, *chéri?*" Alana cooed, her brows furrowed.

I nodded on autopilot but didn't speak.

"A little shocked at all that has happened?" she surmised, her tone concerned, not upset.

Again, I nodded, not wanting to share all the things I was frightened of, lest she kick me out of her fancy auction, costing me the best possible chance I'd ever have at saving my family or living a real life.

Seven million dollars.

"Could it really be true? The money…" I croaked.

She laughed out loud, curved an arm around my shoulders, and eased me toward the side of the stage. Her steps were sure while mine wobbled in heels I could barely walk in.

"It has happened. All your worries will be no longer. I know your bidder personally. It will be an experience to say the least." She gave me a half smile.

Her reassurance helped, but the niggling fear wouldn't abate. "There aren't going to be any cops waiting to arrest me?" I whispered, my voice small and scared.

Abruptly, she turned around and held up a finger to the audience.

Shit, I was losing my cool on stage with the audience still present. I started to tremble, the need to run, to hide, to *escape* tingling at the edges of my nerve endings, demanding action.

"Dear one, I will never let anything bad happen to you." Alana looked me straight in the eyes, and a soothing balm spread over my frayed nerves. "You have my word," she promised.

I held her gaze with my own for as long as it took for me to believe her. And I did. Madam Alana and I were kindred spirits. I didn't have to share the horrors I'd survived, or learn all of hers, in order to know that we'd had similar pasts, or at the very least, shared trauma that contributed to shaping who we were today.

"You're going to be okay." She smiled gently and reached her arm out to Jade who was waiting at the end of the stairs.

"Come on, Maia. I'll be with you the whole way," Jade offered with a rare smile as if she were trying to calm a frightened animal.

I took Jade's hand and looked into her pretty eyes.

"What have I done?" I gulped.

"You've changed the course of your life in every way

possible. Doesn't it feel great?"

Other than being absolutely terrified of what came next, I didn't know how to feel. Maybe after I met the man I was to be married to, and if he was a good guy, I could find some semblance of normalcy again.

I let out a long breath I'd been holding. "Let's get this over with."

Episode 20

Mr. Davenport

MADAM ALANA

I watched Maia accept Jade's hand as she shakily took the steps down from the stage. I mouthed "Thank you" to Jade.

She nodded, wrapped an arm around Maia's shoulders, and lead her to the signing room we'd chosen for her and her bidder. With my coolest, calmest, mask firmly in place, I smoothly turned around and approached the podium.

"That was exciting! I want to thank you all for being here tonight. This concludes the evening's auction. Those of you interested in attending the next event in four months know how to reach me. Now, please, feel free to return to the meet-and-greet room where we have a complimentary beverage service and additional noshes to tantalize those eager palates. Until next time, *merci*! *Au revoir*." I smiled as the stage lighting dimmed and the lights over the audience brightened.

"How dare you talk about a woman like that!" I heard Rhodes holler from the middle of the room.

Christophe stood with his arms outstretched to separate Manny and Rhodes. "Now, now. It's over. You won Maia's hand, Rhodes. Calm down."

"Only because I let him!" Manny blustered, wiping his hand over his balding head. He was laying it on far too thick and continuing his act well beyond what we'd agreed upon.

As the rest of my guests were straggling out of the room, I lifted my hands, fingers forward, and shooed them on like baby chicks. "Nothing to see here, please exit," I called out, waiting until the last person left. "Gentlemen," I called out as I approached.

"Alana!" Rhodes seethed, his face reddened in obvious anger. "This man needs to be kicked off your list of eligible bidders." He pointed a jaunty, accusing finger in Manny's direction. "You should have heard the things he said about Maia," he snarled.

"Oh?" I fluttered my lashes and played along, wanting to hear why Rhodes felt the need to defend her honor.

Manny grinned in my direction. "It worked, didn't it?" He stepped away from Christophe, lifted his hand to his forehead, and ripped off the wig he'd worn. "Ah, yaassssss. That damn thing was itching something fierce." His beautiful black hair was slicked back beneath the wig. He shook his large belly with both hands. "Jesus, this damn thing is soooo heavy," he griped.

"What the hell is going on?" Rhodes snapped, his lips twisted into a snarl as he watched his nemesis.

Manny unbuttoned his blazer and his dress shirt, then dropped both onto an empty chair. "I'm sweatin' buckets in this thing!" he complained.

"You chose the costume, not me." I shook my head and crossed my arms.

Manny removed the large belly and chest mold that was looped around his shoulders and shrugged it off. Then he stood in a white T-shirt and slacks, stretching and arching his back. An audible popping sound filled the room, and he groaned in relief.

Rhodes stood there, eyes wide, hands resting behind his neck. His mouth dropped open in an expression that could only be labeled as shock.

"Darling, how did Manny do?" I asked my Christophe.

He moved to my side, put his arm around my waist, and kissed my temple. "*Mon couer*, Rhodes was ready to start a brawl right in the middle of the auction. He was so angry."

"Nailed it!" Manny laughed, pumping one fist in the air while ripping off the bulging nose prosthetic that covered his much nicer, natural Romanesque one with the other hand.

"Are you fucking kidding me? You played me?" Rhodes gasped while his brows furrowed, anger and sadness marring his expression.

"I wouldn't exactly call it that," I responded gently, trying to be considerate of his currently volatile mood.

"So, this guy acted like a douche for what reason? To get people to up their bids?" He shook his head. "Unbelievable. I thought you ran a legit auction here," he continued, taking the situation in an entirely different direction, one that was sordid and uncouth. A path I hadn't even considered because I wasn't normally the type to deceive. Alas, desperate times had called for desperate measures. If I hadn't intervened, Rhodes wouldn't have even considered bidding on a wife this evening. Something that I knew with my whole heart would do him a world of good.

"Darling, the intent was not to up the bidding price. It was to get you to bid in the first place. Maia already had a buyer who was willing to pay top dollar. I didn't tell Manny to bid on her at all. Just to act as though he would." I narrowed my gaze at Manny. "Bidding was not part of our agreement."

Manny, a thirty-five-year-old method actor, slumped into a chair. "I got caught up in the whole thing. It was really exciting and when I knew I was making Mr. Drag Ass there upset, I had a feeling he wouldn't take the plunge until I went all in. As actors, we have to know when to improvise."

I closed my eyes and inhaled a breath, then slowly let it out, trying to calm my own ire.

"I apologize, Rhodes. The intent was not to raise the bids, nor was that part of my very explicit instructions," I stated with severity in my tone while glaring at Manny. "The plan was only to get you to see what you might miss if you didn't bid on Ms. Fields."

"He called Maia a pint-sized whore!" Rhodes growled between clenched teeth.

I jolted back into my husband's arms. "*Pardon moi?*" I focused my gaze on Manny.

"Improvisation, my friend. You weren't responding to the sexy talk. But when I called her names, you got really hot around the collar. I knew you'd go for it then." He smiled as though he'd done something positive and expected to be praised for it.

I sighed and went over to Rhodes, placing my hands on his arms and looking him directly in the eye. "I'm sorry I deceived you. Please understand my intent was to encourage you to bid on a woman you yourself said you couldn't stop thinking about. If you'd like to terminate your bid, I will allow it because it was done under false pretenses. I'll tell Maia she will have to come back to the auction in a few months."

Rhodes snarled. "Fuck!" He put his hands behind his head again and started to pace. "I can't imagine her going through this again. She looked so happy, and that smile." He sucked in a quick breath. "Men would crawl across hot lava to see that smile every day. Fuck!" he cursed again. "I don't know what to do, but…"

I tried to hold back my smile as he mentally and physically went back and forth between his own needs and his wants.

"Rhodes, it's okay. I'll talk to Maia. I can probably go into the meet and greet and get the other interested party to take over her bid right away. Maybe not for seven million, but I'm sure between him, Maia, and myself, we can come to an agreement that suits all involved."

He suddenly snapped to attention. "The hell you will. I won her fair and square. No other man will touch a single hair on her stunning head," he returned, his chest rising and falling along with his frustration.

"Yes, but technically it was under false pretenses, and I will not hold you to it based on deception. That's not how I run my business." I squinted over at Manny, who winced and looked away, now sullen.

"I-I…" He shook his head and ran his fingers through his hair. "I don't want to back out. Take me to her. Now," he demanded in no uncertain terms.

"As you wish. Follow me," I instructed. "Manny, wait here until I'm ready to deal with you."

"I ain't leaving until I get paid anyway." He grinned happily, not realizing the massive errors he'd made with his deplorable judgement.

When we exited the room, I turned to Rhodes. "I am deeply sorry for what occurred. You are my family. I would never lie to you. I simply wanted to encourage you to consider the opportunity before you." I swallowed against the fear that this could be another person in my life that I might lose due to someone else's ignorance.

He reached out and cupped my shoulder. "Hey, I get it. Your heart was in the right place, and hell…" He looked down at his shoes. "Maybe it's the nudge I needed. I don't know. Things aren't going well with Emily. Her mother could give a rat's ass about her, and I'm so goddamned lonely," he admitted, his shoulders dropping in what could only be defeat.

I pulled him into a hug, pressing my cheek to his chest. "I know you are. You've done everything you could for your daughter, Rhodes. Deep down, she knows that. She also knows you love her to distraction. But there comes a time when you have to put some of your own happiness on your priority list. It can't all be Emily and work, intermingled with Portia's antics. You deserve someone to come home to at the end of a hard workday. Someone to discuss the highs and lows of raising a teenager. Maia could be that for you, if you're willing to take the risk."

He sighed and shifted me out of his arms. "What if it's like what happened with Portia?"

"Being unfaithful is against the contract," I stated with conviction. "Maia will forfeit it all if she betrays you. And I promise that young woman needs this just as much as you. Maybe for different reasons, but I think over time you will see her reasons line up with yours."

He chuckled and looped his arm around my shoulders. "Ever the romantic. You realize she's in this for the money, right? Which is basically the same reason Portia took me for a ride."

I shook my head. "Maia needs the money, yes, but I think she'll surprise you. Get to know her. Take her out. Travel a bit with her. Introduce her to Emily."

"Fuck! Emily is going to shit a brick. This is going to rock her world and not in a good way. Portia just told her yesterday that she wasn't marrying Pablo. I can't introduce her to yet another new person who's going to change her life."

I rolled my eyes. "Portia has more fiancés than I have expensive shoes, and, *mon cher*, I adore my wide variety of footwear," I tutted.

He laughed out loud.

"Besides, you do not give that girl enough credit. She is not unaware of the coming and goings of her mother and the lack of interest she takes in her life. Emily may need you to start treating her like a young adult. Then maybe she'll start acting like one."

He rubbed at his jaw. "Maybe you're right. Still, this is

going to be a major blow. Her dad found a woman and is all of a sudden engaged? After eight years of not even bringing home a single girlfriend? Sure, I had some fun here and there, but nothing that would warrant an introduction to my daughter."

The man had a point. Emily needed some time away from all of them. A little space to blossom, to find herself and mature. And I knew just the way to help make that happen.

"How about this? You were scheduled to come spend a couple weeks with us at the end of your Summer with Emily, *oui*?"

"Yeah," he grumbled.

"Since I'm done with the auction, we'll take Emily for the next couple weeks. Give you the time you need to get to know Maia personally, then you can bring her to France and meet up with your daughter. And Christophe and I can help with the transition."

"Really? You want to take Em for two weeks?" He gulped. "She can be a real handful."

I waved my hand in the air. "Christophe would love nothing more than taking her to every museum and castle in the French countryside. And it would give me one-on-one time with her. You know I live to spend time with my niece."

"I couldn't ask that of you." He worried his bottom lip with his teeth as he considered it.

"You're not asking. I'm offering. She's already at our apartment here. Meet up with your intended, sign the contract, take her out to dinner, and I'll secure Maia a room at Joel's resort. In the meantime, I'll discuss the idea with Emily about her coming to France with us for a couple weeks. Then when you arrive later in the evening to pick Emily up, we'll discuss it further."

"If you're sure," he said while rubbing at his jaw. "Sounds like a plan." He took a breath as I opened the door to the signing room.

Maia spun around to greet us, her eyes as wide as saucers when she saw her bidder for the first time.

"Oh my God, it's you!" Her hand rose to cover her mouth as she blushed deeply.

"Yes, it is, sweetheart. And you can call me Rhodes, your fiancé, or Mr. Davenport."

Episode 21

Third Time's a Charm

MEMPHIS

I paced back and forth in the signing room waiting for my bidder to enter. Energy sizzled up and down my nerve endings like electricity, making me feel buzzed and a little out of control. I shook my hands and jumped up and down a few times trying to shake it off.

"Memphis, get your shit together. You want to impress your bride, not freak her out," I said to my shoes.

"Is that right?" A voice called from the door behind me.

I spun around and could not believe my fucking eyes. Even tried to rub them with my fists to clear away what surely had to be an illusion.

"Naomi? Holy—you can't be here!" I choked out as my eyes widened with worry. "Fuck, this is not good at all." I groaned and looked up at the chandelier hanging from the center of the ceiling, the crystals shooting rainbow rays of light in every direction. "God, seriously!" I snapped.

"I'm afraid God can't help you now," she said moving farther into the room.

I shook my head and lifted my hands in supplication. "Naomi, I'm so sorry to do this to you, but you have to go."

"Why?" She smirked. "You have a hot date? Your fiancée meeting you, perhaps?" She blinked her long eyelashes in a slow, sultry move that was sexy as fuck.

Damn, she was beautiful. The kind of pretty that a man like me could never even hope to score long term.

Why was this happening? Come on, God. I trusted you, I mentally complained. The Big Guy always listened, even when I was having one of the most jacked-up moments of my life. Hopefully He could save me from the embarrassment I was about to befall if my bidder walked in on this situation.

"I am waiting for my fiancée." My shoulders fell as defeat weighed me down. "She's going to be here any minute, and I can't risk her being angry seeing someone like you here."

Her head snapped back with purpose, and she cocked her neck. Uh oh. When a woman cocked her neck to the side, eyes narrowed, you best be careful. In my experience, it was like poking a rattlesnake; you never knew when they were going to strike.

"Someone like me?" Those eyelashes fluttered with even more intent.

"Yeah. Someone who looks as gorgeous as you, talks with that sexy rasp, has the commanding presence you have. You could make anyone feel small in comparison. Yeah, I don't need my fiancée feeling out of place. Especially after what we shared." I lifted my hand to my neck and rubbed at the tension there. "I already feel bad."

Her features softened, and I couldn't help but take her in one last time before I asked her to leave again. She wore a slinky, body-hugging dress that left absolutely zero to the imagination. Her curves were poppin' and on full display. Her height paired with her toned arms and legs had my mouth watering and my hands itching to slide across all that bared skin.

The dress was shiny and gold. One arm was completely

bare as the fabric wrapped around one shoulder, molded to her breasts, and slashed across her collarbone. The sleek material coasted down her small waist and rounded hips and clung to her thighs, falling to a couple inches above her knees.

"You feel bad?" Naomi interrupted my blatant perusal, walking toward me on a pair of heels so high she could have been a model. "Because your fiancée could be here any minute?"

I watched her glossy lips move into a smirk. I had to bite down on my own bottom lip at the desire to see if that shimmer on her lips tasted as good as it looked.

"Mmm-hmm," I managed, lost to her beauty as she moved deeper into the room and went over to the high-top table where the final contract waited for my bidder. I'd already signed my name across the candidate line, knowing I was fully invested in this plan, no matter who purchased me to be their husband.

"What's this? Your prenup?" she asked, fingering the pages, her onyx gaze shrewd and assessing.

Prenup?

Fuck, I was losing my mind. She shouldn't be looking at the contract. No one was supposed to see it besides Madam Alana, Jade, me, and my bidder. I was so excited I didn't even hear the name Alana had called out during my auction. All I'd heard was, "*Sold for ten million,*" and everything else just slipped away.

Kind of like now.

Naomi was a force of nature. Just being in her presence stole points straight off my IQ.

"Uh, something like that." I approached and stopped mid-stride as she lifted the pen, flipped to the end of the contract, and signed her name across the bottom.

"What are you doing?" I barely heard myself speak as the edges of my vision blackened and warped. My heart beat so loud in my chest I thought I could hear the heavy beat echoing around the small room.

She spun around and grinned. She had one hand on her hip while the other tapped the pen against the wooden surface of the table. "Signing my commitment to marry you for ten million dollars."

I stood stone-still, afraid everything she'd just said was a messed-up hallucination my mind had conjured up because of how much I wanted her to be the woman for me.

Was I even awake yet?

Was this all a dream?

Hell, if it was, I never wanted to wake up.

"Is this real?" I croaked, not sure my voice was capable of much more as uncertainty weighed heavily against my subconscious.

She chuckled, and the sound was so sweet I wanted to listen to it for the rest of my life.

"Yeah, it's real. Who needs fate anyway?" She winked, referencing the conversation we'd had the second time we ran into one another. "I guess third time's the charm for us," she beamed.

"I can't believe it." I stared and stared.

"Are you going to keep looking at me like I'm a mirage, or are you going to come over here and greet your fiancée properly?"

Without so much as a single thought, I raced over to her, looped one arm around her waist, and pulled her against my chest, tucking my free hand around her nape. My head came down at the same time she lifted her face.

Our lips met.

Spoiler alert, her fucking lip gloss tasted like peaches. *Delicious.*

I ravaged her mouth like I'd never get another taste. She was just as hungry, her hands clasped on either side of my face, holding me close. As if I might take my mouth off hers any time soon.

Not a chance.

She weighed nothing as I lifted her off her feet and carried her to the nearest wall, pressing her back against it as our fronts touched from chest to knee. Naomi clung to me, our mouths staying sealed.

The sweet little moans and sighs she gave as I devoured her whole lifted my confidence to mountainous heights. As we ate one another, our hands started to roam. She hiked up her skirt indecently and wrapped one long leg around my hips.

I ground my cock against her as my hand gripped her ass firmly, making sure she felt *everything* I had for her. "You want that, my queen?" I whispered against her lips as she sucked in air and moaned.

"Fuck, yes," she groaned, then tightened her leg muscles and dug the point of her high heel into the back of my thigh, forcing my erection to press harder exactly where she wanted it.

I hissed at the small bite of pain, then curled a hand around the front of her throat in a commanding but gentle hold as I gave her another roll of my hips and watched her eyes as the pleasure overtook her.

"Fucking beautiful," I grated through my teeth, loving the desire swimming in those obsidian pools.

Her breath caught and then she whimpered. That needy sound would be my undoing. I was about to fall to my knees and give the woman exactly what she needed, right here, right now, when another voice stopped me cold.

"Oh, wow. Okay, so, this is working out better than expected," Jade spoke from somewhere behind us.

I tightened my hold on Naomi's ass and let go of her neck so I could use that hand to ease the insanely restricting dress back over her luscious form. And ensure my own body protected her modesty as she dropped her leg and shimmied the fabric into place.

I turned around and grinned, looping an arm around Naomi's shoulders protectively, wanting to keep her close.

"Jade, I'd like you to meet Naomi, my fiancée." I said the words with such pride I couldn't contain my very obvious elation.

"We know each other." Jade smirked then waved a finger. "Hi, Naomi. Glad to see you found the perfect man for you."

"Boy, did I ever," Naomi cooed with exuberance and clucked her tongue with a little sass and a snap of her fingers. Praise from my intended, I felt ten feet tall.

Jade moved to the table, scanned the contract and our signatures, then smiled rather sweetly. Surprising for Jade because she was like *The Mona Lisa*. You never really knew what that woman was thinking based on her facial expressions. "Congratulations. I'm looking forward to receiving a wedding invitation," she said.

"You're on the list, lady. And be sure to tell Alana that I could not be happier with my bidder." I ran my hand up and down Naomi's arm. She was unbearably soft. I couldn't wait to feel more of her skin. With my entire body. Preferably naked.

"Kind of got that impression when I walked in on the two of you mauling one another," Jade teased, yet another small smile splitting her lips.

My hand slid down to Naomi's hip where I squeezed it, glorying in the fact that I could touch her freely. She was going to be my wife. "Hey, now, I may have been a wee bit excited about my bidder. It's not every day God answers all your prayers."

Naomi shifted her head so she could look me in the eye while still standing hip to hip. "Are you suggesting you asked God for me?" Her eyes sparkled as she dug her long nails into my ass. "That compliment is going to get you laid for sure," she taunted.

"I heard that! Then again, it's not like I wasn't going to be tappin' that ass the minute we get to one of our rooms," I stated with absolute certainty. There was so much sexual tension in the air, it could have lifted ten hot air balloons into the sky.

"On that note, I'll be filing these documents with the lawyers." Jade tapped the edge of the contract against the table. "Have fun, you two!" She waved and left the room as quickly as she'd entered it.

"Tappin' that ass, hmm?" Naomi placed her hands within my own and started to walk backwards, leading me toward the door where Jade had just exited.

"Unless you had something else in mind. Lady's choice." I licked my lips, wanting to suck on hers and see if there were any peach remnants from her gloss.

"Oh, the lady wants to get right to *business*," she assured, her voice a sultry timber that had a shiver running down my spine.

Then I remembered the item burning a hole right against my heart and I grinned stupidly. "Hold up just a minute."

She puffed out her bottom lip and I swear she became even more fuckable. My pants became infinitely tighter. I'd take a pretty pout when she was on her knees and my cock was tapping that sexy bottom lip playfully, but I was the one who needed to be kneeling for this part.

"Close your eyes. I got something I gotta do," I said.

The pout deepened, and she made a cute huffing noise.

"Trust me to take care of you. Playtime will happen very soon. But there's something I need to do first."

"Right here?" she asked.

I nodded.

Naomi rolled her eyes. "Fine," she sighed as she finally closed them.

I got down on one knee, pulled the velvet box out of my jacket, and opened the lid. The diamond ring I'd maxed out my credit card for sparkled beautifully. I couldn't wait to see it on her finger.

I held the box aloft, the ring nestled against the dark velvet.

"Hold out your hand," I asked, my throat drying out instantly.

She did so without peeking.

I took hold of her hand and looked at the answer to every last one of my prayers.

My gift from God.

Naomi.

"Okay. Open them."

She did so and her hand gripped my fingers tight, clearly surprised at the gesture of me down on my knees before her.

"Naomi, my queen, would you do me the great honor of making me the happiest brotha on the planet by marrying me…in a month…for ten million dollars?" I gave her my best cheeky grin.

"Memphis, I will marry you." She laughed as I put the diamond ring on her finger.

I jumped up, grabbed her cheeks, and kissed her hard and fast then rested my forehead against hers. "Are you sure you want to do this? And for all that money?" I couldn't help but give her one last out. This was all happening so fast and even though it was supposed to be like this, she was a person I actually cared about more than the money. Someone who I could truly see myself with long-term.

Her hands slid up and around the back of my head as we breathed one another in, faces so close our breaths intermingled. Which was why I heard it clear as day when she said, "I would have paid twenty million for you."

"Woman," I chastised teasingly as my throat once again gave out and the emotions swelled between us in large, earth-shattering waves.

She wasn't finished blowing my mind.

Not even close.

With her forehead to mine, her hands cupping my cheeks she whispered, "Hell, I might have even given it all up to have a man like you as my husband."

Episode 22

Elevator Jack

SUMMER

Waiting was the worst. Anticipation sizzled like live electricity across the surface of my skin while I paced the small signing room. The room was pretty bare. Only four walls, one exit, a bar top table with the contract on it and a pretty chandelier hanging from the center. There was some nice crown molding but absolutely nothing else to look at. Not a single thing to hold my attention until my husband-to-be arrived.

I sighed, dug through my small purse, and pulled out my phone. There were already a handful of texts waiting for me. The first three were from my mother. Not at all surprising since she was heavily invested in the idea of me entering The Marriage Auction. She wouldn't let it go until I agreed to do it. I scanned her messages and chuckled at her obvious eagerness.

From: Mom

Did you win a husband?

Ignore that last message. Of course you got a man. My girl is stunning, smart, and a good human.

Sunny, it's been forever. Are you okay? I'm sure you're okay. I'm worrying too much. Send me photo proof you're alive.

I snort-laughed as I went to the camera app and snapped a selfie, then responded to her last message with it. Next, I read my dad's text.

From: Dad

Your mom's worried. I told her you're a grown woman who can take care of herself, but you know how she is. Let us know how everything is going. We're on pins and needles over here.

I rolled my eyes and read my sister's note next.

From: Autumn

Mom's going nuts. She's reaching out to her spirit guides and our ancestors to keep an eye on you. I already had a vision of you sucking face with a hottie. Has that happened yet?

Immediately I started responding, my fingers flying over the keys. When my sister had a detailed vision, it usually was a snapshot of the future. Her visions have never been wrong.

Really? Did you get a good look at him? Is he the tall, dark, handsome man with an accent you saw yesterday?

I waited impatiently, staring intently as the three little dots popped up while my sister responded.

From: Autumn

You bet your ass!

I fist pumped the air and squealed, "Whoo hoo" as I started to shimmy and dance, careful not to fall and break my ankle in my high heels. "I'm about to get *freaky* with a tall, dark, and handsome stranger." I wiggled my fingers and swayed my hips as I continued to celebrate.

"Nice moves. Maybe you can teach them to me one day," an elegant, *accented*, voice said from behind me.

I spun around to find Jack, the hot guy from the elevator

fiasco standing near the doorway, leaning against the wall, his arms crossed, looking ridiculously handsome. He was in a beautifully tailored suit. Though what caught my breath was not how he looked, but the sinful smirk plastered across his face. The kind of smile that indicates they know something important that you don't.

"What are you doing here?" I asked, a frown marring my face.

He pushed off the wall and stalked forward, his large frame full of powerful grace, like an alpha lion approaching his pride.

"Let me introduce myself more fully. I'm Jack Larsen." He put his hand out for me to shake.

I placed my trembling one in his. When our palms touched, a magnet-like swirling vortex drew me a step closer.

His soft hand curled around mine and his rich, addicting scent, of bergamot, pepper and walnut invaded my nose, seeping into my lungs like a warm, comforting hug. I wanted more. Wanted to breathe him in so deep I could taste those flavors on my tongue, gorge on it until I'd had my fill.

"Hello, Jack Larsen," I finally responded. "Giving me your full name doesn't explain why you're here."

"To get freaky with you?" He grinned, using the exact words I'd said after reading my sister's message. Then it dawned on me—the only reason he would be standing right here, is because he's my bidder.

I yanked my hand out of his hold and put it up to cover my mouth as it dropped open. "Noooooooo!" I whispered in pure disbelief. My thoughts ran a million miles an hour.

How could this be? There's just no way. Man, he's good-looking.

"Yes," he smiled wider, one of his perfect eyebrows cocked as if daring me to deny the truth.

"You!" I pointed at him and then at myself without saying another word.

"Well, I do believe I'm tall, dark-haired, and I have been

known to turn a few heads," he said, then chuckled.

"This is unbelievable," I gasped. "You're...YOU! How in the world could this be happening? You're, the— the elevator guy!"

He chuckled. "I'm also bidder number five, your *fiancé.*"

I dropped my purse and phone as both my hands rose to my burning cheeks. "This is so fucking wild! My family is never going to believe this. I'm not sure I believe it!" I scoffed, staring dumbly at his gorgeous, arrogant face.

He put his hands into his pockets and rocked back and forth from heel to toe, a boyish smile across his face. "I will agree this is an unusual circumstance...*Rebecca.*" He drew out my cat's name, reminding me that I'd given him a fake name after he'd talked smack about me smelling like weed when we met.

"Yeah, about that..." I bit into my bottom lip and looked down, suddenly feeling a little ashamed of not being honest. He did take care of me during that small crisis. Everything was fine, and we were always safe, but it didn't feel that way at the time. And he'd been rock solid. Held me close, made sure I didn't go into a full mental spiral, or worse, pass out. Jack even teased me about my backup panties which ultimately took my mind off the very scary realization that we were stuck in an unreliable elevator car.

Jack reached out his hand and lifted my chin gently with a curled knuckle. "You know, I tried to call you to make sure you were okay. Only to find I'd called——"

"Eureka's pizza." My shoulders dropped in defeat before I mumbled, "I worked there when I was a teenager. They have really amazing pies. I'll take you there sometime."

His brown eyes seemed to melt as he traced one of my cheekbones with his thumb. "I'd like that very much," he whispered, his gaze filled with something more than concern. Something I wasn't ready to put a name to or trust, as my entire world was just flipped on its axis.

Still, I couldn't help the shiver that ran down my back at his touch, or the way his minty breath fanned across my face. I licked my lips and shifted from foot to foot as a wave of nervous energy overcame me.

Would he kiss me? Right here? Right now?
Did I want him to kiss me?

Too many questions, too little time. Before I knew it, he'd dropped his hand and went over to the contract and signed his name across the bidder's line.

"I think that's the end of that part. Where to next?" He stated as if it were just another day in the life of a rich guy. You know, wake up, coffee, shower, breakfast, lunch, meetings, bid on a bride, spend eight million dollars, sign a three-year contract, maybe a quickie wedding, and back at the hotel for a good night's sleep.

"What do you mean, where to? I have never done this before, and you bought *me*, buddy! Not the other way around. Technically it's your show. As the bride-to-be, I'm supposed to go wherever you say." I crossed my arms, more as a self-hug than anything else. I still couldn't believe Elevator Jack and my fiancé were now one and the same.

"*Touché*." He rubbed at his scruffy chin and ran his thumb along his bottom lip.

Ugh. That move was aces. Straight up eye-candy to a sex-starved woman like myself. And then my brain immediately switched to thinking about sex. My future husband was absolutely bangable. Top tier hot. His shoulders were broad, his frame solid, and he had an air of pretentiousness that made me want to dirty him up a bit.

"I imagine you'll want to go home, introduce me to your family," he suggested.

"You want to meet my family? Already?" I pressed my lips together and tried desperately to hold back my laughter but it came out in a big gush of air. I laughed so hard at his innocence. My family was freakin' awesome. The problem was, they were totally the opposite of what the average person would consider "normal."

Jack grinned. "What's so funny?"

"I...I...I'm just imagining you meeting my wacky parents, my psychic sister, and turning right around and heading back to Madam Alana to ask for a refund." I replied, through gasping bouts of air.

"Your sister's a psychic?" His eyebrows rose up toward his hairline either in curiosity or incredulity. I wasn't sure which.

"Yeppers. And my mother is a real life, practicing pagan witch." I added with zero voice inflection, so he'd know I was being serious. The worst thing he could do right now was scoff at what I'd shared. If he was going to be one of those people who discriminated against others for their beliefs and lifestyle choices, we could stop everything right there. I hadn't signed my name across the dotted line yet. And I wouldn't marry a man who couldn't accept my family exactly as it is.

"What does your father do?" Jack asked, his expression neutral.

I frowned, expecting him to ask me a hundred questions about the very unusual facts I'd just shared about my sister and mother. "He's a...a botanist. Handles all the science behind our products."

"And you? At the auction, Madam Alana said you were already wealthy and didn't need the money."

"But you're paying up, my friend." I side-eyed him. "I'm earning that eight million by becoming your wifey."

That made him chuckle. "Wifey, I like it. Suits you." His eyes heated as he reached out and pushed a dangling lock of hair behind my ear.

I simply stared at him. Jack Larsen was beautiful. And he smelled good enough to eat.

His hand fell from my neck to my bare shoulder. "Tell me, wifey, what is it you do for a living? What fills you with passion, gets your heart pumping?"

"Right now? You're doing a mighty fine job of getting my heart pumping," I breathlessly responded.

"I'm glad to hear I affect you as much as you affect me. You're a uniquely beautiful woman, Summer. Looking at you is like staring at the sun. If I look too long, I may find myself blinded by your beauty."

I swallowed the sudden lump in my throat. "Um, uh, I'm a horticulturist. I make plants grow." I said robotically. Hating and loving in equal measure the sheer pull this man seemed to have over me.

His thumb caressed the ball of my shoulder. "Plants. How curious. And you have a company that sells these plants you grow?"

I nodded, my entire focus on that small slide of his skin over mine, wishing it was directed somewhere else. I squeezed my legs together as arousal wove through me, a throbbing ache settling between my thighs. Without reason, I stepped closer, placing both of my hands onto his chest. His hand curled around my shoulder and tightened. His other arm wrapped around my waist, holding me close. I could feel the hard press of a very impressive erection digging into my abdomen. So he was as affected as I was.

I lifted my face and smiled as I ran my hands up his chest and around his neck, my fingers weaving into the shorter layers of his hair.

Just as I lifted up onto my toes and he dipped his head down, our lips an inch from one another...

"Oh my! My timing is impeccable this evening," came Jade's voice from the doorway.

Jack and I turned our heads but didn't let go of one another.

"Um, hi, Jade. Just getting to know my fiancé," my voice cracked.

She laughed. The first time I'd heard the serious woman

lose her cool composure. "There must be something in the air tonight."

"Oh yeah," I let my arms fall down Jack's chest, making sure to cop a quick feel of his muscular chest before I winked and shifted to the side.

Jack, surprisingly, kept an arm looped around my waist, keeping me close. It was as though he didn't want to let me get too far away. Swoon.

Jade briskly walked to the table and scanned the contract. "Summer, you haven't signed. This final contract will commit you both to three years of marital bliss from the time you get married. All ceremonies are to take place within thirty days of signing this document. After two weeks of marriage, you must have consummated the marriage."

"I understand the agreement," Jack answered with confidence, absolutely no hesitation in his tone.

"Are you having second thoughts, Summer?" Jade asked, then narrowed her gaze at Jack, likely assuming he might have done something to make me hesitate.

I hustled over to the table. "Not at all. I just wanted to make sure that when I met my future husband, that he understood a few things about my family. My family and I are a package deal."

Jade pursed her lips, waiting for me to continue.

Jack came up behind me and peeked at the contract over my shoulder. "She's waiting for you to sign, or decline."

My eyes widened. "Oh! Sorry." I turned around. "Sooooooo you're good with what I shared about my mom and my sister? I don't want anything to be weird when you meet them."

"*Solskinn*, of course things are going to be weird. I'm meeting your family for the first time, and I've just purchased you in a marriage auction. I'm sure they're going to be more concerned about me being in your life, and what that means for the next three years, than how I perceive them."

I snickered and shook my head. "Oh Jack, you have so many surprises ahead. Hand me that pen, will ya Jade?"

Jade passed me the pen, and I signed my name across the candidate line.

"Thank you. Congratulations. Please do send the details about your wedding. Madam Alana and I would love to attend."

"We shall do that once we've made plans," Jack replied in a stern, professional voice.

I rolled my eyes and waved as Jade left the room. The moment the door closed I spun around and faced my fiancé.

"Now where were we!" I squealed with excitement as I flung myself toward him.

He caught me mid-air with an *oomph*.

"Jesus!" He laughed, and I felt the base of his joy reverberate in my chest.

I tunneled my fingers into his hair and brought my face super close to his. So close I could almost feel our noses touching. "I think we were right about here," I whispered edging closer, giving him time to pull away if he wanted.

One of his hands plunged into the back of my hair and tipped my head to the side as his lips pressed to mine.

Time passed as we kissed, our lips brushing, tongues tangling sweetly, and our sighs intermingling. We held onto one another so tightly, I could no longer determine who was who. Our souls collided in that kiss, and they never wanted to let go of one another.

It was fire. It was passion. It was everything all at once.

The best kiss of my entire life.

Eventually, Jack shifted away, but my soul clung to his. Hesitant to let go. My mother would call it a soul bond. An intense, weighted, all-encompassing neediness I'd never experienced with anyone else. The same bond she had with my father. She claimed it was how she knew he was the one. Because her soul decided for her.

Jack cupped my cheek with his large hand. "Where to next?"

"A bed? The wall? Floor? I'm not really picky," I answered, twirling a finger around a longer lock of his hair at the crown of his head.

"I meant where's home?" He grinned wolfishly.

"Oh, California," I mumbled, my entire focus on the two of us getting somewhere we could take that kiss to the next level.

"Excellent. My jet is waiting. Come, wifey, let's meet the parents."

Episode 23

No Harm No Foul

MAIA

"Oh my God, it's you!" My shaky hand lifted to cover my mouth as a wave of heat rushed to my cheeks.

"Yes, it is, sweetheart. And you can call me Rhodes, your fiancé, or Mr. Davenport," said a man I instantly recognized but could not in my wildest dreams believe was standing next to Madam Alana. The two of them smoothly entered the room I'd been assigned to wait in until my bidder arrived.

My body temp rose as I watched them enter. Gooseflesh pebbled on my skin and my ears burned.

"My fiancé?" I gasped. Rhodes Davenport was the man I'd crashed into and pickpocketed at the airport. A man I was sure I'd never see again. Which meant, if he was here now and standing next to the Madam...Rhodes Davenport was my bidder.

A whooshing sound ripped through my head and cut off everything but the bright lights above. I blinked rapidly as my ears throbbed, the noise of large gusts of wind going through a tunnel the only thing I could hear. My vision blurred. I inhaled desperately as my heart pounded so hard I thought I might be having a heart attack. I covered my aching chest with my fist and backed up as he and Madam Alana stared at me, each with an undecipherable expression.

The room was closing in on me like a mouse trapped in a bucket, with only a dirty stick of peanut butter to nibble on until its fate was decided. Rhodes was the hunter, I, the mouse. Would my hunter eat me whole or set me free to roam the earth again? As I tried to breathe, I realized Rhodes didn't have to do anything. I'd already eaten the poisoned peanut butter and signed the contract. That act would change the trajectory of my life. Now I just had to suffer through the consequences of my decision.

"Are you here to get back at me for stealing from you? It was only a few hundred bucks, man. Rent was due and I was already behind. And besides," I gasped, still sucking in as much air as my suddenly restricted lungs would take in, "I gave back the phone and the credit cards. I could have taken you for a lot more." I banged my fist into my chest as I started to feel dizzy.

Rhodes shook his head as a gentle smile spread across his handsome face. "Stealing is stealing, Maia. We'll have to work on that little habit of yours."

I glared at his insinuation, as if it were a habit I enjoyed. Most people didn't steal because they wanted to. They did it because they were desperate, or just assholes. I was the former, and maybe a bit of the latter, but the streets had taught me to be that way. If I were kind and sweet, people took advantage of me. If I looked like I might be a force they didn't want to tangle with, I was more likely to survive. Not that he'd understand. But if anyone understood, it would be Alana. She once lived on the streets.

Alana approached me, her expression filled with concern. "Darling, come here, have a seat, you look pale," she clucked as if herding her baby chick around the coop. I let her take my elbow and lead me numbly to one of the chairs lined up along the wall. Once seated, I instantly bent over my legs, trying to shake off the buzzy sensation overtaking my mind.

"What's happening to me?" I gulped, my breath sawing in and out of my lungs.

Alana ran her hand up and down my spine in a soothing pattern. "You're having an anxiety attack, *chéri*. Just breathe with me. In for four beats, out for four beats. Follow along," she demanded in a stern voice.

I did as she bade, closing my eyes and focusing entirely on the sound of her voice. Alana had never done anything but help me in the past. She wouldn't have brought this bidder here tonight unless he'd been thoroughly vetted and ready to pay for his bid. She couldn't have known he was someone I'd stolen from.

Man, what did I ever do that was so bad I now had to face my pickpocket? I wasn't prepared to look into the mirror of this sin just yet.

And now I was supposed to marry him.

"Good God, why am I such an idiot!?" I wheezed and then coughed.

"You're not an idiot. You are scared. And I'm right here. Nothing is going to happen to you while I'm here, darling. You are safe."

I nodded, but kept my eyes closed tight, breathing as she instructed.

"In for four *chéri*…good, good, now out for four. Excellent. You're doing great. Just keep breathing, Maia." She cooed, easing the fear clinging to every single one of my cells. I hadn't had such a visceral response to anything since the night Sam saved me in that alley.

Suddenly I felt a warm touch on my bare knees. "Everything is okay, Maia. I'm not mad at you for the stolen cash. You did what you had to do," said a soothing, deep rumble. "It's okay. No harm, no foul, right?" It was the same words he'd said to me when I ran into him. And once I was literally sitting on top of him, my hands directly over his wallet and phone, the desire to snag those items was too much to ignore.

His touch on my knee, and his reminder of what occurred that day, brought me back to the present. I was finally able to breathe more easily as I opened my eyes, only to stare into the prettiest gray eyes I'd ever seen. They were like a frozen lake. Icy in color, but cool and calm in temperament. And so pretty I could stare into them for a lifetime, yet never be able to differentiate each tiny burst of color.

Rhodes smiled gently. "Hey there, you feelin' better, sweetheart?" He cocked his head and rubbed both hands across my knees again. It was nice, a gesture of comfort I hadn't experienced in many years.

I nodded, uncertain how to respond. I felt bamboozled and off-kilter.

Madam Alana suddenly appeared with a glass of water. I hadn't even seen her step away. "Here, Maia, sip on this. Did you eat today?"

I thought about the day from start to finish. My stomach had been in knots since I arrived. If I'd put a single morsel of food into my mouth I'd have been kissing the porcelain gods for sure. I shook my head.

"I can take care of that. How about we go to dinner, and you and I can talk? Determine if going through with this auction is the right thing for you," Rhodes suggested.

My haze of fear and anxiety shattered at his insinuation that I may want to get out of this situation. "No, I need the money. Period. I've already signed the contract."

Rhodes lifted his hands. "Hey, hey, slow down turbo. It's okay. I haven't signed yet. No one is rushing you into anything. You can still get out."

"And I'm telling you that I've already made my decision. If you don't want to be with me, because of what I did, or because of this," I waved a hand in front of me referring to my panic attack or whatever the hell it was. "That's on you. The contract was very clear. I knew exactly what I was signing. It's just seeing you was a huge surprise. You were not at all who I expected would be walking through that door," I said as I pointed to it.

Rhodes rested his hands on his knees and pivoted up to stand before me. He stared into my eyes for a long time, so long I was just about to look away when he nodded abruptly.

"If you're sure you're ready to do this," he walked over to the table where the contract sat. I'd already made my decision. I was in it for the cash. Simple as that. My family's safety depended on it.

"Rhodes, if you'd rather take more time…" Madam Alana offered him another out, which I found irritating.

I stood up abruptly, wobbling on the stupid stilts the stylist put me in. I'd give anything to slide my feet into my well-worn, beloved, Doc Martens right about now.

"Do you two know each other or something??" I rubbed my arms, trying to warm them from the chill in the room. *Did hotels have to keep the temperature at freezing at all times? Damn.* I shivered.

Rhodes clocked my tremble and immediately unbuttoned his suit jacket, shrugged it off, came over to me, then placed it around my shoulders. The scent of a fruity, woodsy-like cologne wafted through the air from the satin inner lining that was pressed against my skin. I clutched the lapels between my breasts and sighed when the heat of his body transferred from the jacket to me.

"Thank you," I whispered feeling shy and awkward after everything that had happened.

"My pleasure, Maia. And in answer to your questions, Alana and I have known one another for many years. Since before my daughter was born."

"And unfortunately, a situation occurred during your

auction that was unfair to my friend. I invited him in the hopes he would see you specifically. I knew based on the information he'd shared about being pick-pocketed in the airport by a stunning, little brunette, that you were very likely the culprit."

I slumped where I stood. "Fuck my luck, man. I'm sorry, Alana. I didn't mean…it's just, the timing was so perfect and…"

She held up a hand. "You do not have to explain yourself to me. You and I have our own past and it is water under the bridge, *oui?*"

"Yeah," I huffed. "Still, I'm sorry I stole from your friend." I turned to Rhodes. "I'm sorry I stole from you. It's just Sam really needed the rent, and he's covered for me too much already." I blabbed, sharing more than I'd ever shared before with Alana or *anyone* for that matter. This situation had me spilling all my secrets and completely out of sorts.

"Who's Sam?" Rhodes growled. "You in some kind of trouble? If a man is messing with you, or making you feel unsafe, I'll handle it right now. Take me to him," Rhodes demanded.

"Whoa!" I lifted one of my hands between us. "You don't even know me. And what you do know of me hasn't exactly been positive and you want to stick up for me? I don't get it."

Rhodes let out a long exhale and rubbed at his temples with his thumb and forefinger. "God damn, this is getting complicated. Is this Sam person threatening you?"

"No. Totally the opposite. Sam has never made me feel unsafe," I assured him.

"Is he a romantic interest?" Rhodes rumbled, his tone rising, nostrils flaring.

I couldn't help my nasty expression as I responded, "Gross. I mean, the biker bunnies love him, but he's more like a brother to me." I imagined my best friend's gruff, wicked smile. His hair swept off his head with a red bandana tied around his forehead like Axl Rose from Guns N' Roses. Which also happened to be his favorite band. Go figure.

Rhodes pursed his lips and crossed his arms. Those were some massive guns. I'd bet I could put both my hands around one bicep and my fingers wouldn't even touch.

"Okay, so do you still owe this Sam, like a brother to you, money?" Rhodes countered.

I shook my head and looked away. "I paid him with the money I stole from you so we're all settled up until next month. But I figured I'd need to pack up my stuff and move it wherever my husband wanted me to move."

"We'll take care of it this week," Rhodes said before grabbing the pen, and signing off on the bid.

"Um okay," I whispered, my eyes wide, my heart back to thundering in my chest. I swallowed and glanced at the contract then back up to the endlessly icy depths of his eyes. "Does this mean we're getting married?"

"Yeah, sweetheart, it means we're getting hitched." Rhodes ran his hand through his hair and sighed. "What else needs to be done, Alana?" he asked the madam who'd been silently standing several feet away.

She walked over, scanned the contract and then held it to her chest. "I'll make sure my team files everything. Maia, the $250,000 deposit will go into your account tonight. When the two of you have gotten officially married, $2,250,000 will be transferred into your account. The second deposit on your first anniversary, and the third on your two-year anniversary. If at any time you break any of the rules as set forth in the contract, including but not limited to being unfaithful to your husband, you will forfeit all monies. This goes both ways."

"Having experienced that pain myself, I would never do that to another person," Rhodes hissed.

"I understand." I murmured then looked at Madam Alana and then to Rhodes. "What do we do now?"

Rhodes closed his eyes, took a deep breath, then held out

his hand to me.

I stared at that hand as if it were a venomous snake about to strike. Still, I summoned up the courage to place mine overtop his and waited for something bad to happen.

It never did.

He curled his fingers around mine. "How's about we get to know one another over dinner? Alana is going to secure a room for you in the same resort where I am staying. As you know, I have a teen daughter. I'm not going to bring you back to my suite until the two of us have figured out more of the future. How's that work for you?"

For the first time today, I smiled.

"That works perfectly." I squeezed his hand to emphasize my relief and appreciation.

"All right then. Let's get you fed, and then we'll talk." His smile, and the way he kept hold of my hand as we exited the room, made me feel cherished.

My intuition told me that Rhodes Davenport, my future husband, would keep me safe.

I could only hope I was right, because Lord knows I've been wrong about men before.

Episode 24

My Life in Shambles

JULIANNE

"Say you'll work with me on getting revenge against Brenden and Bianca," I pleaded and held out my hand, hoping against all odds that Gio would agree. "Say yes to marrying me," I whispered, my heart in my throat, my entire plan depending on his answer.

Gio closed his eyes and sighed deeply. "Fuck me." he rumbled.

"I plan to. But only once we're married, old friend," I chuckled dryly. The situation wasn't funny at all. It was fucking *tragic*, but I didn't see any other way around Bianca and Brenden's betrayal. They couldn't get away with kicking me to the curb of my own family's company. Besides, Giovanni was the standard I compared all other men against. He was the most handsome man I'd ever met. He had a great sense of humor, cared deeply about those he loved, and was a genius in business. I'd learned a lot from him while working at FM Enterprises, and knew I could teach him a few things as well. He'd also been an incredibly attentive and giving lover the one time we'd had sex—a fact he'd forgotten after he passed out in bed beside me all those years ago.

Gio rubbed his face with both hands and slumped over, his elbows resting on his knees as he hung his head.

"Our parents would have a field day with this plan, Jules." He sighed so deeply I could feel the weight in the air pressing against my body like two metal plates squashing me from either side.

I shrugged and pressed my lips together as the reminder of what I'd lost came racing back to the surface. Even thinking of my parents for a moment too long would bring on the waterworks, and I'd already cried a river of tears since their unexpected death. Now I was just so angry.

Angry at my brother.

Angry at Bianca.

Angry at God for taking my parents away.

And frankly, I was angry at *Giovanni* for running away from it all to lick his wounds, leaving me behind. And here I was, my entire plan depending on him.

My life in shambles.

"Look, the parents I knew wouldn't have allowed any of this to happen. I'd still be living my best life at FM Enterprises. You'd still be marrying a backstabbing, unfaithful bitch, and loyal to a friend who clearly wasn't giving the same in return. Perhaps this was meant to show us Brenden and Bianca's true colors. Though I have no clue what it means about my parents and them not leaving me equal shares. That's still something I can't wrap my mind around, no matter how often I run through every possible scenario."

Giovanni nodded. "It doesn't make sense. They loved you deeply, Jules. I find it all hard to believe as well, but marriage…between you and me?" He swallowed, and I watched his Adam's apple bob deliciously along his tanned throat.

"A marriage between you and me would be filled with

trust, respect, hot sex if that kiss was anything to go by, and a whole lot of success in business. And if our marriage has the added bonus of making Brenden and Bianca go nuts?" I grinned wickedly. "All the better."

Giovanni crossed his arms over his chest, his legs spread out wide as he tapped a foot. He looked large and in charge, a king on his throne, ready to crush the enemy.

"Aren't you angry?" I prodded at the simmering beast.

Gio's gaze flashed to mine. "Of course, I'm angry. Brenden betrayed me. I called that man brother."

I nodded. "Yeah, and Bianca. You gave that twat all of your love, time, and planned to give her an amazing life by your side. She not only spat on that gift, she got your best friend to be an accomplice. I know that hurt, Gio, because they both did the very same to me." I scrambled over to him, fell to my knees and rested my hands over the center of his strong quads. I lifted my chin and stared straight into his eyes. "These two people did the unthinkable. I need your help and you need mine. Together we can be such a force."

He reached out and cupped my jaw tenderly. I rubbed my cheek into his palm like a content kitten.

"If we come together, Julianne, and it goes bad, it could break our families' bond forever."

I cupped his hand over where he held my face. "And if what's between us is good, we could be the legacy our parents always wanted for us." I let go and put both of my hands to his thighs again, then ran them up and down the long, muscular length, my touch gliding from soothing to intentional.

Giovanni's gaze heated as my wandering hands moved further up his thighs, my fingertips just barely grazing his hard length, for which I was rewarded with a sharp grunt. He'd been hard since I'd grinded on his lap and kissed him silly. What he didn't know was that I was wet between my thighs and more than ready to show him exactly how much I was attracted to him.

I wanted Giovanni's help, but I also genuinely enjoyed working with him. We were a formidable team. With Brenden, we'd been the three musketeers. Somehow all that changed with the introduction of Bianca and then the deaths of our parents. I wanted to go back to the time it was just us three and our happy parents.

"Giovanni, our new reality has changed." I kept running my hands up and down his quads, my fingers purposely grazing the firm bulge behind his slacks as I forced his legs to open wider.

I crawled on my knees until I was fully between his thighs. Boldly, I cupped his length with my entire hand and smiled devilishly at him when he moaned, the sound bouncing around the too quiet room.

"Jules," he grated, but I felt his hips press forward, pushing his length deeper into my hand, as though he couldn't help himself. Even when I could clearly see the restraint in his expression, I proceeded to stroke him from balls to tip. His jaw was firm, the muscles in his neck and cheeks bulging. He showed his teeth when I shifted my hands to his belt and started to slowly pull the leather through the metal buckle.

"Let me show you how amazing it could be between us, Gio?" I taunted breathily and licked my lips.

His gaze went from heated to a burning inferno. "This isn't smart," he warned, but didn't stop me.

I undid his belt, drew the zipper down, then curled my fingers around the waistband of his slacks. His breath was sawing in and out of his chest as he watched me insert my hand into his black boxer briefs and pull out his thick, long, cock.

"Damn, so not only are you hotter than any man has a right to be, you have a monster cock too?" I teased. I'd barely gotten a glance at it years ago.

He was about to speak when I gripped his length and

swirled my thumb around the glistening tip before stroking him down to the base.

"Fuckin' hell, this is going to be complicated." He grunted but moved his hips in an alternating pattern from my strokes.

I grinned. "Oh Gio, you have no idea." I bent forward and swallowed him whole, all the way down to the base.

One of his hands dove into the back of my hair where he fisted it at the roots and followed my movements up to the head, where I laved at the bulbous crown. A cat lapping up all the cream. I rolled my tongue around the mushroom capped top, sucking at it until more of his arousal seeped at the tip.

"Christ Jules, where the fuck did you learn that?" Gio's hands tightened at the back of my head as he cupped my jaw and pulled me off his cock. I was immobile, my lips just grazing the sticky head. I flicked my tongue out and teased the slit at the top, making sure to get every drop.

"Dirty girl," he hissed, his tone dripping with desire as arousal rippled through me. My entire body ached. My clit pulsated as my lower body clenched with the need to take him inside.

"Let me…" I flicked my tongue, barely getting a taste of him from where he held me hovering at a distance. I gazed up at him from my position on my knees, submissive to his whims, his cock standing hard and proud.

"You want to take this cock down your throat again, Julianne?" He growled. "Taking me so deep you choke on it until I explode?"

I mewled and nodded, suddenly desperate to give that to him. To make him lose his mind so completely that we both got exactly what we needed.

"Tell me what you want?" His grip in my hair tightened almost to the point of pain. But that slight jolt of discomfort set me reeling. He'd stumbled upon a side of me I didn't even know existed but wanted desperately to explore.

"I want you," I whispered.

He shook his head and shoved my head toward his length. Instantly, I gobbled up his cock like it was a feast and I hadn't eaten in days. My throat had barely been breached, my nose nestled against the black trimmed curls at the base as my pussy clenched around nothing, arousal coating my lace undies, when he yanked me off again.

"No, dammit!" I griped, trying to move my head back to my tasty toy, but his hold was strong. I couldn't even stick my tongue out and tease him at that distance.

"You will do as I say, Jules," he bit out, almost as if he was angry but hadn't tipped over the edge. "You suck my cock when I say you can, not when you want. Am I clear?" He commanded in a sexy snarl that made my heart pound and my clit throb.

"But—" He cut me off at the quick.

"When we are being intimate like *this*, you do as I say, or we will never work out. I need control in this. Do you understand?" His nostrils flared as his gaze pierced mine. Those eyes said he was about to give me unspeakable pleasure, the likes of which I'd never experienced before. I simply had to trust him.

I was so turned on, all I could think about was putting my mouth back on my prize until he satisfied me by shooting down my throat. Fuck, I could practically taste it now. I panted, my gaze going from his weeping, hard cock, to his magnificent face. I couldn't help my response. This Jules was suddenly not me. She was *Giovanni's* to mold and play with until we mutually got what we wanted.

"Say you understand, or this stops now," he clenched his teeth.

"I understand." I trembled.

He smiled devilishly, an entirely different Giovanni sitting before me. This man was confident and arrogant, unconcerned that his cock was out, the tip wet with my saliva and his arousal.

He'd never been sexier, even including the single night we'd had. This was a new, mature Giovanni. A man who knew exactly what he wanted, how he wanted it, and just how he expected his woman to tend to him. I couldn't fucking wait to rock his world. Because this whole experience was obliterating mine in ways I wouldn't be able to contemplate until later, after it was all said and done.

A shiver tore through me as I realized in that moment I wanted nothing more than to please him. Knowing if I did, he'd reward me somehow. I needed that reward.

"Good girl. Now use that mouth to take me deep." He loosened his hold on my face, and I instantly took him back in my mouth. I moaned around his erection and did as he'd instructed, taking him all the way down my throat, breathing through my nose and relaxing my tongue.

"Fuck yeah," he roared into the empty room, the sound vibrating in the air around us.

I doubled my efforts and went to town on him. Up and down, flowing with his thrusts. His hand stayed in my hair and would tighten and loosen along with his movements. So much so, I felt like I was a bucking bronco, along for the ride, until he cupped the back of my head and held me down.

"Swallow it all," he demanded, his words a raspy growl.

I hummed low in my throat, and his body went stiff as he came. I did as he'd bade, swallowing like a champ, feeling so unbelievably proud of myself when he groaned and shook. Just as I pulled off his softening length, he hauled me up and over his lap. Suddenly my chest and belly were pressed to his thighs and the silky fabric of my dress was up over my ass. He wasted no time at all ripping the lace fabric of my undies at the seams and tearing them off.

I had no idea what was coming, but screeched when my entire ass became enflamed with white hot fire.

"Ouuch! What the hell!" I yelled as another blow of

Giovanni's hand crashed against my ass jolting me forward.

"Dirty, fucking girl," he smacked me harder, my cheeks bursting with pain that sizzled and spread out before warping into unbelievable tingles of *pleasure*.

What in the…

Another smack, lower on my ass, where the fleshy bit met the back of my thighs.

That time, a moan slipped from my lungs, low and heady. Another fire brand came down on the other fleshy cheek, which had me tilting my ass up higher, desperate for him to hit me lower. To touch me where I wanted him most.

"Look at that pretty round, red ass, begging for more of my touch. Let's see just how much you want release, hmmm…" Giovanni hummed. Then his fingers slid between my thighs, two of them plowing straight inside me.

"Oh my God, yesssssss," I cried out.

"Just as I suspected…*soaked*." He plunged his fingers deep, and I clung to his thighs.

"Please, Gio," I begged and hung my head. I'd never wanted to come so badly in my life. Right then, I was his to play with. His to pleasure. His in everything he wanted.

He hooked his fingers and started to fuck me with them. His thumb maneuvered between my folds, found my clit and circled the hardened bundle of nerves until my body contorted into a silent scream. The orgasm shot through me so fast I wasn't prepared for how huge it was. Giovanni held me across his legs as I bucked, grinding into his hand as the pleasure splintered and spread through my entire form.

I came and came and came until my body went limp on top of him, and I blacked out.

When I woke, my dress was back in place, and I was chest to chest with him. My legs draped over one side of his lap as he held me close with both arms.

"Hey," I spoke gently, feeling emotionally and physically raw.

"Jules, what happened…it wasn't…I just lost my mind after that kiss and…"

"It was so hot, I'll be masturbating to it for years." I chuckled then yawned.

"Wait, you're not mad?" He swallowed slowly, his gaze searing into mine, his expression tortured while I felt sated and content for the first time in months.

"Depends. Are you going to marry me now?" I asked, then pressed my head to his shoulder and sighed, wanting nothing more than to close my eyes and sleep for a week.

"Jules, we need to talk more about that. Especially after what happened." His words were filled with concern and regret.

I sat up and cupped both of his cheeks, forcing him to pay close attention. "What happened was hot as fuck, and I want to do it again and again. You didn't take advantage of me. If anything, I started it by rubbing your hard-on, until, of course, you took the reins and gave me a sexual experience I certainly won't ever forget."

He bit into his bottom lip. I reached forward and used my thumb to remove it from between his teeth. Then, I lowered my head and kissed that spot.

He returned the gentle kiss until I pulled away. I got up, grabbed the panties he'd torn, balled them up and tossed them at him. He caught them midair.

"Hold onto those for me, will ya?" I winked then went over to the contract and signed my name with a flourish. I grabbed the contract and pen, brought it over to him and held both out before him. "We just proved how explosive we can be in the bedroom. Let's spend the next three years kicking ass, taking names, and sticking it to my brother and your ex. How about it?"

His gaze traced my body from head to toe before he closed his eyes and shook his head. "Where do I sign?"

Episode 25

Two Peas in a Pod

GIOVANNI

Julianne handed me the contract right as we heard a knock at the door. Then Madam Alana peeked through before she opened it fully and entered.

"I'm sorry I took so long to return. There was a situation I needed to tend to."

"Everything okay?" Julianne asked, a shaky hand lifting to smooth her hair back into place. It didn't help. Her luscious, shoulder length, red locks were a tumbled mess. She certainly appeared nowhere near as flawless as she had when she'd showed up for the auction earlier in the evening.

I winced at the memory of how tightly I'd tugged at the roots of her hair, working her over my cock. I closed my eyes and took a long, full breath, letting it out slowly. It helped ease the chaotic thoughts thundering through me.

I'd defiled Julianne after she'd sucked me off so good I saw stars. The woman had a mouth on her I would dream of for years to come. There had been none better. Then again, if I signed on the dotted line, I wouldn't be dreaming about the things I wanted to do with and to her. I'd be living them for the next three years.

As her husband.

I fisted one of my hands as I stood, thankfully having already put myself back together after I'd made Jules come like a waterfall. What else could I do when I had her curvy body laid out, naked, and fully under my control?

I shivered at the debauched images my mind so helpfully supplied and clutched the contract as I moved to the table. I scanned the document. Again, I had to give her one last out.

"Jules, is this really necessary? I'd happily give you the money you need. And Brenden can't get away with letting you go without my signature as co-owner. I'll move back to New York. I'll go back to FM Enterprises, and we'll work this out together. You don't have to marry me in order to keep your job."

She shook her head and crossed her arms defiantly. "Marrying me and signing that legally binding contract guarantees you can't go running away when the shit hits the fan again."

"That's a low blow, and you know it. I lost everything! Fucking *everything!*" I growled as the memories of my parents perishing in that plane crash, Bianca's betrayal, and my best friend stealing my fiancée and fucking her on the very night before we were to wed paraded through my mind. A tsunami of pain barreling down over me all over again.

She stomped to where I stood and put her hand on my arm. She looked me dead in the eyes, her face a mask of the same pain I was just barely holding back. "So did I," she breathed, emotion choking her words. Her lips trembled, and her gorgeous blue eyes filled with unshed tears. Jules was not a crier. Even letting me see that much of her true feelings gutted me.

I reached out and cupped her cheek tenderly. "I'm sorry." I ran my thumb over her now wet cheekbone where a single, stubborn tear had appeared. "We really are two peas in a pod, aren't we?" My nostrils flared as I huffed and inhaled sharply. I couldn't get in enough air. The room was stifling with all the things unsaid between us. The many sorrows we did, in fact, share that could, and had, so easily swallowed me whole the past couple months.

Maybe if we worked together, the numbness and anger would eventually fade into something livable. I stared into her beautiful face, so elegant and enchanting. I'd been half in love with the woman since we were children. Brenden made it clear from the day he caught us kissing on the dock that if I so much as laid a finger on his sister ever again, he'd never talk to me. He'd been so angry, he punched me in the face and bloodied my nose. I let him, believing I'd betrayed some cardinal guy code by lusting after my best friend's baby sister.

Instead, I'd loved Julianne from afar. Dated relentlessly in my teens and twenties to forget all about the one girl that was off limits. Until the morning I woke up with her virgin blood on my cock and flashes of the night before invading my hungover brain. I'd not only been drunk that night, but I'd also tried mushrooms for the first time, after my girlfriend back then had broken up with me. Funny enough, Brenden was the one who'd suggested them. We got high on the 'shrooms, drank until we were practically falling over, and then he left to go back to his own room.

My girlfriend at the time was a curvy redhead with light eyes. Obviously, I have a type, and that type is Julianne Myers. Somehow, Jules must have shown up. I can only recall bits and pieces, but at the time, I'd thought it was my girlfriend coming to make amends. I was all too happy in my inebriated state to fuck all of our cares away. Only, when I woke up to the worst hangover of my life, I found Julianne asleep in the bed beside me, not my girlfriend. I freaked out. Pretended to be asleep until Jules woke up and rubbed her supple body along mine in greeting. I murmured my girlfriend's name and, keeping my eyes closed, told her I still loved her. Then faked going back to sleep.

I heard Julianne gasp and choke back a sob. I could practically feel her heartache as she'd scrambled out of the bed and out of my room, then out of my life while she attended college.

She never said a single word about it later that day, or at any time in the many years after. We both acted as if it had never happened.

I'd taken Julianne's innocence without even knowing it, then responded like a coward instead of facing up to my actions. Worse, I let her walk away from me, and for the next *ten years*, we never said a word about it. A ghost between us. Neither one of us willing to set aside our pride and share the truth.

It was the most fucked up moment of my entire life.

And as I stared at the devastation, the hope, and salvation brimming in her eyes, I knew this could very well be the path to my redemption. This time I'd stand at her side, help her with her twisted plan, and maybe, just maybe, build something real. What we shared moments ago felt more real for me than anything else had in a very long time.

I turned around, signed my name on the bidder's line and offered it to Alana. "It's done."

Alana nodded. "I'll have these filed, and the money transferred over as noted in the contract."

"Transfer the entire thirty million and the commission from my accountant tonight," I instructed. "No need to break it into payments."

Alana's brows rose toward her hairline. "*Pardon?*"

Julianne made a gagging screeching noise. "No! Gio, you don't have to do that. I can start with the first ten million after the ceremony. It will be enough to get a new business going if that's what we decide to do."

"My wife will have what she needs." I ground my teeth

while looking at her in the stunning white dress. She already looked the part of a bride. "We wed tonight. Alana, would you do us the honor of witnessing our marriage?"

Alana's eyes widened. "I…but of course. *Oui.* Christophe is waiting in the apartment with Emily. I can have them meet us."

"Emily?" Julianne queried. "Rhodes daughter? That Emily?"

She nodded. "Rhodes Davenport also picked out a bride tonight."

"You're kidding!" Julianne squawked in disbelief. "Now *that* is news. I thought he'd sworn off women forever after that two-bit hussy Portia took him for ride, and left him to raise their daughter alone."

"First, it is none of your business as to whom he chooses to share his life with, *ma petite fleur.* And your mother taught you better than to gossip," Alana chastised.

Jules snorted. "You and I both know that is an outright lie, *marraine.*" She called her *godmother* in French. "My mother was up in everyone's business."

Alana's lips twitched, proving she knew what Julianne claimed as the honest truth. Even I knew Rachel Myers liked to chat about the people she loved. "Be that as it may, she was better at hiding it," Alana finished.

Julianne shrugged. "Well, I've already made an appointment for us to be married at the chapel downstairs. I assumed I'd be marrying someone tonight."

Alana cringed. "You don't want to do a small, lovely ceremony at the family estate? I'd be happy to help coordinate it," she offered.

I reached out and took Julianne's hand, interlacing our fingers. "I will go along with whatever you prefer," I said, my gaze entirely on Jules.

She licked those swollen lips, reminding me of what she'd done with that perfect mouth not a half hour ago, as if goading me into imagining her plans for *after* the ceremony. "I'd rather not wait. Alana and Christophe are here, there's no one else I need present." Her eyes shimmered once again, likely thinking about our lost parents and her brother, the bastard.

I squeezed her hand. "Then it's settled. We marry tonight." I took in every inch of her features. Oh, how I wanted to kiss her again.

Those blue orbs went from sad to fiery in a second flat.

"I'll need a little time to freshen up." I swallowed down the desire obliterating my senses. I needed to retrieve my grandmother's and grandfather's wedding rings from the hotel safe. When I received the email explaining the details of The Marriage Auction, I had my assistant secure the family heirlooms from my Manhattan home. They were couriered to me at my lake house before I came here. I didn't believe at the time that I'd be officially using them, but something had told me to have them on my person.

Just in case.

Now I was glad I had. I wouldn't marry a woman like Julianne with a wedding ring I picked up at the hotel jeweler. No, she would wear my beloved Nana's ring. The one she'd worn for sixty years of wedded bliss with my granddad before she took her last breath only three years ago. The engagement ring was ostentatious as fuck and the exact color of Julianne's eyes. Pride soared through my veins at the thought of placing my grandmother's ring, an eight-carat blue diamond with triangular-cut diamonds on each side, set in platinum, on Julianne's long, dainty fingers. Back in the sixties, the ring had sold for just under four million but had recently been appraised at a whopping eighteen million. Julianne deserved nothing less.

Strangely enough, I'd never planned on giving that ring to Bianca. The newsflash was like a punch to the solar plexus. If I had been truly, madly in love with Bianca, why had the idea of presenting her with my grandmother's ring never entered my mind? Nana's ring was the first thing I thought of after I'd confirmed my seat at the auction to bid on Julianne's hand in marriage.

"Hey, you okay?" Julianne put her hand to my chest, directly over my pounding heart.

I nodded. "Just ready to move forward...in all things."

She wrapped her arm around me and rested her head to my chest. "Me too, Gio. Let's do this."

* * * *

I waited at the entrance to the small resort chapel, pacing the hallway like a caged beast. My nerves were shattered. The ring box was burning a hole in my jacket pocket. I'd changed into my best bespoke suit. A pitch-black Brioni tuxedo with a slim satin lapel that complemented my larger frame. Underneath I wore a black fitted dress shirt that had a slight sheen to it and paired that with a satin tie.

"Gio," I heard my name as Julianne approached.

She was a vision in flowing off-white. Her bountiful curves were sheathed in a breathtaking wedding gown. At first it looked like one piece of see-through fabric that had lace flower bud appliques strategically placed in a cascading pattern. The front of the dress plunged into a deep V, giving an enticing view of tantalizing cleavage that made my mouth water, even though the bulk of her bosom was completely covered. The upper half nipped in at the waist, while the material hugged her generous hips and thighs, flowing all the way to the floor and fanning out. There was another tulle-like fabric attached at the waist that flared, creating the visual of a much larger skirt. Her arms were completely covered in the transparent lace, which allowed her pearly skin to show through. She'd left her titian hair curled and down, brushing against her face, and just touching her shoulders.

"You are breathtaking." I whispered as she approached.

She smiled so radiantly, I knew I'd never forget the way she was looking at me. I seared that expression of pure joy straight into my memory bank.

Madam Alana had also changed from the dress she'd worn earlier into something softer. A pale pink, satin slip dress that moved like oil and fell to her knees. She was wearing a pair of matching stilettos. Christophe was wearing a grey suit and a pink tie. Walking next to them was an excited looking blonde teenager. She, however, was wearing a black sundress and a pair of Chucks. Her lips were stained the same red as Alana's. Even their makeup looked almost identical with the black cat eyeliner.

My Julianne was all soft colors, her freckles dusting her nose and cheeks, not hidden behind concealer. For that I was grateful because the woman I adored was also that freckled-face teenager I'd grown up with. Seeing her like this, taking my hand, about to become my wife was surreal.

Jules rose on her toes and kissed my cheek. "You ready to get hitched?" she teased.

"Seeing you in that dress, standing before me and looking like an angel, I can't imagine anything I'd want to do more than make you mine."

Mine. Not just my wife because we were entering an agreement, but mine.

She reached out and ran her fingers over the sides of my hair, adjusting the longer layers into place. "You are one handsome man, Giovanni Falco. I think I'm going to enjoy being married to you." She leaned closer. "I've even got a surprise underneath all of this lace." She winked.

Arousal tore through my body, making me grit my teeth and fist my hands. If I let myself respond the way I wanted, she'd be up against that wall, her knee hiked around my hip, my hand on her juicy ass, and my tongue down her throat, in two seconds flat.

I cleared my throat and swallowed. "I look forward to what awaits."

"Are we getting this party started or what?" the teenager asked. "Uncle Christo promised me I could pick all the numbers on the roulette wheel after you two got married."

"Shhh, you weren't supposed to share that part, *ma douce*," *my sweet*, he tsked as Alana gave him the side-eye.

Julianne smiled. "I'm ready."

I extended my elbow, and she looped her arm through it. "Let's make you Mrs. Julianne Falco."

"Uh, that would be Julianne Myers-Falco. I was Julianne Myers when you met me, and I'll be Julianne Myers when you marry me. I'm adding you to my family, not losing my identity. You should think about adding Myers to your name too."

I chuckled at her ballsy, take-no-shit attitude I knew all too well. "Maybe I will."

"Let's gooooooo! I'm dying to experience a Vegas wedding in real life. My friends are going to think this is sooooo cool!" Emily prattled. "Oh! I'll be your photographer."

Alana nudged the girl. "*Chéri*, you were not asked to do such things. And that is not how you offer your services."

Emily frowned, her excitement waning. "Um, would you like me to take photos for you guys?" she asked, her spirit lightening up as Julianne smiled and nodded.

"We'd love it. And my new hubby will toss you a hundo or two for a job well done. Right, honey?" She blinked at me grinning and fluttering her long eyelashes playfully.

"Definitely. Just don't get in the way. I plan to have my eyes on nothing else but this beauty becoming my wife."

Julianne gave me that look again, and I melted where I stood. The only thing I would have changed about this moment would be having our parents here to witness the unbelievable…Julianne and Giovanni's wedding.

No one was going to believe it.

Episode 26

Pure Chaos

NAOMI

We held hands as we left the ballroom where I'd signed away three years of my life and ten million dollars. I couldn't help the silly ass grin on my face.

Memphis lifted our hands and kissed the back of mine, his warm brown gaze on me. "I feel like I'm walking on air."

"Oh?"

He grinned and nibbled on my pinky finger, his top lip teasing against the ring he'd presented me. It was an emerald cut, two carat diamond with almost no inclusions, maybe a VVS1 on the clarity scale. The color wasn't anywhere near as flawless as I'd demand for my elite clientele, but there was something unbelievably charming about the slight yellow hint in the natural stone. It was attractive and rather dazzling against my skin. I wouldn't have ever pictured myself with such a dainty engagement ring that couldn't have cost more than ten thousand retail. Being in the precious gems business, bigger and meticulous quality was always better, but there was something extraordinary about seeing this ring on my finger that made my heart beat faster and a shiver run down my spine.

Had he been thinking about me when he purchased it?

"I'd fallen on some hard times recently, but finally, today, all of that changed. For me and my family." He smiled gently.

My eyebrows rose as I processed his declaration and remembered that he had a big family. Five sisters, if memory served. "Is that why you entered into the auction? For your family?"

He nodded as we moved toward the elevator to make our way down. Neither of us were staying in this casino hotel like the other candidates or bidders. Even with the excitement and arousal flowing through my veins, the time it took to get back to The Alexandra where we were both staying, would allow us to cool off a bit. Gather a little perspective on what we had just entered into.

Me, I'd thrown out the rule book. He'd had time to make this life-altering decision. And technically, I could have been anyone. Ultimately, it wasn't me that he chose, regardless of our connection before the auction occurred.

My heart squeezed as I thought about another woman winning this man as her husband. I gritted my teeth.

Not a chance.

Once I'd seen him strut across that stage, it was as if God Himself had shown the light down over him as a beacon, calling me to answer. But hot damn, the adrenaline and sheer joy that Memphis was all mine had me wanting nothing more than to jump straight into bed with him. From his beautiful eyes to his mouthwatering footballer's physique, and up to those lips I wanted all over me, the man was lethal to my libido. Still, I was no hussy, even though I'd acted rather uninhibited thus far.

"My sisters need schooling. More than that, every last one of 'em deserves to have the best chance at a great life. An intelligent woman like yourself probably knows a thing or two about dreaming big."

"I sure do." I swung our arms, thinking back to my college years.

They were fun as hell, but also filled with hard work. And I didn't have to worry about where tuition came from. My educational path had been laid out for me by my parents before I even turned a year old. By three, I was already in the most prestigious preschool in the nation. I took that life path all the way through undergrad, then got my master's in business at the Ivy League school my father demanded I attend. Once I'd completed my schooling on my family's terms, I broke Daddy's heart. Instead of going to work for him within his empire, I changed my destiny and signed up and completed a yearlong gemology program. Using the trust they'd provided me, I went into business for myself. Now I'm the best at what I do, in spite of my father's plans for me.

Once we were in the elevator, Memphis pressed up against the back wall, his hands around my waist, head dipping to my neck where he placed a sweet kiss. "We have two choices: We can take this back to our hotel and hit your room or mine," he breathed hotly against my ear, then trailed his lips and teeth along my jaw.

My lady bits throbbed, and I was loath to deny them or me. Fuck it all to hell. Tonight, I'd be a proud flag waving member of the hussy fan club.

"Mine, please," I murmured.

He kissed me breathless, and we didn't stop until we heard the elevator ding and a man clearing his throat.

"Getting off?" an older male voice stated from somewhere beyond the lust haze Memphis had me in.

Memphis shifted just his head. "Not yet." I gasped in delighted horror at the innuendo as he winked at whomever was behind us. He turned and nestled me up against his strong body. "Sorry, newly engaged." He grinned.

The older man was all teeth as he held up two glasses of

champagne. "I remember those days. Got my beautiful wife of thirty years waiting a few floors up for her bubbly as we speak. Have fun you two!" He smiled as Memphis led me out of the elevator and onto the casino lobby level.

"Thirty years," I said in awe. "Can you imagine?"

Memphis looked at me in such a way that I thought I could see his very heart shining through his eyes.

"To a woman like you? Abso-fucking-lutely."

I nudged his shoulder with my own. "Sweet talker."

He chuckled. "Nope. Just a man who knows what he's got when he has it staring him straight in the face. My momma didn't raise no fool."

I rolled my eyes. "You barely know me."

He stopped in the middle of the casino floor before we reached the exit. The lights blinked all around us, alarms blared, and people celebrated with endless hoots and hollers. It was chaos.

Everything that had happened so far. Everything that was sure to come. All of it, pure chaos.

"I know what I *feel* when I look at you. I know what I *feel* when I'm pressed up against you. I know what I *feel* when you let down that cool exterior and show me the heat underneath." He cupped my cheek, and I let out a weighted sigh. "Naomi, I think I already know you better than most people. And baby, I don't get bored or tired of things that feel good. Three years or thirty, neither will be near enough time with you."

I swallowed down the fear that suddenly encroached, making my throat as dry as the Sahara. I hadn't exactly had the best track record with men. Especially the alpha types that I tended to be drawn toward like a moth to a flame. And I wasn't fooled by this man either. He was as alpha as they came. Old fashioned. Direct. A footballer. You didn't attempt to go pro in that field if you weren't dedicated, fearless, and exceptionally hard-headed. He may have swagger and romantic tendencies but that didn't mean he'd roll over and become what I needed in a partner. And my needs ran hot or cold, depending on what I was working on or what mountain I was set to climb careerwise. That was the appeal of the auction in the first place. A man I could mold and shape into what I wanted. Someone who could fit smoothly into the neat little place I left open for a man.

Memphis didn't seem like the type that would fit into anything. Definitely not the tiny space I'd left available. No, he was a storm. Wild, untamed, an act of God. An entity that would smoothly appear, kiss a woman with soft whispering rain, then wreak havoc in the most earth-shattering ways.

He was going to change everything.

For the first time, I was willing to take a chance on something wild. Embrace the experience with my eyes wide open, my hands above my head, and the roller coaster of life speeding to a destination unknown.

Today, standing before this man, I felt more alive, cherished, and desired than I ever had before.

Nothing was going to prevent me from walking straight into the eye of the storm and learning exactly what awaited me there.

"Come on, let's get this party started back at our hotel." His gaze heated, desire oozing around us like a wind tunnel.

I smiled wide, wrapped my arms around his neck, and kissed him, hard and fast. Then I turned around and slid my hand down the length of his arm until he gripped my fingers. I glanced at him over my shoulder coyly, my lips pressed in a sultry pout.

"Come on, future husband. It's time to feast…and then maybe we'll eat." I winked saucily.

He closed his eyes, face turned to the ceiling, when he grinned and said, "Good Lord, what on Earth did I do to deserve such a blessing?"

* * * *

Memphis had me up against the entry wall, hands on my ass, mouth to mine the second the door clicked shut in my hotel room.

His mouth slid down my neck. "Woman, you are going to be the death of me."

I moaned as he pressed closer, his big body plastered to mine like a warm blanket on a freezing cold day. "You die on me before giving up the goods and there will be hell to pay." I clung harder to the muscles of his back.

His hands scaled along the skintight fabric of my dress. When he got to the hem, he curled his fingers and yanked it up past my hips, over my ribs until I got with the program and held my arms aloft. "That's not how you remove it—zipper."

"Fuck unzipping. This is faster." He lifted the dress over my head, taking my long curls with it. I burst out laughing when he cupped both mounds and pressed them together, and with his tongue flat, licked between them, leaving me to untangle my hair from the damn dress before tossing it to the ground.

"God damn you smell good. What is that scent?"

"Baby, I'm not wearing perfume."

He groaned so deep in his chest, I felt the rumble between my thighs.

His fingers shoved down my strapless bra until it was hanging around my waist. "Fuck me, Nay…I've never seen prettier titties. Jesus!" He grunted as he sucked my nipple into the fiery heat of his mouth. I arched with the pleasure, panting like I'd run a marathon. My hands shook as I held his head to my chest, feeding him more of me.

He sucked and swirled that magnificent tongue, and finished with small biting nips against the now tender, erect tip. "Next," he hummed, switching to my other breast.

My legs trembled, my knees weakening. "I'm going to

slide down this wall if you don't find a bed soon."

He released my breast with a plop, then shook his head, went back and sucked it again for another couple seconds as if he couldn't bear to stop even to take a breather.

Before I knew it, I was down on the floor, his big body over mine. "Better?"

"Fuck yessssss!" I kissed him, our tongues tangling magically. He tasted like my peach lip gloss along with a subtle hint of salt and spice. I shoved off his suitcoat, discarding the item. My fingers went to the buttons of his shirt. I got one undone before he straightened up.

He was breathing just fine, an athlete in his prime, ready to take down his opponent in a battle to the goal, while I was a panting, blubbering mess of exposed nerves and needy moans.

He undid his shirt smoothly, and tossed it aside, putting his massive, sculpted chest on full display. The man wasn't just fine from top to toe, his body was living, breathing art.

I watched with anticipation as he undid his belt, unzipped his fly and shoved his pants off until he was clad only in his boxer briefs.

"Naomi…" He fisted and unfisted his hands. He seemed desperate to stay in control of himself, possibly even moments away from snapping. "If you want to slow down, let me make love to you good and proper in a bed now's your chance to make that known. Because, woman, the second I get my mouth between those thighs, all bets are off."

I ran my hands over my breasts, tweaking my nipples as I went, curving my body towards him. His nostrils flared, and he inhaled sharply as he flicked his tongue out to lick his bottom lip.

"I want you to fuck me now. Make love to me later."

"Thank Christ!" And then his mouth was on me. Right over the simple satin thong I wore. His tongue teased over the damp fabric as he maneuvered his shoulders between my thighs, spreading me so wide my hips smarted, but I didn't care. The pleasure was worth the ache.

He snapped the itty-bitty line of fabric on each side of my hips as if it was as easy as ripping a tissue. Then his mouth was *there*. His tongue went straight for the promised land, driving as deep as he could go. So much that his teeth grated along my clit, and I saw stars. He placed both hands close to my sex and held me open as he devoured me whole.

I was so strung up, the foreplay having lasted the past hour, I came instantly, my body quaking like a six-point-four earthquake, destroying me further with every second he drew it out. The orgasm spiked, soared, and ravaged the heart of me.

Once I came down from my high, he reached for his pants, pulled out his wallet, and fingered a condom. His hands trembled as he ripped the foil, shoved his briefs down, and presented me with one monster-sized cock.

"Have mercy," I gasped as he slid the rubber over that behemoth.

"Don't worry, it will fit. You were made for me." He groaned as he ran his large hand up and down his dick, working his length, hissing with pleasure.

"There's those pretty words again. Now give me the goods," I snapped, losing my ever-loving mind.

"Mmm…" He grunted as he notched the wide head to my slippery slit. He thrust straight in.

My entire body bowed as I held back a scream by covering my mouth with my forearm and biting down on the fleshy muscle.

"Fucking hell, you're tight. Damn." He slid out and glided back in. "Come on, baby, open wider. Take all of me," he cooed.

"All of you?" I croaked and glanced down, realizing that there was another couple inches between us. "Oh hell, no," I wrapped my legs around his body, took a deep breath and used my core muscles to take him to the hilt.

"Perfect damn woman," he fell on top of me, gripped my ass, tilted my hips to the most beautiful angle and pounded me straight into the floor.

"Yessssss!" I cried and hung on for dear life.

He went to town on me, fucking me hard and deep. I gave back as good as I got, spearing myself on that titan between his thighs until he swirled those hips, prodding that secret space inside, and I lost it.

I was pretty sure I screamed like a fucking hyena as his mouth covered mine, stealing the sound straight from the source.

He owned me so completely, I didn't know which way was up or down, whether I was alive or dead. All I knew was a woman would walk to the ends of the earth and back for an experience like this.

Memphis ripped his mouth away, and pressed his face to my neck as I held on. "I'm gonna blow, baby."

"Give it to me," I begged and tightened my internal muscles until I had a chokehold on his cock.

"*Naomi.*" He sped up, plowing me so good the edges of my vision blurred as another orgasm rocketed through me. "Fucking beautiful, Naomi." he murmured, his hips working overtime. Then his entire body locked into place, his fingers dug into my ass so firmly I knew I'd have ten grape-sized fingerprints on my booty when this was all said and done.

Every muscle I caressed on him was flexed, veins popping, and the surface of his skin misted with sweet smelling sweat as he convulsed, moaning into my neck. "*Naomi*, my fiancée," he murmured with such pride and relief, I actually teared up.

My emotions were at a twenty out of ten. I was worked over, wrung out, and sated beyond compare.

For a full five minutes, we stayed there locked together, our sweat drying in the cool air of the room, while our bodies calmed.

I ran my fingers up and down his wide back, tracing patterns, becoming intimately familiar with this part of him. He eventually eased into a one-armed pushup then grinned like the Cheshire Cat that had just lapped up all the cream.

I smiled back, feeling a bit shy, lying with his dick sliding out of me, my bra still hung up around my waist, and both of us naked on the entryway floor.

"How you doin', gorgeous?"

I reached up and put both of my hands to his shoulders. "Um, good. Cold. A little emotional. Happy. And ready to eat my weight in steak and french fries."

"Bed, blanket, food, and cuddle time. Coming right up." He grinned.

"Then round two?" I ran my finger down his sumptuous neck teasingly.

"Then round two."

Episode 27

Meet the Parents Part 1

JACK

Summer slept like the dead the entire flight to California. The second she sat down, she yawned, kicked off her heels, curled her legs up into the supple leather seat, and claimed she needed a few winks. Then the woman crashed. It was mind-boggling. I'd never seen anyone who could slip into dreamland so quickly. Then again, I'd never met anyone like Summer Belanger. Not only was she a true beauty, physically speaking, she had an ease about her that called to me. Made me want to be closer to her. Almost like a gravitational pull.

When the plane landed in Humboldt County right outside of Eureka, which is, apparently, where her family lived, she popped up and out of her seat, grabbed her heels, and took my hand.

"Let's go! They'll be expecting us." She grinned, nearly vibrating with excitement.

I frowned. "How will they be expecting us?"

She shrugged and her eyebrows lifted. "They just will be."

I led her into the Land Rover I'd rented, and she

navigated since she was familiar with the area.

"Oh!" She pointed out the window in Old Town Eureka. "There's my favorite restaurant. I'll take you there tomorrow maybe," she gushed, clearly happy to be home.

It was a gorgeous area. The houses were incredibly unique, each building a different color, reminding me of Nyhavn in Denmark. Only the architectural style was completely opposite. The homes here were Craftsman, beachy, or looked like doll houses with jutting spiral lookouts and pointed roofs. The location had a free-spirited, artsy feel that put my mind at ease.

The coastline spread out parallel to the town, the breeze off the channel making the air feel crisp and fresh. The pine trees surrounding the area enhanced the clean, nature-focused atmosphere.

"This place is magical," I stated, admiring a bright yellow house with burnt orange trim. It shouldn't work together but somehow, it did.

As we stopped at the crosswalk to let a family walk by, I spied a familiar name on a cute little building. "Eureka's Pizza. Should I pop in and see if you're there?" I teased.

Summer's cheeks turned hot pink. "I'm sorry I lied. That was uncool of me. But in my defense, we'd just survived a very harrowing experience, I'd melted down, had a panic attack, and thought you were stuck up and snobby about me smelling like weed."

"Mmmhmm," I clicked the turn signal and followed the road out of the main part of town toward a mountain blanketed with large pine trees in the distance.

"It was pretty nice of you to try and check up on me. Proves you're a good guy, Jack Larsen."

I chuckled. "If I'm being honest, I did want to check up on you, but my intentions weren't pure of heart."

She grinned wickedly. "Oh. Are you admitting to being into me?"

"If *into you* means I think you're gorgeous, your eyes are the prettiest I've ever seen in my life, and your body makes me want to fuck you into next week. Then yes, I am most certainly *into you*, Summer."

"Hot damn. Don't hold back or anything." She snorted playfully then suddenly started bouncing in her seat. "Pull in right there. That's the driveway to my parents' house." Summer wiggled like a brand new puppy who'd just met its new owner. She was so excited she could hardly contain it. A lightness filled and expanded my chest watching her, my fingers tingling with the desire to reach out and touch the living, breathing energy this woman exuded. I held back but just barely. There would be time to connect. Three years of time.

I tamped down the urge to touch her as we continued down a long dirt road that eventually ended on the top of a hill. A sprawling one-story white, wooden, ranch style home greeted us. There was a tree line surrounding the property miles off in the distance. It reminded me a lot of what Erik's parents had back in Oslo. This home, however, had a wraparound porch with several rocking chairs, pots of every color bursting with flowers, and lush greenery trailing the banisters.

"Wow," I whispered as Summer bolted out of the car.

Before her feet even hit the steps leading up to the porch a flash of color raced out of the house. A woman with blonde, waist-length hair spread her arms out wide, the fabric of her dress draped to the sides like a butterfly's wings in flight as Summer crashed into her.

The woman curled her arms around Summer and swung her from side to side. As I exited the car, a tall, slender, redheaded man approached the two. He cupped the back of Summer's head, closed his eyes and kissed the crown of her golden hair. His red beard and mustache combo disappearing into her hair.

I leaned against the front of the car to give them some time. The door to the house opened and a tall, slender, fair redhead with corkscrew curls and bare feet padded down the steps. She wore a tie-dyed skirt and a black strappy tank. Hanging from her neck were at least ten different necklaces, and her wrists were circled by stacks of beaded bracelets. On her long fingers were a plethora of silver rings of various designs I couldn't make out from such a distance.

Summer let go of the woman who had to be her mother, and plowed into the younger woman's arms. The redhead ducked her head straight against Summer's neck and held on.

I waited a few minutes for the group to pull themselves together. The entire spectacle was astonishing. This homecoming was one you'd expect to see when someone returned after having been away for months or years, not a two-hour flight away in a neighboring state. It said a lot about how connected this family was to one another.

What if they found me lacking?

Would Summer terminate our agreement?

Technically, she didn't need the money.

I scowled as the thought of her not wanting to take this adventure with me wove into my psyche. She could leave me at any time. There wasn't anything tying her to me until after we officially married. I made a mental note to speed up the wedding date to as soon as possible. Maybe there was a justice of the peace around Eureka I could speak to. I'd have my assistant look into it.

"Jack! Come here, silly!" Summer's voice cut through the uncertainly clouding my mind.

I shook off the haze and ran my fingers through my messy, windblown hair while focusing on my fiancée who was waving me over. I adjusted my suit, closing the center button of the jacket.

When I got close, Summer looped her arm with mine and pressed to my side. "And this is Jack Larsen, my fiancé. Jack, this is my mama Ann, my sister Autumn, and my father Bernie."

Ann stepped forward, reached up, and cupped both of my cheeks. Her eyes were the color of emeralds. Freckles dotted her creamy skin in pretty patterns. Her lips were plump, pink, and looked exactly like Summer's.

"Oh, I see you, dear. So much loss." Her thumbs traced over my brow ridge, down my nose, and over my cheeks the way a blind person might scan the topography of a person's features. "We'll help you, son. The light always shines bright around here." Her gaze flicked to Summer as she smiled. "Sunshine year-round. Stick with my girl, and she'll rid you of any darkness." She patted my face lovingly, reminding me of Erik's mother Irene. "Come, you both need to eat. It's well past dinner time."

I shook Bernie's hand. "It's nice to meet you, Sir."

"You can call me Bernie, Dad, or Pops. I don't answer to anything else." He gave a wonky sideways grin before he took his wife's hand, and they made their way up the porch and into the house.

Autumn waited patiently for them to leave before she smiled wide. "You are even hotter than in my vision." She nudged Summer's shoulder. "Lucky ducky!" she teased. "Come on, let's get in there. Mom already made tea for all of us."

As we made it to the top of the stairs, following a few steps behind Autumn, the woman abruptly stopped, turned around and tipped her head to the side. "Where's your son?" She asked pointedly.

I jolted my head back. "Uh, my son?" I croaked. No clue what she was talking about.

"Yeah, the little boy. About two or three years old?" She frowned and then squinted. "No…yeah, I see you with a small child. A boy. I assumed you had one? The vision is very clear."

Summer grasped my arm and pressed her cheek to my

bicep, her gaze concerned. "You have a child," she whispered with uncertainty.

I shook my head. "No. I don't know what's going on here, but I do not have a child. I swear. Some friends of mine are having twin girls. And a very close friend back home has a young boy."

Autumn said the one name that sliced straight through my heart. "Troy."

I winced and inhaled sharply. "Yes, the boy's name is Troy Jack, but we call him TJ," I clenched my teeth. Summer ran her hands up and down my arm. "But he's not my son. He's…" I let out a long breath. I didn't want to go into everything regarding the helicopter accident, losing Troy, then his wife having her baby without my best friend there to see it. Erik in the hospital and then practically disappearing off the face of the earth for two years, leaving me to be the only one looking after Troy's wife and kid. It was all so complicated and chock full of some intense feelings I'd pushed way into the back of my mind and didn't want to resurface now. Especially after Erik finally found happiness and started to heal. Erik, Troy's wife, Ellen, and I were finally moving on from Troy's loss. The last thing I wanted was to bring it all to the surface again.

"Hey, hey, it's okay. Autumn…um…she has visions that are hard to decipher. She obviously got your connection to the boy mixed up."

Autumn tried again, her lips pursed into an expression of intense concentration. "Uh, not exactly…"

Summer cut her sister off. "Enough. Obviously you're upsetting Jack. Lay off a bit, yeah? Maybe go ground yourself."

"But…" Autumn breathed.

Summer held up her hand. "Enough! Can we come in? Get Jack some tea and a seat. We've both had an incredible day. We could use some time to decompress."

Autumn's shoulders slumped. "I'm sorry if I overstepped.

You know how it is sometimes. I can't unsee things, and they push and push. And they just come out."

I firmed my jaw and gave her a hint of a smile. It was all I could muster after she mentioned Troy and his son. It was a very sore subject and not one I was planning to discuss with Summer's family. Heck, I wasn't even sure I'd discuss it with her. Troy and Ellen were an important part of my life, but I was trying to build something of my own too. Ellen made me promise I'd try for her and for the friend I'd lost.

Autumn entered the house, and before I could grab the screen door handle, Summer stopped me. "Hey, you okay? I saw your face when she mentioned Troy and TJ."

I closed my eyes and nodded. "Honestly, Summer, I really don't want to talk about it right now. I just want to spend a little time getting to know your family over tea and then maybe find a hotel where we can crash. It's been a very long day."

She took my hand, put it to her cheek and rubbed against my palm. "Okay. But we'll stay at my house back in the middle of town, if it's okay with you."

"I'd love to see your house."

She grinned. "Remember you said that," she teased before opening the door and dragging me behind her.

We went through a massive living space that had big picture windows. There were bookshelves from floor to ceiling across almost every wall. Books, knickknacks, picture frames, crystals, and plants filled every shelf, everything meticulously placed.

Candles burned on small tables that weren't already lit with warm lamps in varying colors. The smell of frankincense mixed liberally with lavender in the air. It wasn't overbearing, but we'd definitely leave here smelling like a walking stick of potpourri.

I followed Summer through the kitchen where her father was dishing out heaping bowls of stew. Steam wafted in the air above each large bowl, and my mouth watered.

My stomach growled and Summer chuckled. "He's definitely hungry, Dad," Summer announced as she walked me past him to a well-lit covered patio. Here the lighting matched the environment. Moody, charming, and relaxing.

Autumn and Ann were already seated at a large round table with a loaf of bread on a cutting board placed in the center. Next to Ann was a side cart that held a pot of tea and several dainty teacups, a bowl with sugar cubes, and a metal pitcher that I imagined contained milk.

"Sit you two. Take a load off," Ann suggested. "Bernie's ladling up the stew as we speak. We figured if you were coming straight from Vegas and the auction, you might not have eaten."

The auction.

How did she already know about that?

I gripped the chair closest to Ann and held it out for Summer to take her seat. Her mother smiled, obviously approving of the gesture.

I took my own chair. "So, you know about the auction?"

"Tea, Mama?" Summer interrupted.

Her mother pushed the cart over to Summer, then picked up a stack of worn looking cards and started to shuffle them.

"Sugar and milk?" Summer asked me.

"However you make it will be fine, *solskinn*," I answered, then focused on Ann. "The auction? You're aware I purchased your daughter's hand in marriage tonight?" I wanted to get right to the truth. If she knew, there was no reason to pussy-foot around our current situation. And I preferred to plot every possible move on the chess board even before I played.

Ann smirked. "I was the one who suggested she enter. A beautiful girl like my Sunny can't spend her life hiding in the greenhouse with her plants and her old man."

"And why not?" Bernie touted playfully as he entered with a tray of steaming bowls. He set the food down and passed out each bowl, then offered napkins and silverware. "She's a chip off the old block."

Ann sighed as she stirred her stew. "Yes, love of my life, but my daughter needs a man of her own. Passion. Friends. Kids. She can't spend all of her days in the fields or locked up with her father in the greenhouses. It's not healthy. She needs more."

"She needs dick is what she needs," Autumn grumbled around a bite of bread.

"That too," her mother agreed wholeheartedly.

I choked on a sip of tea. "*Jesus Kristos!*" I cursed and wiped at my mouth, shocked at the candor of this family.

Summer laughed and pointed her spoon at her sister. "So do you. How's Raquel anyway...the *bitch*." She whispered the last part.

"I heard that!" Autumn fired back, anger suffusing her pale cheeks. "You never liked my girlfriend. Not ever. Admit it!" she snapped.

"Because she's a bitch who doesn't deserve you!" Summer snarled and leaned back, crossing her arms over her chest.

"Well, that is the truth," Bernie grumbled, agreeing with Summer.

"Bernie," Ann countered. "Do not get involved in their squabbles."

"I'm just saying, Raquel has never treated you the way you should be treated. That's all. And she hates me. She also doesn't like coming here. That's a sign right there that she's not good for you," Summer stated.

Autumn rolled her eyes. "Puh-leeese. She doesn't hate you. She's afraid of how smart you are. Says you talk to her like she's stupid."

"Because she *is* stupid," Summer fired back. "The woman knows how to play pool, drink beer, watch sports, and boss you around like you're her personal maid. And you put up with it. Why? Because she knows how to finger the G-spot!" Summer crooked her index finger in a mocking manner.

My mouth dropped open at the same time Autumn's did.

"How dare you! You wish you had a person to fuck you stupid like Raquel does me."

"Being good in bed isn't everything," Summer sneered.

"No but it's a damn good start! Maybe try it with your own man and lay off my girlfriend, why don't ya," Autumn huffed.

"Fine! I'm sorry. I just love you and want more for you." Summer huffed.

"Let's change the subject, shall we?" Ann interrupted. "So, how much did you pay for my daughter in the auction?"

"Eight million, but I would have paid more. Please pass the bread," I pointed to the loaf in the center.

"Eight million dollars?" Ann croaked disbelieving. "Whoopie!" She squealed and the entire table burst into laughter.

Episode 28

Meet the Parents Part 2

SUMMER

"Eight million dollars," my father gasped then slumped into one of the open patio chairs between Jack and my sister Autumn. "Well, I'll be damned. We'll be able to get that state-of-the-art HVAC system in place for the next growing cycle on the indoor crops."

I fist pumped the air and wiggled in my seat. "I know, right? It's going to be amazing. My babies are going to love a perfectly cooled and heated space. Pair that with the hydroponic system we set up last quarter, and we'll have some incredible new products to offer."

"Your babies?" Jack leaned over, a hunk of bread dangling between his fingers.

"My plant babies. I'll introduce you tomorrow." I grinned and scooped up a spoonful of Dad's homemade soy and vegetable stew. When the delicious, familiar taste of the broth hit my tastebuds, I sighed dreamily. "Sure is good to be home," I hummed.

"Okay, about that, when are we going to talk about the

ceremony?" Jack announced.

"The ceremony?" I blinked, uncertain of what he was referring to.

"For the wedding. We have a month to get married, or the contract is null and void." Jack's tone was all business.

I waved my hand in the air. "Oh, *that* ceremony. Pish posh. A month is plenty of time. No worries."

"A month is no time at all," he countered. "And if it's okay with you, I'd prefer we plan accordingly. I can have my assistant find us a wedding planner who can handle all the details on our behalf."

I shrugged. "Cool. Whatever you want works for me."

Jack reached over and covered my hand with his and squeezed. He was openly smiling from ear to ear, obviously pleased with my carefree approach to our impending nuptials. Which boded well for our future. I often let the chips fall where they may. The universe always provided the best course of action. Most people just ignored the signs.

"Sunny," Mom cut in, her tone one of concern. "Honey, this may have started as a business transaction, but no daughter of mine is going to have a haphazard wedding. We need to involve the town, the coven, Jack's family and friends. You can't start wedded bliss on a 'whatever works' mentality," Mom insisted. "We can have the wedding here on the property. Your sister and I can plan it while you, your father, and Jack evaluate the future of Humble Buds."

"Humble Buds?" Jack interrupted. "What is that?"

"The name of our company. Isn't it clever? It's kind of a play off of humble beginnings, and being humble in life, and of course the plants...buds. Get it?" I bit my bottom lip as Jack chuckled.

"I do. Very clever indeed." His warm, jovial gaze turned my heart into mush.

As I stared into his handsome face, I realized Jack had a sweet side. I looked forward to bringing that trait out more often. Every interaction with him to date had been so serious. Loosening up my future husband would be one of my goals. Alongside climbing the hunk like a tree. It had been too long since my last sexual encounter. Even though my sister was trying to get under my skin with the "she needs dick" comment, she wasn't wrong. It has been close to a year since my last romp.

I turned my hand over and interlaced our fingers. I was about to suggest we take this little party to my house when Mom started shuffling her tarot cards again. Once she got the bug to do a reading, there was no stopping her.

Jack's gaze flitted from me to my mother.

"So Jack, tell me about your family. Big? Small?" Mom asked.

"Uh very small, seeing as I have no biological family to speak of," he answered briskly.

I immediately lifted his hand up to my face and rubbed my cheek on the back. "What do you mean? Did they pass?" I whispered, my entire focus on him. Even Mom stopped shuffling her cards, and Dad and Autumn put down their spoons to give Jack their attention. The tension swirled in the air around us.

He shook his head. "I was orphaned as a baby. Lived in a variety of foster homes as a small boy. Then was placed in an institution for boys at the age of ten. Which is when I attended the same school as Erik Johansen, my best friend. His family practically took care of me as Erik and I were glued to one another's side. He owns Johansen Brewing, which is the company I run."

"Johansen Brewing!" Dad breathed. "That's the top performing alcoholic beverage company in the world."

Jack grinned. "I know. We've worked hard to make it the success it is today."

"But, you have no parents? No aunts, uncles, no one to call your own?" My eyes filled with tears as I took in his solemn expression.

"Hey, now. Don't cry for me, *solskinn*. I live a very charmed life. My upbringing wasn't ideal, but I turned all of that around. And the Johansens are the family I chose. And so are you." He cupped my face and wiped away a tear as it fell down my cheek.

I cupped his jaw and pressed my forehead to his. "I choose you, too," I whispered and then pecked him on the lips.

His hand tunneled into my hair, and he deepened the kiss. The moment our lips touched, we both forgot the world around us. For a few beautiful seconds, there was only Jack and Summer. Everything and everyone else just slipped away.

"Um, hello? Still eating dinner here," Autumn teased.

Jack's fist tightened in my hair when Autumn spoke and then loosened as he gently pulled away. He cleared his throat and adjusted his jacket. "I'm sorry. That was inappropriate."

I grinned stupidly. "I like that you forget where you are when you kiss me." I admitted, not giving two figs that my parents and sister were present.

"Me too." Mom sighed, her tarot cards held to her heart, a big silly grin plastered to her face. "All right, Jack, let's see what the Universe wants you to know today."

"I'm not sure I'm following," he said.

"She's going to do your tarot cards, just go with it." I placed my hand to his thigh, instantly appreciating the hard quad as I did. "Damn, baby, you work out?"

He smirked. "Every day. You?"

I snorted. "Have you seen this body?" I gestured up and down my frame.

His gaze heated once more as he leaned over until he could whisper in my ear. "Not nearly enough of it, no."

I shivered and my mouth went dry. "Uh, well, I didn't get these curves by hitting the gym on the regular. That's more my sister's speed."

"Ew. Gyms, no thank you. Yoga, Pilates, hiking, walking, yes. Gyms are icky and stinky. All that clanging of weights against one another messes with my Zen space. No thank you," Autumn scrunched up her nose.

I sighed. "True. I meant that you exercise regularly. Must you be so literal?"

"Yes, actually, I must, and you know that," Autumn bit out.

"Girls," Mom warned.

We both clamped our mouths shut.

"Okay, Jack, pick a card," Mom instructed.

He picked one off the table where she'd spread them out then flipped it over. It was the Five of Wands.

"Oh, fives are teaching cards. They are meant to teach us lessons about ourselves that the Universe would like us to put more focus and attention on. The image on this particular card is a clash of the fairy folk…"

"I don't believe in fairies."

The three women at the table gasped simultaneously. Dad, on the other hand, started laughing out loud while I reached over and put my hand over Jack's mouth. "He didn't mean it!" I announced, looking around the garden. "Don't pull any shenanigans to prove your existence. Pretty please. The rest of us will educate him," I assured the fairies, lest they strike out.

"What did I say?"

Mom shook her head. "Don't repeat it. Summer will explain later. Let me finish your reading." Her attention returned to the cards. "Oddly enough this card tends to appear when there is conflict, confusion about moving forward, lively debate, and combustible energy. All of which you will certainly experience being a part of this family. But don't fret, the card also shows passion and action. You seem very much to be a man of action, and my daughter has more passion in her pinky toe than most people have in their entire bodies. Together, you'll balance one another out."

"Except for when I mention my disbelief in the fairies." Jack snickered.

"No!" Mom, Autumn, and I shouted at the same time. He was so fucked and didn't even know it. The fairies could be ruthless but mostly they were tricksters. He had no idea what was coming.

Dad continued to laugh and shake his head. He'd learned all of this when he started dating my mother thirty years ago. It was probably like watching himself from the past.

"Now you've done it. Once can be considered an accident...twice a challenge. Good luck, son." Mom picked up his card and put it back into the deck.

Jack smiled and reached for his water glass. Just as his fingers barely touched it, the entire glass tipped over. Water sloshed straight into his lap, soaking him from the waist down.

"*Faen!*" he cried out as he stood abruptly, wiping the ice and chilly water from his lap. His thighs and groin were fully covered, looking exactly like he'd peed himself.

"And that, my friend, is why you don't fuck with the fairy folk," my sister tutted arrogantly.

I glared in her direction. "He doesn't know any better," I snapped. "Give him a break."

"This was not the fairy folk. It was me being an idiot and not gripping the glass properly. The condensation from the ice made the glass slippery, and I knocked it over. Simple science."

"Whatever you say," Autumn cackled.

I lashed out. "Shut up, Autumn!"

My father handed Jack the towel he still had hanging over his shoulder from when he was cooking. "Here, son."

Jack wiped at the worst of it. "Sorry everyone. I guess I'm a bit off kilter. It's been a long day." He shifted the chair, turned around, and moved to sit back down. Somehow he missed the mark, and the chair fell backward as he hit the floor.

Well, he'd been warned.

"*Helvete*, what in the world is happening?" He barked what I believed was another curse word. I'd ask him later what those words meant in Norwegian.

Autumn went into full belly laughter. Through her giggles, she panted, "Like I said…don't fuck with the fairies." She burst into another round of laughter as I got up to help Jack. This time, I put the chair in the right place and held it there while he took a seat.

"Autumn, I swear if you don't shush up, I will summon Hecate so I can spite your ass myself."

"You wouldn't dare," she growled.

"Try me!" I gave her my patented big sister, don't mess with me look.

She rolled her eyes and sat back in her chair and, blessedly, kept her big mouth closed.

"You okay?" I ran my hand up and down Jack's arm. "That had to hurt your tailbone."

He firmed his jaw and gave me a fake smile. "I'm fine. Are you about ready to head out? I wasn't kidding about it being a long day."

"Totally. Let's get you home and into bed." I waggled my eyebrows playfully and started to pick up our bowls and silverware.

"No, no, you both go on ahead. Dad and I will take care of the dishes. Go get some rest. We'll see you tomorrow." My mom ushered us away from the table.

"It was really nice meeting all of you. The stew was delicious. Thank you." Jack shook my father's hand.

Dad clapped Jack on the shoulder. "Our family can be a lot on a new person, but I promise you'll never meet a more devoted group of people. We back one another up in all things and share our woes and successes. It's my honor to welcome you to the family."

"Thank you, Bernie. I look forward to getting to know all

of you better in the coming weeks." He went over to Mom and leaned over and kissed her cheek. "Thank you for the hospitality and the…interesting card reading."

"You're welcome, son." She smiled as she pulled him into a hug and winked at me, then fanned her face.

I grinned and shook my head as Jack shook my sister's hand. "Until next time."

"What do you mean next time? I need a ride home."

"Autumn, no. Stay here," I attempted.

"Sunny, I have to open the store in the morning. Come on, I'll be quiet."

"Fine," I grumbled. "Let's go." I took Jack's hand and led him back through the house. "Autumn lives in the connected guest house and storefront. Don't worry, there's a long breezeway to the main house, which will be bolted and chained," I said louder than necessary so she could hear.

"Like I want to catch you and your new beau walking naked around the house, banging on every surface." Then she glanced over her shoulder at Jack. "Actually, he is pretty hot…"

"Autumn…*Hecate*… Remember?" I warned for the second time.

She made the gesture of tying her lips into a knot, basically promising to keep silent. I doubted that promise, but she actually came through because the car ride home was uneventful.

Jack pulled up in front of my house, and squinted at the rather large Victorian home. It had been built on a corner lot and faced the ocean in the distance. The guest house and storefront were on the corner part where Autumn headed immediately. She waved over her shoulder. "Night-night. Glad you're home and scored yourself a hot fiancé."

I stood at Jack's side and cuddled under his arm. He was staring at my house. "Is it my eyes, or is the entire house pink?"

I snickered. "It is pink. It's called The Pink Lady, and I've been in love with her since I was a small child. The very second our business became successful and I could afford to buy her, I made the owners an offer. It's been the love of my life ever since."

"Guess I've got some serious competition for your affections then." He rubbed my arm and stared at my home.

"Guess you do. Let's head in." I let him go and raced up the steps like I did every day. Jack got our bags out of the trunk and carried them up the stairs and followed me inside.

I flicked on the lights, and the crystal chandelier in the entryway reflected sparkles of light all over the space, making it seem even more inviting.

"Come, let me show you our room. Unless you want a tour now."

"I'm beat, Summer. Sleep first. Tour tomorrow."

"You got it. Though it's three flights up, which should be nothing on those firm quads." I teased.

"*Touché.*" He murmured and followed me up the three flights to the master bedroom.

"Go ahead and use the bathroom first, and I'll get everything situated," I offered, pointing to the bathroom door.

He nodded, and his shoulders seemed to slump as the lines around his eyes deepened. He really was beat. He took his suitcase into the bathroom while I grabbed mine and tossed the entire thing in the closet. I'd deal with unpacking later, or in a week or two, depending on my mood.

I turned on the end table lights and pulled back the coverlet to make my queen-sized bed seem more inviting. I wanted him to feel comfortable here. Then maybe he'd want to stay in Eureka for a while instead of carting me off to his homeland. Not that I didn't want to see Oslo, that would be awesome. I just wanted to share more of my home with him while we got to know one another better.

Jack exited the bathroom, wearing a white t-shirt and a

pair of loose burgundy sleep pants. "It's free. Which side do you sleep on?"

"I usually sleep in the middle so pick a side." I offered then skittered into the bathroom. Once inside, I brushed my teeth, peed, washed my face, brushed my hair and removed all my clothing before putting on my black silk robe with the badass peacock on the back; its feathers even fanned out and trailed across the arms.

I exited the bathroom to find Jack already in bed, the covers up to his waist. His shirt still on. Weird.

His gaze fell to my bare legs and then up to my face. "You're one beautiful woman, Summer."

"Thank you," I said while untying my robe. I let the satin drop, revealing my naked body.

Jack made a choking sound as he sat straight up in bed. "*You're naked*," he breathed, his eyes tracing all over my bare curves like a caress.

"Yes, I know. That's how I sleep."

"*Helvete!*"

"What's that mean?" I yawned, pulled the covers back and then slipped underneath.

He swallowed, closed his eyes and inhaled slowly. "It…uh…means *fucking hell*."

"Nice. Goodnight, Jack. Sleep well." I tucked my hands into prayer position under my cheek and immediately fell asleep.

Episode 29

All You Can Eat

RHODES

"Whoa sweetheart, slow down," I suggested as Maia shoveled a huge mouthful of mashed potatoes and took a monster bite of a buttery roll almost simultaneously. Her cheeks were puffed up like a chipmunk, which was rather cute, but also concerning. "The food isn't going anywhere. It's a buffet, you can eat as much as you want."

Her eyes widened as she chewed and swallowed. She lifted her water and drank deeply before wiping her mouth with her napkin. "Uh, sorry. I haven't eaten today."

I chuckled and reached for my glass of red wine. Maia hadn't taken so much as a single sip from the glass I'd poured for her. Perhaps she didn't like wine.

"So, why this place?" I gestured to the all-you-could-eat buffet in Caesars Palace. It wasn't my regular dining preference. Everywhere I looked there were tourists loading their plates to the gills, some not even waiting to start eating until they'd gotten back to their table, sampling items while picking through what was available.

Maia cut a large chunk of steak. The damn thing was practically burnt, it was so overdone. If she'd wanted a good steak, I could have taken her to the steakhouse in The Alexandra. Joel's resort catered to those who could afford the best. Something I'd worked very hard to ensure I could have at my leisure. I certainly would have enjoyed the experience more. Except, when I asked Maia if there was someplace in particular she wanted to eat, she'd chosen the buffet at Caesars Palace.

"I've always wanted to sit down and eat here officially, like a real customer. The food always smells and tastes great."

"What do you mean it tastes great? If you haven't eaten here officially, how have you tasted it?" I asked, confused by her response.

She bit down on her bottom lip and focused on her food. She pushed a cooked carrot around her plate randomly before tilting her head and looking up at me through her lashes. Shame and sadness filled the air around our table.

My heart cracked at the desperation I saw in her eyes.

"I...uh...well, the cooks and waitstaff hang out in the alley to make calls, smoke, take their breaks. Over the years, they'd see me...um...digging through the trash." Her jaw firmed, and her lips pressed together as she looked away. "They'd often leave me a doggie bag full of items that remained in the buffet at the end of the night. They were going to toss it anyway, which is why I was there waiting. One night, I found a brown bag on top of the main garbage can. The bag had a note. 'For the girl with sad eyes.'" She sighed and scooped up more potatoes. "I survived on the kindness of the crew here for a very long time. Almost every night there'd be a bag of food there. Some days it was all I had to eat." She shrugged.

"So you wanted to eat here for what reason?" I pushed, knowing she'd already likely shared more than her pride would allow.

"Maybe to prove I'd made it somehow. Even after Sam found me and gave me a place to live, and I'd done a bit better for myself, I still relied on their kindness more often than not. Food is expensive. And I didn't always find what I needed."

"Through pickpocketing," I teased, trying to lighten the moment.

She smirked. "That, but I also did odd jobs for the motorcycle club. They've been really good to me too. To this day, I still clean the clubhouse once a week, and if I do their bedrooms, which are disgusting by the way, men are dogs." She laughed, and the sound was so pretty, I vowed I'd find more ways to make her laugh regularly. "They'd each leave me whatever money they deemed the job warranted. Some were more generous than others. But I did it even if it was ten bucks. Because ten bucks was ten bucks. And I couldn't be choosy."

"Jesus," I sucked back the rest of my wine in one gulp then refilled my glass. The woman had eaten garbage and cleaned up after bikers in order to survive and have a roof over her head. "You've had some life," I said.

She shook her head. "No. I've had a shit life. Cleaning up after the club and living in the room above Sam's garage has been the absolute best I've ever had. So don't knock it," she finished, a bit of venom in her tone.

"Until now it's the best you've had. All that's changing, Maia. I promise, you'll never have to live that way again. You can trust me."

"Yeah, well, I've been promised a lot of things in life, none of which has ever come true. And there are only two people in the whole world I trust. Sam and Alana. Frankly, Mr. Davenport…" She said my last name in a husky timbre that made my cock take notice. I gritted my teeth and breathed through my nose. My heart pumped wildly. This woman did things to me. Made me feel unsettled and a little heated around the collar. "I don't know what to think about you," she finished.

I reached out and put my hand around her small forearm. She was too thin for her size and age. Regular food, sleep, and lack of worries would do wonders for this beautiful woman. "I'll earn your trust."

She jerked her arm away and glared. "Excuse me if I don't hold my breath, and please don't grip me like that. It scares me."

I snatched my hand away, giving her space. "Sorry." I felt like a total heel.

"Thank you," she mumbled and grabbed another roll from the basket on the table, slathered it with butter, and took a huge bite. Maia had already cleared the mountain of food on her plate and was still eating. The woman must have a hollow leg, because I had no idea where she'd put so much food.

I leaned back, having not touched the overcooked steak, the baked potato, or the grilled asparagus on my plate. None of it looked appealing in the least. And after our conversation, my appetite was nonexistent.

I leaned forward and planted my elbows on the table, resting my chin on top of my clasped hands, and doing my best to appear nonthreatening. The way she snatched her arm away from my grip said she'd been hurt physically, probably by a man. I wanted my future wife to open up to me, allow me in, not fear me. It was the only way this relationship would work, going forward. "Tell me more."

"I've done nothing but answer your questions since we arrived. How about you tell me about you. Why's your daughter such a brat?" she stated with zero diplomacy.

I winced. "Emily is thirteen going on thirty. She thinks she knows everything, worships her mother, who's a terrible influence, and hates me."

"Why does she hate you?" she asked around a mouthful of bread.

"Because I'm her dad. I don't let her get away with things.

I make her pick up after herself. She has to tell me where she's going and with whom. I insist that she has to introduce me to her friends and their parents before she's allowed to hang out. I check her grades and ensure she's doing her homework and keeping up with school assignments."

"Normal stuff then. She seemed to have a chip on her shoulder at the airport. Why?"

"Again, because she's a teenager. You know how it is. Think back to when you were a teenager."

Maia's expression seemed to contain elements of cynicism and derision as she reached for two more rolls. "When I was a teenager, I was on the streets sleeping under cardboard, if I was lucky. You, your daughter, the lifestyle you have—we are not the same." Her voice lowered as the punch to my gut hit true.

Maia Fields had been living on the streets since she was a child.

Fury rose up my chest like a wave of fire, tingling and spitting embers along the surface of my skin. The image of her cold, shivering, and hungry while sleeping on the streets had me spitting mad. What kind of people allowed that to happen to a child? There was a special place in hell for people like that.

"Where are your parents in all this?" I asked bluntly, putting my hands into my lap as I fisted them so hard my knuckles turned white, and my palms ached at the extreme pressure.

"My mother and half-siblings are in Colorado. That's all you need to know." And like flipping a switch, her demeanor changed. "Can we go? I'm really tired."

Damn this woman was a whirlwind of contradictions. One minute she's sharing and eating happily, the next she's snapping at me like an abused and frightened animal.

I stood up and laid four hundred-dollar bills on the table.

Her eyes widened at the sight of the money. "That's too

much. Each meal was $50.99 and already included tax. The bottle of wine you chose was listed at $88. That's exactly $189.98. An appropriate tip would be fifteen percent, twenty if you enjoyed your meal, which you clearly did not since you didn't eat any of it. The tip should be no less than $28.48. That means your total with fifteen percent tip is $218.46. You're overpaying by $181.54. That's a lot of money." She sucked her lips between her teeth and cradled one of the white linen napkins in a ball along with a small sparky purse.

The woman knew her math. Interesting.

"Let's just consider it an extra tip for the kindness the staff has shown you in the past." I held out my arm, encouraging her to go first. "After you."

She clutched whatever she'd wrapped in the napkin as though hiding it and high-tailed it out of the restaurant and into the bright flashing lights and roar of a busy casino.

I sidled up to her and placed my hand lightly at her lower back. She stiffened for a moment and then glanced over her shoulder.

"Let's get back to the hotel. I need to meet up with my daughter before she takes off with Alana and Christophe for two weeks."

"Alana is taking your daughter somewhere?"

"Yeah." I sighed. "Purchasing a bride in the auction wasn't part of my summer plans, or any future plan really. We need some time to figure things out, wouldn't you agree?"

She nodded silently.

I led her into a waiting taxi then ducked in next to her. "The Alexandra, please."

We were both quiet during the ride to our hotel. After I paid the driver, we visited the reception desk and got her room key. No surprise, Alana had secured Maia a room on the same floor as mine.

I walked her to room number 1820 and handed her one of the keys. I don't know why, but for some reason, I pocketed the extra. "I'm in 1826, just down a couple doors on the same side." I gestured with a chin lift down the hall. "If you need me for any reason, just call or knock, okay?" I dipped my head and made sure she looked me straight in the eyes.

"Okay. Thank you, um, for tonight. For dinner and you know, for the…uh auction." She grimaced.

I reached out to grab her shoulder, but before I could lay a hand on her, she'd twisted away as though it were a natural reflex. I let my arm fall to my side. "I'm never going to hurt you, Maia."

"That remains to be seen. People have told me the same and done the opposite," she admitted and then her eyes widened, suggesting she didn't mean to share that bit of information. Though I'm glad she did. It proved I needed to handle her with kid gloves in all things. Including my incessant desire to touch her.

"Another thing I'll earn then." I smiled.

She shrugged, disbelief written across her expression.

"Okay. Well, let's connect for a late breakfast. Say, ten o'clock?" I asked.

"You're the boss. I go where you say, right?"

I growled under my breath. "We'll talk more tomorrow. Sleep well."

She unlocked her door and slipped behind it. I waited until the lock clicked into place before heading to the elevator to chat with Emily.

* * * *

The door to Alana and Christophe's penthouse apartment opened with a flourish.

"Dad! I love you so much!" Emily screeched and flung herself into my arms.

I caught her and held her tight, soaking up this shocking

moment of pure affection from my normally surly teen.

"I love you too, Em. What's got you so happy?"

"Aunt Alana and Uncle Christophe are taking me to France with them! She said you told her I could go. Auntie is going to take me shopping, and Uncle Christo is going to show me his favorite pieces of art. And get this!" She glued herself to my side, her spindly arm wrapped around my waist. "Uncle Christo said he's going to teach me how to paint. Aaaaaand," she drew out the word in her excitement. "Aunt Alana said we'd castle hop! Castles, Dad. Real life castles, like, from a hundred years ago."

"More like several hundred years ago, *chéri*," Christo corrected, his face all smiles as we entered the living space. Alana was already wrapped in a red satin robe, her hair tied into a pristine bun at the top of her head, a dainty teacup held aloft in her hand. Emily was dressed similarly, in a pale blue matching robe. Her long blonde waves captured in the messier bun I was used to seeing.

"That sounds very exciting. Are you sure you're going to be okay being away from your old man for a couple weeks?"

Emily rolled her eyes. "Daaaaaad, I'm almost fourteen! I can handle being away from my parents. Besides, I'll be with family. I even have my own room at their house, remember? Auntie says we can redecorate it to whatever I want now that I'm older."

"You spoil her," I addressed Alana, then Christo, who grinned and nodded, completely unashamed.

"*Oui*, and that is a problem why?" Alana sipped on her tea, her legs crossed, her body perfectly poised as usual.

I shook my head. "It's not." Having people that loved and cared about my daughter was a gift. I wouldn't tell them how to parent in my absence. They knew I was strict with good reason. In my world, when you made the kind of money I did, me and my family could be a target. We hadn't been, thankfully, as I stayed out of the limelight as much as possible, but it was always a concern. One I know Christophe and Alana shared, so they'd be mindful of her safety at all times.

Emily sat on the floor and picked up a teacup, her pinky finger pointed way out. The cup had so much cream in the tea it likely tasted like sugary milk. "We're having tea."

"Caffeine free," Christo added.

"We already transferred her luggage to our room so you could have a night alone. We're leaving tomorrow first thing. Unless you wanted more time?" Alana asked.

"I…"

"Dad, it will be okay." Emily got up and then plopped into my lap.

"Oomph!" I wrapped my arms around my baby girl. "I'll miss you so much."

She actually hugged me back and rubbed her forehead against my temple. "I'll miss you too, but I really want this, Dad. It's going to be so much fun. And, don't be mad, but Alana told me you've made a lady friend recently."

I held Emily tighter. "She shouldn't have shared that," I growled and glared at Alana who calmly sipped her tea, not a concern in sight.

"I'm glad she did. You never go out with women. You're, like, the loneliest Dad on the planet. Mom meets guys and falls in love all the time."

"You realize that isn't how it's normally done, honey."

"Yeah, Mom is always heartbroken. But at least she tries to find someone to make her happy. You expect me to be the only source of your happiness, and Dad, I'm not always going to be around. Soon I'll have college, and I'll move away."

"College? You haven't even started high school yet. Slow down, take it down a notch."

"You know what I mean. Alana says you're going to spend this time getting to know someone special. And that is soooooooo cool. I look forward to meeting her."

I ground my molars. "Alana has been all kinds of chatty

this evening it seems."

Alana stood and came over and put her hand on Emily's cheek. "Emily is not a baby or a small child. She's a young lady and can handle her father entering a relationship." She then squeezed the ball of my shoulder before going over to the tea cart and pouring herself another cup.

"You sure you'll be all right?" I looked intently into Emily's pretty eyes. "You want to come home, I'm on the first plane."

Another eye roll. "I'm a big girl. I can handle hanging out with my aunt and uncle for two weeks. Relax, Dad. Have some fun for once in your life." Already my daughter was beginning to sound like Alana. Which usually was a good thing, and maybe it was now too.

"Bedtime, *chéri*," Christo announced. "Early flight."

I got up, hugged my girl tightly and kissed her forehead. "I love you, Em."

"I love you too, Dad."

"See you in two weeks."

Episode 30
A Family Unit

JULIANNE

"Do you Julianne Marie Myers take Giovanni Valentino Falco as your lawfully wedded husband, through sickness and in health, for as long as you both shall live?"

"I do," I whispered, disbelieving my own voice as I said the two words. I gazed into Giovanni's beloved face. His lips were sumptuous and pressed together. His entire expression set at sensual, yet calm, while I was a bundle of mashed up nerve endings ready to fire off in every direction with the slightest disturbance.

"And do you Giovanni Valentino Falco, take Julianne Marie Myers as your lawfully wedded wife, through sickness and in health, for as long as you both shall live?"

"I do." Gio squeezed both of my hands in what felt like support. Instantly a sense of calm floated across those rampant nerves, coating the fear with a layer of peace and understanding.

I was not alone. We would handle anything that came our way…together.

A family unit.

"Now, by the power vested in me by the state of Nevada, I

pronounce you husband and wife. Giovanni, you may kiss the bride."

"Hey there, you sleeping?" Giovanni's deep voice was a low murmur against my hairline as I stuttered awake.

The back of the limo was dark. Gio's tuxedo coat covered my upper body, the top tucked against my neck and shoulders, keeping me warm.

"We're at the airport?" I frowned as I looked out the window.

"After the wedding, you said you wanted to go home. I assumed you meant Manhattan," he lifted his chin to where his private plane was parked. *Falco Corporation* was scrawled along the fuselage. The pilot and crew were waiting by the stairs for us to board.

"What about our things?"

"I had management at the hotel pack our bags and prepare them for our departure. I hope I didn't overstep," he said, worry in his tone.

I shook my head. "No, it's great. I do want to go back to New York. We have a lot of work to get done there."

He cupped my face and caressed my cheekbone with his thumb. "Yes, we do. But let us not forget, it's our wedding night." He grinned.

My heart started pounding. "Oh?"

"Come Mrs. Myers-Falco, dinner and a flight await," he said in that smooth way that always made me and the rest of the single office staffers back at work want to sigh like the smitten Giovanni fan club we were.

My new husband was ridiculously handsome, über rich, and incredibly intelligent. Which was why he was constantly on the media's radar for Best In Business, Man Of The Year, and often talked about as the most sought-after bachelor in New York.

People were going to flip when they realized he was officially off the market. Especially after all the crap the tabloids posted about him and Bianca when the wedding cancellation announcement went out, and again when they found out she'd married my brother only a month later.

Gio got out of the limo, walked around to my side, opened the door, and offered me his hand. I placed my hand in his, knowing I'd probably follow him anywhere. Things changed after the intimacy we shared in that auction room and when we said, *I do*. I no longer thought of Gio as my brother's best friend or my business associate.

He was now my husband.

My husband.

I followed closely as he led me up the stairs of the plane. A table with a white linen cloth and silverware had already been set so I chose a seat there. He sat directly across from me.

"Buckle up, baby. It's going to be quite the ride." He winked.

Before I could ask why, the flight attendant approached with a bottle of champagne and two glasses.

"Congratulations, Mr. and Mrs. Falco," the petite woman offered as she set the flutes on the table, opened the champagne, and poured us each a glass. "Your dinner will be brought when we reach cruising altitude. I've already turned down the bed and stowed your luggage in the wardrobe."

"Thank you, we won't be needing anything until dinner," Gio stated.

"I'll make myself scarce until then," she smiled softly, and disappeared behind a curtain near the cockpit.

Giovanni lifted his glass. "To us?" He tilted his head in question, his gaze laser-focused on me.

"To finding the truth," I reminded him about what was at stake for me, but then realized he was attempting to be romantic, and I was screwing it up. "And to us." I tapped my flute against his.

We both sipped the cool, crisp champagne as we took off.

* * * *

We chatted about nothing and everything mundane as our dinner was served. Seared, herb crusted halibut with a delicious lemon-based cream sauce, and grilled vegetables paired with a polenta cake, all to die for.

"Everything was exceptional," I complimented as the attendant came in carrying a single plate with my very favorite dessert of all time. Chocolate dipped strawberries. I licked my lips. "Is that what I think it is?"

He grinned. "I know how you love the simple pleasures in life. And you have made it no secret how much you enjoy this dessert." He stood the moment the plate touched the table.

I pouted. "Where are you going?"

He lifted the dessert just as I was about to reach for a giant strawberry coated in dark chocolate and a dusting of crystalized specs that I assumed was sea salt.

"We're taking this to the bedroom." He stated with a coy smile.

I unclipped my belt so fast it clacked loudly against the chair arms as I stood. "Lead the way, Mr. Falco."

He cocked a brow, and I swear my lady bits sighed. He was sex incarnate, and I couldn't wait to ride him all the way to New York City.

When we entered the small room, I noticed the sheets were a blush-colored satin. Rose petals dotted the surface making the room smell sweet and floral. There were two bedside sconces that must have been on a dimmer because the light was bright enough to see, but not so much that I could discern fine details. Which, if I was a woman who didn't like the ample curves that good genetics and God Himself had seen fit to gift me with, the lighting would soften any hills and valleys. Since I treated the body I was given like the voluptuous temple it was, I didn't care either way. And based on how Giovanni's gaze seemed to covet every inch of me, I knew he very much enjoyed what I had to offer.

"Julianne." His voice was gruff and thick, sending a shiver down my spine as he stared at me.

"Yes, Gio?" My voice was a needy rasp.

"Take off your dress. I want you naked."

I smiled and brought my hands to my waist before sliding them up the sides of my breasts and then back down to my hips. "No foreplay?" I teased.

"I never said anything about there being no foreplay," he growled while tugging at his tie. He tossed the black bit of fabric on the bed.

"Maybe I need help?" I presented him my back and glanced coyly at him over my shoulder.

His gaze traveled down to my rounded ass, and his jaw tightened. It reminded me of the exquisite heat he'd brought to the surface of my skin when he spanked me earlier. A kink I had no idea I was into, but now craved with every shallow breath I took.

He set down the plate of strawberries on one of the bedside tables before he approached, unbuttoning his dress shirt and pulling it from his pants.

My mouth went dry at the washboard abs and tanned skin that greeted my eyes. Not to mention the light smattering of dark hair that spread across his toned chest.

"Eyes forward," he commanded. And it was a *command*, not a suggestion. The grit in his tone made me do exactly as he said, knowing that if I did, I'd be rewarded with another mind-melting orgasm.

He released the small buttons and then the zipper of my wedding gown, removing the fabric so slowly I trembled when two of his fingers traced the open, bare skin of my spine all the way down to the crack of my ass.

"You're not wearing anything underneath. I thought you

said there was a surprise hiding beneath the lace." His breath was hot against the shell of my ear as he curled his hands around my shoulders and slipped the fabric over and down my arms. I shimmied just enough for the dress to fall all the way to the floor in a puddle of lace.

"*Surprise.*" I taunted. "I'm naked underneath."

"My favorite kind of surprise." His breath fanned across the exposed skin of my neck, hands curling around my hips, then up to my waist and higher. He stopped at my ribcage, and I let out the breath I was holding. I wanted him to keep going, to mold his hands over my breasts and tease me until I begged him for more.

But he didn't. Instead, he allowed just the tips of his fingers to graze the underside of both breasts. My legs shook, and I fisted my hands, a small mewl leaving my lips as I arched in a desperate attempt to get him to touch me.

"Eager, wife?" He pressed a warm kiss to the base of my neck, and I sighed.

"Yes," I admitted, knowing he wanted to hear me panting for it.

The air between us was energized, suffused with carnal pheromones and lust I could practically taste.

His fingers moved to my shoulders where he traced my skin in a featherlight caress all the way down to where I'd fisted my hands as he pressed the entire front of his body to my bare backside. His erection, still clothed behind his slacks, nestled between my ass cheeks.

I rubbed my bum against him.

"Dirty girl." He sank his teeth against the space where neck and shoulder met.

I arched into his bite, bringing my arm up and behind me so I could hold on to him. "Please," I begged.

"Please what, Jules? What do you want me to do to this beautiful body?"

"Touch me." I rotated my hips in response.

"Oh, I plan to touch every inch of you, especially now that it's all mine to do whatever I want with it."

"Yessssss," I agreed, lifting my other arm and linking them around his neck.

Finally, one of his hands cupped a breast and went straight for my nipple, plucking it like a guitar string, making me moan, as if I was the instrument and my moans, sighs, and pleas the music. His other hand came around the front, and he gripped my rounded stomach, digging his fingers into my flesh.

"Every inch," he growled as he let go of my belly and shifted his touch down past my pelvis, through the neatly trimmed auburn triangle of hair and straight over my clit. He twirled and teased the tight knot in tandem with his other fingers tugging my nipple, until I was a mewling, panting mess of feral neediness.

"Do you feel how wet I make you?" He nipped at my ear, and I rose up on my toes, thankful for the heels I was still wearing as he plunged his fingers deep inside. "You think you're ready to take my cock here?" he thrust in and out as he spoke.

"Oh my God." I was losing my mind and my patience. I wanted his dick, but I was going to come standing in his arms if he didn't fuck me soon.

"Come for me, Jules. Fuck my fingers until you come, and then I'll give you my cock and make you sing for me all over again."

"I can't twice…" I breathed as I rode those fingers the same way I had earlier.

He chuckled as he thumbed my clit.

I moaned so loud he had to cover my mouth, leaving my nipple with a burning sensation that only added to the intensity of the pleasure I was receiving.

"That's preposterous. I'm going to make you come many, many times in a row, wife. Just let go and leave your pleasure to me."

I sighed and rode the waves of the impending orgasm. "Okay," I breathed, then gasped as he pinched my clit and plunged his fingers so deep and high, I'm pretty sure my toes left the floor. He held me against his body as the orgasm crested and flooded my system. I convulsed wildly, my body twisting with wave after wave of pure Giovanni-induced bliss.

Before I could even realize what was happening, he'd turned me around and backed me onto the bed. I fell onto a cloud of satin, my hair fanning out, my entire body twitching with aftershocks.

That was when he upped the ante, by kicking off his shoes, removing his pants, and shucking off his underwear.

His cock stood powerfully at attention, the tip glistening in the dim light. I watched as a single pearl beaded at the tip and then slid slowly down the length of him.

I groaned and licked my lips.

"You want to put your mouth on my cock, don't you?" He growled.

"Fuck yeah, gimme." I reached out, wiggling my fingers, my gaze zeroed in on the dewy, bulbous tip. My mouth watered as Gio wrapped his hand around his length and stroked up and down.

I fucking whimpered at the sight. Not because he wasn't touching me, but because he was denying me the chance to touch him in this state. The desire to please *him*, to put my mouth on that cock, to make him cry out in pleasure was all consuming.

"I want it," I griped, watching intently as he stroked himself leisurely.

"And you shall have it. When I say. Now spread your legs, Julianne. I want to see you weeping for me."

"*Giovanni*," I arched, and as my head fell back, I spread my thighs wide open, letting him see everything.

"So damn pretty. You make me want to kneel and worship you. Would you like that, dirty girl? For me to postpone my pleasure and make you come with my mouth?" His voice was like gravel—raw and jagged.

"Gio...*please*. Your cock." I swallowed and shifted restlessly.

"Fuck, I love to hear you beg." He put a knee to the bed, centered just the head of his cock inside me and stopped. "Squeeze the tip, Jules."

I tightened my vaginal muscles, and he hissed, nostrils flaring, jaw tight. "Good fucking girl. Goddamn you please me." He panted roughly, then reached for my knee and hiked it up toward my armpit. "Hold on, Jules. I'm going to fuck you into next week."

He did not lie.

Before I could even get a good grip around his shoulder, he thrust home.

I cried out to God, to Gio, to anyone who would listen as he pounded in and out of me. Pleasure soared straight from where he ground down against my clit and splintered out into a rainbow of euphoric ribbons that glided through my body.

It was raw.

It was wild.

It was the best sex of my life.

And it ended with his mouth over mine, muffling my cries when I screamed as the second unbelievable orgasm flowed over me. He lost himself then, groaning against my skin, pumping furiously until he filled me with his own release.

Boneless and sticky seemingly everywhere, Gio hooked me around the ribs and hiked me up toward the headboard, kissed me deeply, then pushed up and out of me. I shivered at the loss of his warm skin as he went to the small en suite. I heard water running and then stop before he came back with a damp washcloth.

Without even asking, taking every privilege as if it was his right, he opened my legs and wiped his release from between my thighs. When he was done, he covered me with the sheet and went back to the bathroom, disposed of the cloth, then walked completely naked, his cock still half-hard, over to the nightstand.

He lifted a single chocolate covered strawberry and grinned boyishly.

I bit down on my bottom lip with delight and renewed excitement.

"Wife, you absolutely earned more than this delectable treat as a reward, but I'm thinking the two orgasms kind of covered any debts I may owe you for allowing me control in the bedroom."

"Wow, you think pretty highly of your skills, husband."

"Let me remind you who was begging whom." He grinned, reached out and held the strawberry just over my lips.

I lunged and took a huge bite, the sweetness of the chocolate and the tart of the fruit blasting my tastebuds magically.

"Amazing!" I hummed as he leaned over and kissed me, stealing the juice with his nimble tongue.

"I couldn't agree more," he murmured, his eyes on me, not the fruit.

Suddenly his phone buzzed.

"Go ahead and get it," I said as I got up and snatched another berry.

He chuckled and shook his head as he reached for his cellphone. His entire body went completely rigid and not in the good way.

"What is it?" I asked as he slumped onto the bed, his head in his hands, the phone clutched between his fingers.

I grabbed the phone and scanned the message he just read. It was from his ex-fiancée, bitchface Bianca.

My entire body went ice-cold as I read the devastating words.

Gio, we need to talk.
I'm pregnant. Eight weeks.
You may be the father.

The Marriage Auction, Season 2, continues in Book 2. You can read book 2 now!

Also, if you haven't read Madam Alana (A Marriage Auction Novella) you might want to rectify that. Madam Alana will continue to be featured in the coming books throughout the rest of this season and it's more exciting to have read her beginning but it is in no way required to continue reading the novels.

Acknowledgements

This has been a wild three years my friends. I had no idea when I told my agent Amy Tannenbaum that I wanted to write a filthy soap opera that she'd actually find a way for me to do just that. This series started on Kindle Vella exactly three years from when The Marriage Auction 2 releases. In that time, I had no idea what I was getting myself into or that I'd find an entirely new way to approach storytelling. I'd always been known for my serials such as Calendar Girl and International Guy, but I wouldn't have expected that skill would transition into having eight full-length novels and two novellas all in the same universe…and counting! I'm so grateful to all of you TMA readers who read every episode week by week as it releases as well as to those of you that binge read the series when it's done and published in book format. Thank you, thank you, thank you. I endeavor to continue to give you the absolute best story possible while continuing to keep it fresh and engaging. And there is so much more to come! Follow me on my socials and my newsletter to stay up to date with the most current TMA news.

To **Team AC**, for those of you that don't know, these women read everything I write in DRAFT format at the same time it's being edited professionally. They receive no less than two chapters a week, read it, write out their feedback, suggestions, concerns and send it to me within a day of receiving it. They are the baddest, coolest, most talented, loving, and supportive women I know. And they are NOT paid. They do all of this out of their love for the stories, me, each other, and the sisterhood at large. I am nothing without them. I love each and every one of you to the deepest depths of my soul.

Tracey Wilson-Vuolo – Alpha Beta, Disney Freak, Proofer, ADA Expert

Tammy Hamilton-Green – Alpha Beta, Rock Chick, Plot Hole Finder, Educational Expert

Elaine Hennig – Alpha Beta, Brazilian Goddess, Medical Expert

Gabby McEachern - Alpha Beta, Dancing Queen, Spanish Expert

Dorothy Bircher – Alpha Beta, Mom Boss, Sensitivity Expert

Dannica Chiverrell – Admin Assistant, Niece, Gen Z Expert

To **Ekaterina Sayanova**, can you believe I roped you into editing another serial? Lol I just want to thank you for being a constant source of advice, intelligence, and always being willing to help me out of a writing corner I've put myself in. Your knowledge of the written word and my voice as a writer is unmatched. You get me, you get my storytelling, you just get it. You are one of a kind, my friend.

To my literary agent, **Amy Tannenbaum** with Jane Rotrosen Agency, you are my rock. You protect me, encourage me, and see my storytelling as something special. I think you're special. I wouldn't want to do this job without you at my back. I am constantly impressed by your business prowess, tact, and exceptional ability to find my babies homes. Let's do this together until we're old and gray. <wink>

To **Liz Berry**, **Jillian Stein**, and **MJ Rose** from Blue Box Press, you ladies are a triple threat of badassery and class. I've told you before and I'll say it again louder for those sitting in the back, you are a dream publisher to work for. On a personal note:

Liz Berry – I have never known a woman whose sole purpose on this Earth was to lift other women up and make them shine. Not only do you excel at it, you make it look easy when I know for a fact it's not. You set a beautiful example for the rest of us of what it means to be classy, confident, and successful. All of which you've done without walking over others to get there. I am in awe of you. You are true beauty inside and out.

Jillian Stein – I'm not sure I've ever known a cooler chick in my life. I aspire to be everyone's friend, but you just are. You have an uncanny ability to connect to people on a business and personal level that is genuine and everlasting. I aspire to be as well-rounded, hip, and considerate as you are with everyone you meet. Your ideas and excitement for the books you publish is as infectious and endearing as you are. Never change.

MJ Rose – At first, I was a little scared of you…in a good way. You're such a veteran of the industry I wanted to bow before the Queen upon meeting you the first time. Having the benefit of speaking to you about writing books and promoting them was like receiving a masterclass by a guru. Your knowledge and intellect is a gift to behold, and I'm honored you share it with me. One day, I hope to have such business savvy with the reputation to match. (Also, you remind me of Stevie Nicks and that's just cool AF.)

Last but not least, thank you to **Stacey Tardif** and **Suzy Baldwin**, you make sure my stories shine as brightly as possible. Thank you for your editing prowess and considerate feedback and suggestions. Knowing I have you two at the finish line making sure my stories read well is an enormous relief. I'm grateful for both of you. Our team ROCKS!

About Audrey Carlan

Audrey Carlan is a No. 1 *New York Times*, *USA Today*, and *Wall Street Journal* best-selling author. She writes stories that help the reader find themselves while falling in love. Some of her works include the worldwide phenomenon Calendar Girl serial, Trinity series and the International Guy series. Her books have been translated into over thirty-five languages across the globe. Recently her bestselling novel Resisting Roots was made into a PassionFlix movie.

NEWSLETTER
For new release updates and giveaway news, sign up for Audrey's newsletter: https://audreycarlan.com/sign-up

SOCIAL MEDIA
Audrey loves communicating with her readers. You can follow or contact her on any of the following:
Website: www.audreycarlan.com
Email: audrey.carlanpa@gmail.com
Facebook: https://www.facebook.com/AudreyCarlan/
Twitter: https://twitter.com/AudreyCarlan
Pinterest: https://www.pinterest.com/audreycarlan1/
Instagram: https://www.instagram.com/audreycarlan/
Tik Tok: https://www.tiktok.com/@audreycarlan
Readers Group:
https://www.facebook.com/groups/AudreyCarlanWickedHotReaders/
Book Bub:
https://www.bookbub.com/authors/audrey-carlan
Goodreads:
https://www.goodreads.com/author/show/7831156.Audrey_Carlan
Amazon:
https://www.amazon.com/Audrey-Carlan/e/B00JAVVG8U/

Discover 1001 Dark Nights Collection Eleven

DRAGON KISS by Donna Grant
A Dragon Kings Novella

THE WILD CARD by Dylan Allen
A Rivers Wilde Novella

ROCK CHICK REMATCH by Kristen Ashley
A Rock Chick Novella

JUST ONE SUMMER by Carly Phillips
A Dirty Dare Series Novella

HAPPILY EVER MAYBE by Carrie Ann Ryan
A Montgomery Ink Legacy Novella

BLUE MOON by Skye Warren
A Cirque des Moroirs Novella

A VAMPIRE'S MATE by Rebecca Zanetti
A Dark Protectors/Rebels Novella

LOVE HAZARD by Rachel Van Dyken

BRODIE by Aurora Rose Reynolds
An Until Her Novella

THE BODYGUARD AND THE BOMBSHELL by Lexi Blake
A Masters and Mercenaries: New Recruits Novella

THE SUBSTITUTE by Kristen Proby
A Single in Seattle Novella

CRAVED BY YOU by J. Kenner
A Stark Security Novella

GRAVEYARD DOG by Darynda Jones
A Charley Davidson Novella

A CHRISTMAS AUCTION by Audrey Carlan
A Marriage Auction Novella

THE GHOST OF A CHANCE by Heather Graham
A Krewe of Hunters Novella

Also from Blue Box Press

LEGACY OF TEMPTATION by Larissa Ione
A Demonica Birthright Novel

VISIONS OF FLESH AND BLOOD by Jennifer L. Armentrout
and Ravyn Salvador
A Blood & Ash and Fire & Flesh Compendium

FORGETTING TO REMEMBER by M.J. Rose

TOUCH ME by J. Kenner
A Stark International Novella

BORN OF BLOOD AND ASH by Jennifer L. Armentrout
A Flesh and Fire Novel

MY ROYAL SHOWMANCE by Lexi Blake
A Park Avenue Promise Novel

SAPPHIRE DAWN by Christopher Rice writing as C. Travis Rice
A Sapphire Cove Novel

IN THE AIR TONIGHT by Marie Force

EMBRACING THE CHANGE by Kristen Ashley
A River Rain Novel

LEGACY OF CHAOS by Larissa Ione
A Demonica Birthright Novel

On Behalf of Blue Box Press,

Liz Berry, M.J. Rose, and Jillian Stein would like to thank ~

Steve Berry
Doug Scofield
Benjamin Stein
Kim Guidroz
Tanaka Kangara
Asha Hossain
Chris Graham
Chelle Olson
Jessica Saunders
Stacey Tardif
Suzy Baldwin
Ann-Marie Nieves
Grace Wenk
Dylan Stockton
Kate Boggs
Richard Blake
and Simon Lipskar